THE RADIANT ROAD

Also by Katherine Catmull:
Summer and Bird

THE RADIANT ROAD

A Novel

KATHERINE CATMULL

DUTTON BOOKS

DUTTON BOOKS
An imprint of Penguin Random House LLC
375 Hudson Street
New York, NY 10014

Library of Congress Cataloging-in-Publication Data
Catmull, Katherine, author.
The radiant road : a novel / by Katherine Catmull.
pages cm
Summary: After nine years Clare Macleod and her father are finally returning to their old home in Ireland, a house by the sea, with a yew tree growing inside it, a tree with its roots in both the human and fairy world—and soon Clare, who has always been able to sense the "Strange," meets the boy Finn, and discovers that she must battle against the forces of evil in to restore order to both worlds.

ISBN 978-0-525-95347-0 (hardcover)

1. Fairies—Juvenile fiction. 2. Magic—Juvenile fiction. 3. Identity (Psychology)—Juvenile fiction. 4. Good and evil—Juvenile fiction. [1. Fairies—Fiction. 2. Magic—Fiction. 3. Identity—Fiction. 4. Good and evil—Fiction.] I. Title.
PZ7.C2697Rad 2016 [Fic]—dc23 2015020678

Printed in the United States of America
10 9 8 7 6 5 4 3 2 1

Design by Vanessa Han
Text set in Arno Pro

For Ken, my best and truest companion,
and for Emma and her interesting dreams

Eternity is in love with the productions of time.

—WILLIAM BLAKE

I too will something make

And joy in the making;

Altho' to-morrow it seem

Like the empty words of a dream

Remembered on waking.

—ROBERT BRIDGES

1

Not My Home, No Place Is

Clare was a strange girl, solitary and shy. She was a stranger to the place she lived, and a stranger to the place she was born. And sometimes the Strange came to visit Clare, and dreams walked through her waking life.

You know the Strange, too. It comes to everyone in different ways and times and flavors.

It's that feeling when you're alone at twilight, and the birds go suddenly silent, and a wind lifts up the leaves and drops them, and you listen, but you don't know what for.

Or that odd sense, when the light shifts a certain way, and you say, "Oh, this feels like a dream, I feel like I'm dreaming"—that's the Strange.

Or the Halloween feeling—you must know that one—the feeling of dead leaves and chill and early dark, when a burning orange mask, freshly cut, bars the way to a familiar door. The breath of the Strange slips under your own mask as you walk down the dark street, carrying your trick-or-treat bag, pretending it's only fun and not scary at all. The Strange swells and sighs beside you, almost close enough to touch.

Clare passed through patches of Strange often, much more than just at Halloween. She passed through them the way you swim through patches of surprising cold in a summer lake: with a shiver, but swimming on. It was her mother who had taught her that word, when Clare was small, that word for it among others. "The Strange has been here—do you feel it?" she would say.

Or "The Other Crowd is passing through."

Or "Throw a pebble in that whirlwind for the fairies."

Fairies. Obviously, the world and time had ruined that word for Clare, to the point where she felt herself flush to hear it. But even at almost-fifteen—when she no longer believed in fairies (in the Strange, the Other Crowd: *whatever*)—even now, when she caught sight of something extraordinary, and Strange, she would hear her mother's words: *Ah, look—a fairy-making.*

It was the only name she knew, for what no one seemed to notice, but her.

For example, one day, not long before this story begins, as Clare sat alone in the living room, a book fell from a shelf all on its own. Its pages fluttered for a moment, like a butterfly balancing on a flower. Then the book settled open.

From a vase on a shelf above the book, one pink rose petal drifted down and landed on the open page.

Clare bent to look. The petal had fallen on a line of poetry: "Eternity is in love with the productions of time," it read.

"Ah, look," she said softly. "Ah, look, a fairy-making."

The breath of the Strange cooled the air around her.

The night this story begins was not Halloween, but late spring. Clare was in her backyard, swinging on a rough board hung by two knotted ropes from a high cottonwood tree. Her bare feet swept up high, straining toward the silhouette of a dead limb that, for no special reason, she was trying to knock down. After a while, the pull and push of the swing lulled her. She forgot the dead branch and dropped her head back into the dark. Her hair, red as a leaf, not quite curly, fell back, then fell around her face, then fell back, over and over. Her body in white shorts and T-shirt made a ghostly diagonal trail in the night, back and forth, back and forth.

This would be her last time on this swing. Today had been the last day of school. Tomorrow, she and her father were moving to Ireland to live in a house with a tree inside it.

Clare had been born in that tree-inside house, fourteen years, eleven months, and ten and eleven days earlier. She had two birthdays, because her head emerged just before midnight on June 20, and her feet right after midnight on June 21. On birthdays, her mother used to make her two cakes, give her two presents, two birthday kisses, and so on.

When Clare was almost six, when the family still lived in that peculiar Irish house, Clare's mother died. It was the worst thing that had ever happened, or ever could happen. For a long time after, the pain was like a fire that never went out, and sometimes flared up hot and raging.

That was too much pain for such a small girl. So Clare smothered her blazing grief, and she did it little by little, by forgetting her mother and their life together. That flower of pain wouldn't stop blooming, and she was only little, and knew no other way. She built brick walls of other thoughts, other memories, between herself and her mother and their life.

After a while, instead of a blazing bonfire, her grief was like the evening sun behind the trees when you ride your bicycle west: sometimes you get a glimpse between the branches, or you hit a bump in the road, and the sudden blaze of sun in your eyes hurts so much, it blinds you. But mostly you're just riding quietly along in the dusk.

She always wore a little silver star on a silver chain around her neck, which her mother had given her, which had been her mother's necklace when she was small, and her grandmother's before that, and back and back. But by now, by this night in the swing, she hardly remembered her mother at all. She remembered a hand on her hair; and she recalled a scent of wild orchids and roses, a scent that meant kindness and joy, a scent that was there, and then was gone.

Clare also hardly remembered that Irish house she was born in—except that it was by the sea, under a green hill, with a tree running up one wall like a spine. She did remember the tree; she remembered her surprise when other people's houses did not have trees inside them. And she remembered walking up to the hill-roof to visit the top of the tree, where it lived with its face to the sky.

After her mother died, Clare and her father rattled around the empty house like two dried beans, and the sound they made was all wrong. She remembered that. The sound was wrong, and that was why they had to move away. Or that was how it felt to Clare, when she was not quite six years old.

So one day they packed their clothes, locked the door of the Irish house, and moved far away. They left Clare's mother's ashes in a wooden box over the fireplace, because her father could not bear to release them to wind or earth or water, and could not bear to keep them near. They moved, and then they moved again and again, as he tried to escape the grief that chased him on. He was too old to build walls to hide his pain behind, and so he ran.

Although he was born in a place called Skye, his work took him deep beneath the earth; he was a geologist, an excellent one, a genius of all that lies hot and still beneath the world we walk on. Rich men in dark suits digging for gold or coal or oil wanted that genius and would pay for it. So the two sad beans could move whenever they liked; there was always a new place to go, a new job to do. They never stayed anywhere more than a year. After a while, they got used to the new sound they made, rattling together alone.

But now, after nine years, her father had given up running. Tomorrow, they would move back to the house where Clare was born, where her mother was born, where her grandmother and great-grandmother were born, and back and back, before there were photographs, before people remember.

"And I've even found work, before our plane lands," her father had said just this morning. He pointed to a contract on the kitchen counter. "There's been a partial collapse of a mine I once worked on—thank God, no one was hurt—and the new owner has asked me in to consult." Clare had squinted at a thick, black, antique-looking signature next to her father's familiar scribble, and smiled to herself. *Maybe that's how they write in Ireland.*

Ireland was tomorrow. This was tonight. Clare let the swing slow, leaped off, misjudged the leap, fell to her knees. She lay back on the grass in the warm night. The streetlight was out, and the moon was low, and the stars' small lights shone clear. The grass itched.

Watching the stars, she thought how they wheeled above her like a flock of birds. *But the sky wheels slowly, slow and slow*, she thought, *too slow for me to see.*

She thought: *I'll write that down, about the slow wheel of the stars.* But she didn't move. Instead she watched the brightest star, closest to the moon, and murmured a soft "Star light, star bright."

When she got to "wish tonight," she paused, searching her heart, then found and said her wish: "A friend."

Then Clare stopped thinking and watched the constellations, her mind as wordless as the night.

That's when a fairy-making slipped in. The Strange often waits until words have died away.

Clare frowned. There was an extra star on Orion's knife.

All her hair pricked up. That fast, Clare was alert as a cat, eyes wide, fingers tense against the grass. More stars, now, blinked off, then on, then off.

But then she saw, and almost laughed: they were not stars—the blinking lights were fireflies.

So . . . was it nothing Strange, then? But it was, for still her skin prickled cold in the warm night as she watched the fireflies blinking among the stars.

The blinking became more regular.

Then it became perfectly regular. The fireflies were blinking off and on together in unison. Each time the fireflies blinked back on, they were closer together. They positioned themselves precisely against the distant, steady stars. It was as if the fireflies meant to complete a picture that the stars had only begun; to make a new, blinking constellation of fireflies and stars.

It felt like a dream. *Ah*, thought Clare—though less in wonder, this time, than fear—*a fairy-making*. Her legs on the grass were damp with cold sweat.

Off, on, off.

A picture.

Off, on, off.

A picture like a face—a terrible face. A glowing fright mask, blinking *off, on, off* above her.

The face was long and narrow.

Off, on, off.

It had one eye, and a huge mouth, gaping wide, as if to swallow or scream.

Off, on, off.

And where the other eye should be (*off, on, off*)—where the other eye should be, instead of an eye, was a swirling chaos.

Clare's heart was beating fast, fast, fast. One arm flew up defensively to shield her face.

The mask lowered itself toward her, and the glowing mouth hovered closer: visible, invisible, visible again. Invisible was worse. *It's insects and stars, that's all it is*, she said to her thundering heart. But her heart did not believe her.

The picture vanished. Clare waited, arm still flung over her face, too frightened to blink or breathe. But the mask and the fireflies were gone. Only the stars in their familiar shapes remained.

The dark was darker now, and the stars were farther away. Clare stood, brushed off her clothes with trembling hands, and ran inside to write it down, as she always did with fairy-makings, just in case.

Clare was always writing things down. It was the last remnant of her making childhood. "Dad, see my making on the refrideragor," she would say of a blobby watercolor, which was perhaps a hairy cow on hind legs. Or "Mam, look at my making, look what I MADE," of a cardboard windmill that almost really worked.

Clare's making continued even in sleep, in her glorious, exultant dreams, where she modeled pink shoes before a crowd of interested birds; where huge golden animals moved toward her at dusk, because she was their queen; where she sat at a campfire, looking through the flames at a dark boy wearing a long scarf like a Candy Land rainbow, looped around and around his neck. In her dreams, she often played with smiling people who could sprout wings or beaks or elephant trunks, who made her laugh, whom she called *the fairies.*

And back then, in waking life, fairy-makings abounded. Her world was the broad refrigerator door where the Strange posted their art, just like she posted hers at home.

Once on a stony beach, she found an oyster encrusted with

pearls, pearls on the *outside*, a cluster of tiny summer moons, and the oyster still tucked inside. Her mother admired it, then waded out into the water, carrying Clare, so that they could throw it safely home.

Another time, under a lake's thick ice, Clare saw a hawk frozen in mid-flight, wings back, talons outstretched, reaching for the fish frozen just out of reach.

In those days, Clare dreamed, and Clare made, and the Strange made, too, and left their makings everywhere for her to see.

But that was before her mother died, before she was a fledgling fallen from the nest too soon, downy and vulnerable and hiding.

Maybe it was the hiding that made her making-wells dry up. Or perhaps they clogged with grief. Or perhaps it was only growing up. Certainly, as she grew older, she learned from others that she was strange, and her makings were strange, and not to be shared on pain of mockery or worse. In time, the wells of making became a bare trickle. Clare even forgot to remember her glorious dreams.

But the fairy-makings never left her; those followed even as she and her father moved and moved again.

She soon learned to keep those to herself as well. One day, on a Michigan grade school playground, nine-year-old Clare saw the wind whirl a pile of autumn leaves into a ruby-colored spout, from which exploded a small flock of sparrows. Unthinking, she cried, "Ah, look, a fairy-making!"

There was silence. No one else had noticed. Then a girl said, "Do you actually, like, *believe* in fairies?"

Clare didn't know what to say. Everyone started laughing, and after that they always asked her about the fairy-makings—in a mean way, not a nice one, as if it were a baby thing.

That evening, Clare asked her father straight out: "Are fairies real?"

He was putting dishes away in the kitchen, and didn't turn to look at her. "Oh now, fairies," he said. "Many stories of them in your mother's country. And Skye was great with stories of the Good People, too, when I was a boy. You're a Macleod—the Macleod castle on Skye still has a fairy flag, you know, given to my many-greats-grandfather by his wife, who was a fairy herself, they say. When the Macleods needed extra help in battle, they'd raise that flag. I've seen it. It's a bit shredded now. In fact . . ." He turned to her, looking pleased, said, "Wait," and went off to his room.

He returned with a tiny shred of dirty, graying cloth, and laid it on the palm of her hand.

"That's a bit of the flag itself," he said. "Or so my granda swore. He swiped a scrap for luck in the war. And he came out of some bloody battles without a scratch. So perhaps it works."

Now he looked up, saw her troubled face. "It's just stories, my girl," he said gently. "Don't let it weigh on your heart."

So Clare put fairy-makings into a special category in her thoughts. Of course they were not actually made by fairies (*fairies*, god, that word), not made by the Strange, obviously she knew that. She *knew* that: but she never stopped believing in them.

Meanwhile the fairies left her dreams, and were replaced by dreams of I-forgot-to-study, or gross bathrooms, or teeth falling out, the same dreams everyone has—though Clare's dream classrooms and bathrooms were haunted by the heavy tread and snuffling breath of some ever-unseen monster.

As for her making, by almost-fifteen, Clare had closed up nearly as tight as a green bud.

Nearly, but not quite. She always carried a small notebook with her, one that had been her mother's, one she had found two years earlier while irritably searching the backs of closets for a missing pair of gloves. The notebook was pocket-sized, bound in a faded gray-green, rather institutional cloth. *Áine Quinn, ~~Fifth~~ Class*, said the first page. Áine Quinn was Clare's mother's name before she was married. Áine was pronounced "Ahn-ya." *Fifth* was crossed out in a different ink color, and *Sixth* written above it. *Commonplace Book*, it said below that.

This was my mother's. It felt warm in her hand.

She questioned her father, without telling him the reason, and learned that *class* meant "grade" in Ireland ("In Scotland we call it 'form.'" Okay, Dad, whatever). She also learned that commonplace book didn't mean "ordinary book" or "you-could-find-it-anywhere book."

"It's where you write down things you've read that you want to remember," he said, "or draw or paste pictures you want to save, like that. Thinking of starting one?"

Clare shrugged.

"Ah well, you needn't tell me, you stubborn child," he said cheerfully, and left it at that.

Clare kept that notebook always with her. When she saw a fairy-making, she wrote it down. When she read a scrap of poetry or prose she loved (which was almost as good as a fairy-making, to her), she wrote that down as well.

And sometimes Clare turned the notebook upside down, and in the back, in her tiniest handwriting, she wrote poems of her own.

Hiding her poems upside down in the back made her feel as if they weren't really there. *Anyway they aren't real poems*, she told herself. *They're notes for poems I might write some day.*

Although she was almost too embarrassed to reread them, and would never have told anyone about them, ever—still, privately, and never aloud—she called those tiny scraps of poetry "my makings."

During the year before this story begins, Clare and her father lived in Texas. It was as if they had come around the world to the exact opposite of Ireland: a hot sun blaring from squint-bright sky, ground flat and dry with patches of prickly grass. Her father would say, "It has its own great beauty here, and the winters are kind," but Clare thought he secretly missed wet and green.

In Texas, no one knew about Clare and her fairy-makings, or knew to laugh at her. But by now she was so Strange-haunted and solitary that no one talked to her at all, except to say, after a long stare, "You talk funny," and walk away.

Clare knew it was true, about how she talked. She sounded neither Irish, like her mother, nor Scottish, like her father. But she didn't sound American, either. Clare didn't sound right for anywhere in the world, but especially not for Midland, Texas.

On the first day of school in Midland, the teacher had asked them each to stand up and say what made them special. Clare made a small list on a page of her notebook as she waited her turn.

1. Dead mam.

2. I used to play with fairies in my dreams, ha-ha.

3. And all the fairy-makings.

God. She started to crumple the paper, but stopped. That second line felt like . . . something.

She chewed for a moment on her chewed-up pen.

Before my mother died, she wrote,

I used to play with fairies in my dreams.

She paused.

And fairy-makings ~~wound through every day~~ drifted through our days

Like curious boats, whose pilots were unseen.

But now—

"Clare Macleod?" called the teacher.

Clare's pen skidded, startled.

"Do you have something to share with us, Clare?"

Hastily, Clare crumpled the paper into a hard, damp ball and shoved it in her pocket, her face on fire. She didn't answer.

My strangeness is all I have, she vowed at that moment—meaning all I have left of Ireland, of childhood, of home, though she never said it to herself that way. *I have to keep it to myself, so no one knows, or they'll try to take it away from me. They'll try to make me like everyone else.*

So Clare kept her strangeness to herself. She kept herself safe; and she kept herself tightly locked. She was her own protector and her own jailer.

It didn't matter much. Combined with her placeless, homeless accent, her silence in class that day was not a good start. She spent her Texas year, like most of her other years, alone.

The morning after she saw the terrible mask made of fireflies and stars, Clare sat in a crowded airplane, still haunted by that gaping mouth and chaos-eye. Her father sat beside her, haunted by a box of ashes he had not seen in nine years, for ashes will pursue you, wherever you go, until you put them to rest. That's why they sat on this plane, not talking, those two lonely beans, flying over a cold dark sea, returning home.

They did not know—but I know—that Clare was a magic bean, sprouting soon, the seed of a great story and the winning or the losing of a great battle. She sat still and silent, but she flew through air and space, and her life was turning as the green globe turned beneath her.

When the plane arrived in Ireland, time seemed to stumble. Was it early morning? Late at night? Clare herself stumbled behind her father through customs. A man in a uniform looked at her passport and said, "Welcome home then, miss."

It's not my home, no place is, thought Clare.

"How long did it take to get here?" Clare asked while they waited for their rental car. "I can't find the right feeling about what time it is."

He rubbed her shoulder gently with one hand. "The flight was nine hours, but we also lost six hours in the time change. The flight is longer going back," he added, "because coming here we flew with the wind, and going back the plane will fly with its nose pushing hard against the way the wind wishes to go."

Clare stopped listening as her father talked on. She felt irritable and afraid.

Soon they were on their way, driving through a tangle of freeways that looked like any country at all, nothing special, nothing that said "home." Then the road dipped, and their car entered a tunnel, a long, dark one, darker and longer than any tunnel Clare had ever known. She thought: *I don't know where I'm going, and I will never come out to the light again.*

That's the feeling of tunnels. But they did come out; you always do. And once they were on the highway, the green rolling past, it started to rain, steady and swishing. The thunder was soft and far away. Clare slipped into the backseat to lie down, and her father didn't say no. She fell asleep.

Maybe Ireland will remind me of my mother, Clare thought. *Maybe the water will taste like her. Maybe the wind will feel like a hand in my hair.* She did feel that somehow, somehow, something was waiting for her here.

And she was right.

2

The Stars Inside It

Clare woke when the car-sound changed from pavement to dirt. They were winding up a soft, green hill. At the top of the hill was a single tree and a pile of stones.

A single tree, a pile of stones, and no house.

Disoriented, she leaned forward to ask where they were. Just then the road twisted around to the left side of the hill and stopped. Clare's father turned off the engine, and they sat in silence, looking out over the Atlantic Ocean.

The sea makes new colors in every new light, but on the day Clare arrived, it was chalkboard green, with greeny-white foam churning against the rough, dark rocks thirty feet below, rocks like a chocolate cake someone's had a handful of. At the foot of the rocks was a small, curving, pebbled beach.

That's our beach. The oyster. Feet dangling in cold water, safe in Mam's arms: "Send it home now, girl! Ah, good throw!"

"Do you remember this?" her father asked.

"Now I do." Not only did Clare remember this beach, this sea: she remembered she loved the sea. To see it, and smell it, and feel its great salt body moving slow beneath them—it filled up a part of her heart she hadn't known was empty.

"That's west," her father said, gesturing to the sea. "The sun sets red and lovely over that sea." He sat still for a moment, then abruptly opened his door and got out. Clare followed him around to the cliff's edge, feeling wet salt air on her face: she had forgotten that, too. How many things had she forgotten? She was shaken, disoriented, by how familiar and right it was.

The sea wind swept around her, lifted up her hair, and dropped it again. Her hair began to curl in random wisps.

"You do have your mother's hair," said her father, running a hand through it as he walked back to the trunk.

"But your eyes," said Clare automatically. It was what they always said.

"As brown as trees," her father agreed, as he always did. His shoulders were hunched in a little, as if he were warding off a blow.

Protected from the ocean, set into the grassy north side of the hill, was a narrow black door, old and thick. Clare turned back to watch the changing sea as her father opened the trunk and began unloading suitcases.

"Give a working man a hand, here, princess?"

Clare slipped on her backpack and picked up a suitcase, waiting as her father unlocked the narrow door with an old-fashioned iron key, long and toothed. The door opened, smooth and silent.

Right away came the rich, complicated smell of earth and stone, a smell so familiar that Clare's eyes surprised her by blurring wet.

They entered a dim passageway, much narrower than a hall, made of enormous slabs of gray stone beside and above them. The floor was dirt. Clare's father, who was not tall, almost had to duck his head in the passage. They held their suitcases in front of them, edging inward.

More like a cave than a house, thought Clare. She did not remember this, it was nothing she knew, and for a moment, she had the bad tunnel feeling again. *I won't know this place, and I won't belong here.*

But they emerged into a huge round room, airy and cool, with curving walls of gray stone and a high, domed ceiling. To her right, high in the wall, was a small opening, lined with stones—a window, but with no glass. Clare remembered, with shocking clarity, asking why their only window had no glass. Her mother's reply, as she looked up from painting a toenail, smiling: "We leave that window always open for the fairies."

Fairies, thought Clare. *Story for a kid.* But she did remember this place, or at least, her bones remembered it, or her blood did. It was unfamiliar, and it was the most familiar place there had ever been. And that was odd, because this place was wreathed in Strange. It was almost as if it were *made* of Strange. All the fairy-makings she had seen all her life, all the patches of Strange she passed through—it's as if they had all been fragments or echoes of this place, this *home.*

She realized something. With only that one small window, it

should be dark inside. And yet soft white light, soft as starlight, filled the room. She looked up and saw, somehow without surprise, that yes, of course: the ceiling was thick with stars.

That's right, I remember: my house has the stars inside it.

But when Clare looked more closely, she saw that the old gray stones of the ceiling were studded not with stars, but with some sort of clear rock that carried the sunlight from the outside to in.

"Very clever, that," said her father, pointing up, "clever for now, astounding for the ancient times when this place was made. It's fused quartz—somehow they found all these long chunks of quartz that had been heated hot enough to become clear as glass. The pieces hang down to bring the light from outside in. Can you see?"

She did see. The light poured through the lovely quartz like water through a straw. By that sunny starlight, she saw a great stone room, like a cathedral, but older, softer edged. The walls were made of gray rock, piled on each other—huge ones near the bottom, smaller and smaller as they went up, all different shapes and sizes.

Her father was watching her. "They didn't use mortar between the stones," he said. Clare looked closer. It was true: nothing stuck the stones together. Whoever had built this place had chosen the stones carefully, and laid them just right to fit. Then they buried the whole thing inside a mound of grassy earth, like a pregnant belly.

And then one day, Clare thought, *I was the baby inside my mother's belly, inside the belly of my house.*

Some of the rocks bore faint carvings: spirals, waves, diamonds, eyes. They looked older than old. Clare knelt and traced her finger across one spiral, remembering her three-year-old hand tracing that same spiral. That small tangled-hair girl, fearless and happy, meeting the silent, uncertain, clamped-down person she was today. The cold stone rough under her finger, then and now.

"You know how they built it without mortar?" her father called as he ducked down the passageway. "It's their own weight and closeness that hold the stones together."

"How long ago?"

Her father put his head back in the room. "At least many hundreds of years," he said, "but more likely a thousand or more. You should know about this house, sweet," he added gently. "It will be yours one day."

Clare turned to the house with new eyes. As she tested that thought—*mine one day*—her eyes fell on the tree. In that instant, she knew that this home was right, and every other home she'd ever lived in had been wrong. And it would not be hers *one day.* It was hers now.

The tree's fat trunk seemed part of the stone, knotty and hard as it was; and yet it was also alive, the bark a pink-patched brown, like peeling skin against the gray stone. It was ancient and innocent, deep rooted and wise, but as vulnerable and childlike as a skinned knee. It was *her* tree—how could she ever have forgotten her tree? Clare walked toward it, not fast, but feeling fast inside.

"It may be a thousand years old, that tree," she remembered her mother saying one cold morning. "Do you know how many a thousand is? How many?" For a moment Clare could almost see herself that day, runny nose making her upper lip cold, a giant wool sweater dragging down to her feet, staring up at the tree, listening to her mother.

"That old you," Clare's father said as he entered with the last bag, and she thought for a moment he had read her mind. Sometimes she had wondered if he could, the way he always seemed to know what she was feeling.

But no: it turned out he had said "old yew." The tree was a yew tree, one of the oldest tree species, her father said. Yews had roots in the oldest world, when dinosaurs brushed beneath their leaves. During the Ice Age their roots held tighter, turned gnarled and hard.

Her father told her all this as he unpacked. He didn't ask her to help—*princess*—as he normally would, perhaps because he saw all she was feeling. There was little enough to unpack anyway, besides suitcases and a few shipped-in-advance boxes stacked neatly against the wall. Most of their possessions, especially the books, had been packed by movers that the mining company had paid for, and were still on their way from Texas.

"Do you remember that they're poisonous?" he said. "I tried to drive that into your head when you were a toddler, because they're quite poisonous, yews—wood and needles and seed and all. I worried over my small teething girl. But your mother never worried, and she was right."

Clare walked back to the center of the room and closed her eyes. It wasn't just the Strange so thick in the air, it was something else as well: something that was kindness, and sweet clear light, and above all was *Mother, Mother, Mother*, so strong that she almost wept. Like the aromas of two savory pots on the same stove, *Strange* and *Mother* wove together to make a new scent, a fragrance she had forgotten could exist: the fragrance of *Home*.

Her father came up beside her, his hands in his pockets. "When we first married, I thought we couldn't really live here, with a dirt floor and an open window and no rooms but this one big one. I thought we might camp out for a week or two until we sorted proper digs. And your mother didn't argue, she never pointed out, as well she might have, that people have lived here quite happily for many a century. But that first week passed, and another, and I . . . It was easy here. It was easy to live here. It wanted us here. And so we stayed." He nudged her elbow lightly with his own. "I think you'll like it, too. Now: come with me, because I need you for this."

They walked to the fireplace, where a fire was already burning, warming the room (*But who lit the fire?* Clare wondered, then forgot to wonder). Above the fire, on a long stone mantel, sat a wooden box, all alone. Her father took it down and held it between himself and his daughter. His hand, strong and lean, traced the carvings on the box, and her hand, smaller, paler, did so, too, tracing the same spirals and stars and diamonds as on the walls.

"So these are her ashes," he said, soft.

Clare nodded. She felt her arm tremble, so she put her hand down.

"And I'm sorry I left them here alone all these years," he said, and was he talking to Clare, or to the ashes, neither of them knew. "There is always one girl born in this house, only a girl, and only one, or that's the story. And as far as the records go, that's what it shows. One girl is born here, one in every generation, as you were, and your mother, and her mother. When we married, she said we'd have a girl born in this house, and she was right. And she always said you'd come back here, if you left." His voice went wrong for a minute. "She always said you'd come home," he continued, "and so you have. I made sure that was right. You have come home." He was silent a long time, his head turned so Clare could not see his face. Then he cleared his throat.

"We'll do something right by those ashes soon, shall we? Give them over to the ocean or what may be. We'll decide together. All right?"

Clare nodded again.

Her father placed the box on the mantelpiece and put an arm around her shoulders. They stood looking at it for a while. "We're all together now, back in your house," he said, and now Clare was almost sure that he wasn't speaking to her. "So that's all right, then," he concluded. Then he gave Clare's shoulders an extra squeeze, and returned to the unpacking.

Clare looked around. She saw chairs for sprawling beside the fire. Saw the boxes they had shipped, stacked neatly against one wall. Saw a cooking area, with sink and stove, which, though older than any sink or stove she had ever seen, looked new and alien here. She saw—oh, and she *recognized*—the long wooden table with five chairs around it, and the wardrobes and cupboards, and the rumpled, dark green couch. Clare ran to the couch and pressed her face into that remembered scent of sweet and smoky wood.

And even with the furniture and kitchen, the great domed room still felt spacious and free, as if you were outside under the stars. She remembered that, too.

The memories came faster—yes, that old wooden screen, painted all over with spirals and diamonds like the walls, but also with stranger things, like three legs bent into a wheel, or triple bird heads all looking at one another, or a man whose body turned into a rope that then tied itself in complicated knots. *That man, those crazy birds, I forgot about them, but I remember now.* Behind the screen was her parents' big bed, where they all used to sleep together.

Well, her father's now. And she saw no other bed.

"So . . . but where do I sleep?" she asked.

"Look up," said her father, smiling into the box he was slicing open.

Clare looked up and saw rocky dome, quartz stars—and something she hadn't noticed before: a platform of pale, rough planks, built high against the wall where the tree grew, the wall that faced the ocean. A ladder led up through a hole in the platform.

Like a tree house, but inside.

"Your room," said her father. "It was your mother's room, too, when she was a girl. That loft always belongs to the girl who lives in this house, your mother used to say, as soon as she's old enough to climb the ladder, and until the house becomes her own."

He climbed the ladder himself partway and, with effort, lifted Clare's suitcase onto the platform. But he didn't go in. "Your room, chocolate éclair," he said. "All yours."

Clare slung on her backpack and climbed the ladder's smooth-worn rungs.

She found herself standing on bare, broad planks, much closer to the starry, arching roof; and yet it felt all air and space, clean and cool. One side of the platform hugged the curving walls of the dome, and the other curved out into the air, so that the floor was shaped like a wide-open eye or the deck of a ship. Where the platform jutted into space was a half wall, up to her chest.

Clare walked around the room, trailing a hand to touch each object. The yew trunk sprouted a few leafy twigs here, making it even more like a tree house. A single bed with a giant pillow and a thick, sky-colored comforter pushed its head against the tree. Beside it sat a small blue table with one drawer and one lamp.

My mother's bed, when she was my age, thought Clare. She lay on it carefully, and found herself looking at blue sky through a hole made of stones. Her room faced the window, which looked out to a green pasture; and the green and the sky looked in. Farther down the green, she could see something that might be a ruin of some kind, like an old church or a castle. Her mother had looked through that window at that sky, at those old stones. *Wearing this silver necklace, just like I am now.*

Clare unpacked her clothes into a worn white wardrobe to the left of the bed. Against the wall near the foot of the bed was a wooden table, stained pale yellow, with other, more accidental-looking stains—ink? crayon? paints? all of these?—in various colors. She set a few books and pens there, and her commonplace book. It looked right there.

Clare sat back on the bed, leaning against the tree, and looked around at her room, her tree house, this empty, airy space that had been her mother's and grandmother's. She felt happy there, happy and secret and free, just herself and the stone and the sky and the green beyond. In Texas, her room had been crammed with things, books and old stuffed animals and boxes of hair ornaments and notecards and posters on the walls. Most of that she and her father had thrown out, given away, or put in storage. At the time, it was hard to do. But now she wondered why she had ever thought she needed that. Only having what she had brought in her suitcase made her feel light and free. She had been given a gift she never thought to ask for: a way back into the great stone egg she had been hatched from before she was ready.

I'm home. I'm the girl who lives in this house. This is who I was always supposed to be. If I don't want to, I never have to leave again.

Clare's father made lunch with groceries he'd bought on the way from the airport. For a Scottish person, he made excellent Italian food, and with sudden and delicious hunger, Clare ate pasta with lots of Parmesan and meatballs on the side. After they finished the dishes, he sat on the couch to read. She stretched out on the other end of the couch. "We just had lunch," murmured Clare, "but I feel tired as midnight."

"You didn't sleep on the plane," said her father, patting her ankle, "and only a bit in the car. The time change is confusing your body." Flipping another page, he began to sing, a soft song about sky or Skye. *I hope that's not supposed to be a lullaby*, thought Clare with sleepy annoyance. But whatever it was, it was nice. Her feet in thick gray socks just touched her father's leg, and that was nice, too. He sang to himself until she fell asleep.

Clare hardly remembered climbing the ladder up to bed, but once in bed she lay awake for a few minutes, disoriented. She could hear the ocean, a long crash and surge that never stopped. It reminded her of the early morning sounds of traffic in one of their New Mexico houses, when they lived near a freeway. But traffic is a single sound that never takes a breath, and this sound, the ocean sound, breathed in and out, in and out.

Clare's grandmothers had died before she was born, but she thought that this was what it must feel like, sleeping beside your kindest grandmother. Holding that thought close, she drifted toward sleep.

A thought drifted alongside her: *One girl in every generation.*

And then she was asleep.

It was a sort of grandmother to Clare, that sighing, breathing sea. So was the belly of earth around this house, protecting the broken family within. So was the wind that carried her here and harried and questioned every stranger who approached this place with bad intent.

The sea and wind and earth all guarded and helped her as they could.

But a dark brute was moving toward this place. And the help of sea and wind and stone was not half the help Clare needed.

But wind had borne her home on its wings; earth bears her now in its belly; and the sea will bear her, too, before this hard time is done.

~

When Clare woke up, it was pitch-black. Above the rush of the sea she could hear her father's soft snore below. Middle of the night, and she was wide-awake. This must be jet lag, this out-of-time feeling, this private darkness while the world snored and the ocean rushed on.

She kind of liked it.

Clare got up, put on socks and a robe over her pajamas, and because it was cold for June, wrapped a scarf around her neck for good measure. She sat at the yellow desk, switched on its lamp, and in its little pool of light tried to guess the origin of those stains. A curve of crimson—a glass of grape juice, dripping? A blue-black blotch—that was spilled ink, a leaky pen. Dashes of grass green and bright lemon that outlined the edge of an invisible corner—oh, someone was painting and ran off the edge of the paper.

My mother's inks. My grandmother's paints.

She opened the commonplace book and began to leaf through the familiar pages, looking for blue-black ink to match that blotch. On its first page, she read, in looping blue ink,

He heard high up in the air

A piper piping away,

And never was piping so sad,

And never was piping so gay.

—WBY

On the facing page, in the same handwriting—*my mother's handwriting*—but in violet ink, Clare read:

Be not afeard. The isle is full of noises,

Sounds and sweet airs that give delight and hurt not.

Sometimes a thousand twangling instruments

Will hum about mine ears, and sometime voices

That, if I then had waked after long sleep,

Will make me sleep again; and then, in dreaming,

The clouds methought would open, and show riches

Ready to drop upon me, that when I waked,

I cried to dream again.

Underneath was written, in the same handwriting, and underlined twice: *Shakespeare was there.*

Something about that sentence—*Shakespeare was there*—made her shiver.

A few pages in, she found a passage in ink just the color of the stain:

Fair seedtime had my soul, and I grew up

Fostered alike by beauty and by fear.

"Fair seedtime had my soul" was nice, though she wasn't sure what it meant. She turned to the back, turned the book upside down, and took up her pen. She had waked up with an image in her head: a girl running across the sea, on a path made by moonlight. But where was the girl running? Bent over her desk, her hair touching the page, Clare began to write. As she wrote—but not before—she understood the answer. That was the miracle of writing, how she did not know what she knew, until she began to write it.

The stone window was black; her tiny lamp put out the stars. But the stars watched, anyway, as Clare wrote, and paused, and wrote. After numerous hesitations, cross-outs, and emendations, she had this:

Along the sea, the moonlight spills

A kind of path

For one with feet, not fins.

Bare feet and cold

Splash this radiant road.

On water and light she runs

Toward stone and tree,

Toward home.

Toward stone and tree. Clare looked up. Yes, the tree—because there was something so *important* about that tree, something she hadn't quite remembered yet. In fact . . .

Without conscious decision, she stood and moved toward the ladder. She would be very quiet. She just had to see.

The tree squatted against the wall in the dark like an ancient, lumpy toad. Clare put her hand against the bark and felt a flash of memory: *the way in.* Yes—how could she have forgotten? There was a way into the tree, a crack or space between two of the ropy trunks, small, too small for a grown-up.

But when she was a red-haired toddler, Clare had often hidden inside that tree.

Probably too small for me now, too. The thought made her anxious, and she had to see. The crack in the tree was close to the wall, she remembered, feeling along—and yes, almost immediately: there it was, the long sideways mouth of it, like a slender leaf.

Looking at the dim shape, Clare was suddenly unsure: Was it one tree that divided? Or was it two trees that grew together? *Either way, I might still fit that space between.* She slipped her arm in and turned sideways to see.

And the room fell silent, as if it, too, were waiting to see. And her arm inside the tree felt cool and prickly, the hair rising up.

And Clare's mind filled with—not pictures, exactly, but feelings, and near-pictures, near-memories, of what was inside that tree.

Her heart started beating fast. She pulled her arm out.

I will see if I fit some other time.

3

Four for a Boy

The next morning, half asleep, Clare heard voices drifting up from below. Wrapping herself in the sky-blue comforter, Clare walked to the edge of the platform and peered down.

She could just see her father's hands gesturing as he talked to a woman. The woman was shorter than he was, quite short, with dark, thick, gray-spattered hair, just curling in at her jaw. When she talked, her hands moved, too, thick and square and strong. Her voice was warm and husky as a clarinet, but not so sad as a clarinet: friendlier. When she laughed, it was like a clarinet blowing bubbles.

The woman said, "I'll be so glad to see Clare again, if she comes down soon." As she spoke, she looked straight up at Clare and winked. Her smile made her face round as a friendly bowl, and her eyes were bright and black. Clare's father said, "Is she up, then? Clare?" and was leaning in to look as blushing Clare drew back into her room. But she didn't feel bad; she felt like laughing, too.

A minute later she climbed down, dressed and uncombed. Her father said, "Oatmeal warming in the pot for you, sleepy. And this is Mrs. Dunn."

"Mary Joseph Dunn," said the smiling, black-eyed woman.

Although she was no taller than Clare, she looked solid and strong as the yew trunk. "But please call me Jo," she added.

"Oh, now—" began Clare's father, who preferred Clare to call adults by Mr. or Ms.

But Jo interrupted him. "Or Aunt Jo, if your father prefers, though I am not your true aunt, of course. But we can't have formalities between two who have known each other as long as we."

Clare glanced at her father for help.

"I'm teasing you, my little red leaf," said Jo. "I delivered you into this mad world; I was your mother's midwife. I was your grandmother's midwife in her time, too, and delivered your mother's red head into this house just as I did yours. And I am so sorry that you lost her, Clare," she added, "so sorry indeed."

And the way she said it didn't make Clare feel embarrassed and sad, as it usually did. It made her feel warm.

Jo was persuaded to stay for breakfast, where Clare learned that she was also the house's caretaker. All the years that they had been gone, it was Jo who kept the house repaired, stoked fires every winter to warm the pipes, chased birds out of the fireplace. It was Jo who had stacked their boxes and lit the fire to welcome them home.

"It's the modern things here, the wiring and pipes and such, that need the babying," she said. "It's not the old stones. They're strong." Jo put an admiring hand on the wall. In the morning quartz-light, the stones were many colors, not just gray—pinkish-violet and purple-gray and a kind of clayey blue.

Conscious that she would own the house someday, Clare said, "Thank you."

"It was my pleasure," Jo replied. "I was a nurse and midwife all my life, and when they pensioned me off I didn't know what to do with myself. It wasn't the money, only I'm up and about at four a.m. and have my own house and garden seen to by ten. That leaves a lot of empty day."

She asked Clare how she liked her room—whether she wanted a rug on the floor or hangings to cover the bare stone. Clare said she liked it as it was, and Jo seemed to find that the right answer.

"And are you still a maker?" she asked, buttering a piece of toast. When Clare didn't answer right away, Jo glanced up at her, her dark eyes crinkling like a smile. "I remember you well for a making child, songs and stories and little forts you would make, all the time. A writer, by now, are you?"

Clare tightened. "Not really," she said. To write hidden, upside-down poems—notes for poems—was one thing. To talk about it was unthinkable. With her spoon, she pushed a lump of cold oatmeal from one side of the bowl to another. "No. I guess I grew out of it."

Jo laughed. "You never grow out of making. At the least, what about in your dreams? Don't you make every night, in your dreams?"

"That's not me, though," Clare said. "I'm not, like, *making* my dreams."

"Ah," said Jo, with a friendly smile. "Who is, though, if not you?" She stood up to clear her plate. "Tell me this: have you been up to visit the top of the tree yet? Let's go and greet it, then. I always pay my respects to the tree when I come."

"Breakfast dishes waiting for you when you come back in," said her father as they left.

The sea that morning was dusty blue and calm. Clare and Jo scrambled up the green hill, still slippery from yesterday's rain, on rough steps made by rocky ground. Up at the top, they stepped carefully around the chunks of quartz that salted the grass, drinking the sunlight. What Clare had taken for a pile of stones the day before turned out to be her own chimney.

They stood with their backs to the yew and the ocean, looking over fields of green pasture that ran up to those stony ruins of a castle or church, and on beyond to the edge of a distant forest.

Feeling the damp on her shoes, Clare thought of a question. "Why doesn't the rain come in the window?" she asked. "It rained yesterday, and the hill is wet, but the house stayed dry, even though there's no glass in that window."

"The window was made that way," said Jo. "Look and you'll see that the stones slant outward. The wind could still blow it in, if the wind so chose, but I've never seen it happen."

"When I was little, Mam used to say it was left open so the fairies could fly through," Clare said. "What's the real reason?"

Jo gave her a sideways look. "What makes you think that's not the real reason?" she said.

Clare looked down. She wanted to be polite, but she wasn't going to pretend to believe in fairies. Also, she'd been starting to like Jo. "Um, okay," she said, her voice tight.

A warm hand pressed her arm.

"I'm not teasing you," said Jo. "Sit down beside me—this sunny patch looks dry, or dry enough—and let an old woman rattle on for a bit."

They sat on the ground looking out over the green. "Well," Jo began. Clare felt, from how she said that one word, that Jo would talk for a while, and she was glad. She lay back on the wet grass to listen and watch the changing sky.

"Here in Ireland, we believe, or we used to believe," Jo began (and Clare wondered which it was), "that when the Good People travel together, they travel on certain paths, and always straight ones. It's hard to see anything but sky from that stone hole when you're inside the house, but—"

"From my room you can," Clare said. "I saw the pasture, and some woods, and those ruins or whatever, over there. It's like the window's a telescope pointed straight at those ruins."

"So it is," said Jo, "that's exactly what it is. You understood that on your first day. Well, well." She was silent for a moment, then continued. "That twelve-hundred-year-old castle is one landmark of the fairy road. Your yew tree here is one landmark, and the ruins is another. And can you almost see," Jo asked, "a good ways beyond the castle, that dolmen?"

"What's a—" Clare began, but Jo interrupted.

"Of course you wouldn't know, my apologies. A dolmen is—well, no one really knows for sure. They say they might be tombs, because at some point people were buried under some of 'em, but it's only a guess. A dolmen is most often two great rocks standing on end, and a third one laid across them, like you made your forts, when you were a child. Only this child would have to be the size of this hill, because the stones are that big, and that heavy—heavy enough to have stayed in place for thousands of years. Can you see it?"

Clare sat up. She thought she might see something, something white in the grass out far past the castle, but she wasn't sure.

"Well, it's hard, at this distance, if you don't know what you're looking for," said Jo. "But that dolmen is called Finn's Cap. They're all over this country, I can tell you, dolmens and standing stones and—oh, much more. And beyond Finn's Cap, which you can't see, is a hawthorn tree—a fairy thorn, as we used to call them here."

"Why *fairy* thorn?" Without meaning to, Clare sounded peevish.

Jo laughed. "You don't care for that word, I see. They are also called the Good People, you know, and other words as well. Fairy thorn because hawthorns are favorites of the fairies, I suppose. I was walking near there yesterday. That tree is fully dressed in flowers still, even though we're past May. It's the fourth landmark, all in a straight line with the others. Inside the forest is the fifth landmark, but you can't see that from here. The point is, when the landmarks go in a straight line, it makes a road for the . . . for the Good People to travel as a host, leaping from one to the next, and through your window to the yew tree—and behind the tree, of course, the sea itself. The sea is the beginning and end of all roads, if you travel long enough, even fairy roads. There are paths like that all over this country."

"Only Ireland, supposedly?"

"Oh no. In every country, everywhere. But most places, people have forgotten the roads, or how to tend them. Here we remember better than most."

Clare squinted into the distance. She wondered why they called it Finn's Cap. Maybe she would walk there later.

"I will tell you something else about that window, though," said Jo. "One day a year, at Midsummer only, the sunrise shines straight through that window."

"Midsummer?" Clare asked. "Like the middle of summer, you mean?"

"Well, it is called Midsummer because it's the longest day, when the sun is in its greatest glory, before the long decline into autumn. But scientifically, my scientific girl, it's the first day of summer, the summer solstice. That's usually June twentieth or twenty-first—twenty-first this year, at the new moon."

"My birthdays," Clare said.

Jo smiled. "That I know," she said, "for I remember that long day and short night well." She brushed her hands again, decisively. "It's time we pay our respects to the yew."

They turned around to face the yew, where the deep green of its leaves flourished against the two blues of sky and sea. But Clare stopped, put her hand out to Jo's arm.

In the branches of the yew were four identical birds, large and thick-beaked, black and white in big patches. The four birds sat straight and still, staring at Jo and Clare.

The hair on Clare's arms rose electrically. The birds were Strange. A fairy-making? But they were just sitting there.

"Well, well," said Jo softly. "Four for a boy."

Clare thought she hadn't understood Jo's accent, because "four for a boy" made no sense. "*What* now?" she said, and immediately blushed at the phrase: *You're in Ireland, not Midland, Texas.*

"One for sorrow, two for joy," said Jo. "Do you not know about counting magpies?"

"Is that bird a magpie?"

"It is," said Jo. "And there's an old belief that magpies are an omen—an omen of what, it depends how many you see. The rhyme for it goes, 'One for sorrow / two for joy / three for a girl / and four for a boy.' There's more, too—I think, 'Five for silver, six for gold—' Ah, I don't remember the rest. But let's both look out sharp for a boy today, and see which of us the omen was meant for."

Clare wasn't sure if she was serious or not. They stood for a long moment, watching the magpies watch them. Then all four birds at once, with no visible signal, no preliminary shifting, launched from their four branches and flapped away.

"Then in we go," said Jo.

The yew's branches spread wide and free here aboveground, and Jo and Clare ducked beneath their green umbrella. Within the shade, the hard boughs twisted and bent to make a little bench, and after Jo refused it, Clare sat. She felt safe; the tree held her in its arms. She felt that she could tell the tree her troubles. She rested her head on the hard wood, the rough brown and the smooth, peeling pink, and stroked a green frond with flat, pointed leaves, like a fir tree.

Jo watched her with a funny expression. "Poison," she said carefully.

"I know." Clare felt compelled to add, "Also, but just: I don't eat *leaves* anymore, actually."

Jo laughed her deep-bubble laugh.

Clare wondered if she could climb higher, and tested one branch by hanging from it.

"Some of the branches are hollow," said Jo, "the tree is as old as that. So be careful."

Clare pulled herself up the branch. Hidden in the leaves above Jo, she spoke. "Jo. Why do people here call fairies 'the Good People'? My father called them that once, too."

"Ah well," came Jo's voice, soft. Clare could just see her, leaning against the yew, looking out through the branches toward the sea. "We say it the same way that if you see a great dog, a large and powerful one, whose tail is not necessarily wagging—then you say, 'Good dog, good dog.'"

When Jo left, and after she had finished washing the breakfast dishes, Clare went outside to see what she could see. Her father said, "Be careful, and take your phone."

"I don't have one that works here yet," she said.

"Oh yes," said her father. "Well, still, then, be careful." He smiled in a crinkly way that he hadn't for a long time. "It's like my own childhood, your running all over the countryside phonelessly."

"Not that I'm a *child* anymore, actually," said Clare,

"Not that you're a child anymore," her father agreed. "Almost a woman, Miss Almost-Fifteen."

Clare made a face. "Not a child. Almost a woman. I really think you have to pick one."

Her father threw back his head and laughed. "Be back for dinner, my bullheaded girl. And stay safe."

The world was green with the new June. Jo had called it "lovely warm," but to Clare it was lovely, lovely cool. She wore jeans and boots, which in Midland meant January. She was going to explore her home.

At the foot of the hill she paused, looking down the twisty one-lane road lined with low stone walls, stone piled on stone, with no mortar in between, like her home. Cars come fast in Ireland and on the wrong side, and there was no sidewalk or shoulder, so she did not want to walk along that road for long. But down toward her left, she spotted a break in the wall she could squeeze through to enter the pasture.

Green hills rose up behind her, hiding the sea, and clouds were crowding around the sun. Clare stood facing the pasture in the changing light. To her left was the woods, and down the pasture a half mile or so was the castle. She set out in that direction. War and knights, battle and blood.

Gradually the castle turned from distant lumps of rock into itself, and she stood before what had once, perhaps, been a door of thickest wood and bound with iron. This cool afternoon it was only a curtain of vines that looked easily pushed through. From within, a faint tingling of Strange drifted through the curtained door.

Clare turned around. Yes: this vine-covered door exactly faced the stone window in the side of her hill. So this was the first landmark—according to some ridiculous kid's story, which of course it was.

Suddenly, the whole thing irritated her in ways she couldn't say. Her mother's silver necklace was scratching her neck, so she unhooked it and balled it up inside her fist, pressing the points of the star painfully into her palm. There were no fairies, and Strange or no Strange, this was just an old castle that belonged to some, no doubt, warmongering king who was long and deservedly dead. This fairy thing was going to ruin the whole country. Forget it. She turned to walk back to the twisting, wrong-sided Irish road.

And then, from the forest to the north, she heard music.

No, a wren's song, she thought. At least, perhaps it was a wren;

it had the shape of a wren song, complicated, wreathing up, down, and around.

But the longer Clare stood listening, the less it sounded like birdsong at all, and the more it seemed a song made on the thinnest flute. Still, it was not quite like human music, either. It seemed both human and made, but also not-made, as complicated and inhuman as birdsong or falling water.

She ran toward the woods, following the music. And a pathway opened up, and welcomed her in.

When she stepped out of the sun, everything changed. The light grew complicated and shifty, the air cooled, the colors deepened. It seemed as if the sweet music bubbled more clearly, the wind sighed more loudly, and the leaves along the path rustled as loud as papers dropped in a church.

Or maybe in the woods, Clare was a better listener. She thought of a line from the commonplace book: "The poetry of the earth is never dead."

The music sang her down the path, and the cool air touched her face like the breath of a ghost. A long-forgotten woods-walk popped into her mind: herself short and worried, holding tight to her mother's hand, and her mother saying, "No fear, girl. We have friends in every woods we walk through, though we walk through them not knowing." Small Clare had thought she meant animals and birds; but older Clare was not so sure. Oh, that Strange song drew her deeper in. She loved its made-and-unmade tune, so sweet and high and wild.

The song began to fade, so Clare walked faster, listening to find it again, her heart beating hard.

And off to her right, she heard something: but not a song.

A snort.

When you are listening to silence to find a flute like a bird, then the snort of an animal, a big animal—well, *snort* is a small word. It doesn't say how a sound can make you cold, make your stomach turn over once, twice. A large animal was very close, and Clare felt very small.

She stood still. She heard a confusion of leaves up ahead, which gathered into a great stamping: one, two, three.

And then, on the path ahead, in the dappled, slanting morning light, she saw the snorting creature. It was an enormous deer, a buck—*a stag, they call it here*—almost the size of a moose, with a thick shaggy throat and muscled chest.

More than the creature's size made Clare's breath catch and stop. This stag was white: all white, every inch, like a ghost or a snowstorm, except only for gray-blue eyes. Its white antlers rose up twining and tangled, as twining and tangled as the high, wild, lovely song that Clare had followed, as if somehow the music had become this other thing, this complicated whiteness twisting and rising into the air.

The white stag held still across the path, looking off to the left. He raised his head and roared or groaned. To Clare, it sounded like both. And she was frightened, truly frightened, especially when he turned to look at her with his rain-cloud eyes.

Silence.

The white stag lifted his head again, gave his terrible, groaning roar, and turned to her again.

Should I say something back?

But Clare didn't know what to say.

One more time the white stag roared, tossing his head, and Clare felt the proud sound inside her, filling all her cells.

And now Clare saw, dangling from one of the stag's white horns, flashing in the sun, her own silver chain, with its silver star.

She looked in her hand; the chain was gone. She must have dropped it as she ran.

The stag turned on his pale, slender legs and galloped away down the path.

Clare ran after.

For the next hour, Clare saw the stag and lost the stag, over and over, in the changing light of the changing trees. She heard its hooves, sometimes, and she heard the music, others. She was tiring fast; if it hadn't been for the silver necklace, she might have given up. But that chain had been her mother's, and her grandmother's, so she listened for hooves or music and ran on.

But in the end, Clare lost the sound of the hooves and the music both; she lost her ghostly stag. In frustration, she stopped, to catch her breath, to look behind her, to be sure she knew the way home, to be safe. Necklace or not, she almost put her feet back on the path home. But she heard a few more notes from the flute—or maybe it was a wren this time, after all. Either way, it was enough to make her turn around again and take a few steps toward a small, stony brook that ran across the path.

Across the brook, behind the trees, she could see that the forest drew back to make an open space of canopied light.

Clare backed up, took her longest running steps, and leaped across the brook. The momentum carried her stumbling forward through the trees and into the open meadow on the other side.

What she saw in the meadow could not be right; made her blink, and blink again.

It was a vast rainbow, curled in on itself, asleep on the ground.

A third blink, but the vivid coil of color remained, a many-colored labyrinth, paths of color turning in and around and back on themselves, filling up the whole wide meadow.

Then Clare said, "Oh," out loud. Now she saw: the twisting, spiraling colors were not a grounded rainbow. They were mushrooms—*mushrooms*, how strange, how Strange—thousands of them, sprouting in every color. The mushrooms of the outer rings were bright and brilliant red, but as the circle spiraled inward, the red softened to brick, then rust, then heart-of-sun orange, then sunshine yellow, lemon yellow, goldy-green, lime—and spiraling closer and closer to the center, the mushrooms were mint, then morning sky, then evening sky, almost night, and a deeper and deeper violet.

And in the center of the mushroom rainbow-labyrinth stood a boy, all in black and gray with long, wild black hair. He was looking straight at Clare, holding a thin silver flute.

And from the end of the flute dangled Clare's silver chain.

4

A Sky Holding Snow

The boy standing in the earth-rainbow radiated Strange like an electrical storm. Oh, but the sight of him felt dark and sweet and familiar to Clare, a cup of hot chocolate inside that storm.

She thought of the word *elflocks*. "Ach, you've got elflocks," her mother would say when her hair tangled, when she had to tug the comb through hard. Clare remembered that word as she looked at the dark, silent boy, with his long dark face under long, tangled black hair. Elflocks. Not even tangled, more than tangled, and all different lengths, some twisted into ropy strands that hung lightly around his face.

He was about her age. His clothes were dark, old-fashioned, and coarse, like someone in a black-and-white movie, and his eyes were cool blues and grays.

"I know you," said the boy.

His accent was not Irish or Scottish but thicker and older than them, like the root of the tree that bore them. Clare recognized that way of talking, but she could not think from where.

"I don't know you," she replied; though she did, she knew she did.

He smiled a smile that was warm July to his December eyes. "Four for a boy," he said. "Did you see the message?"

"You sent those birds?"

"Not 'sent,' no, I am no king to *send*," he said. "I asked in the proper way."

Clare tried again. "Did you make—did you make, this, this—" A question rose to her tongue; seemed unbelievably stupid; was asked anyway. "Is it a fairy ring?" She had read about those, and weren't they made of mushrooms?

He smiled one half of a smile. "They say we make the rings for dancing in," he said. "But it isn't your idea of dancing we're doing."

We make the rings. We?

"And no, it is not," he added. "But I did help the mushrooms make it, I did that."

"How did you—" Clare didn't even know how to start this question. "Did you, did you dig up this clearing and then spread—"

"We don't make with tools," he said. "You know that, you know it, oh, Clare. All you've known you've lost. Gone too long, too long." A shadow slipped across the boy's eyes, a cloud across the winter sun.

"Well, I'm sorry," said Clare, stubborn. "But—"

"We made it together, for you, the mushrooms and I," said the boy. "Just as the birds and I made your morning message. That is how we make."

"Well, it's . . . incredibly beautiful," she said, flushing at the weakness of the words. *Lame.*

He smiled down at the colored rings rippling away from his feet. Clare broke the silence, speaking in a rush. "I don't know you. Only I do."

"You do," the boy agreed. His voice was low for a boy; not like a man's, but deeper and richer than a boy's should be. "You know me, Clare. You've only forgotten. Girl," he said. "Un-forget."

And saying that, he reached out as if to touch her. He was too far away to touch her—he at the center of the hundred colored rings, she at the edge—but then he wasn't, suddenly, he was quite near, and Clare stumbled back.

But he caught her, he steadied her, and into her hand, he placed her own silver chain.

With the boy's touch, with the green, woody scent of him, Clare's heart startled, as wild as a bird. She did remember. She saw two babies, once, and then two toddlers, and now the same two in this meadow, nearly grown, and all of them superimposed, all layered against each other. *That's me*, thought Clare. *That's me, once, then, now, all orange-red and warm and autumn. That's him, now, once, then, all cold and winter branches and eyes like a sky holding snow. That's us, facing each other on this path. I know this boy, oh, I know him.*

And she knew with certainty that this boy was winter to her autumn, and that as winter and autumn go hand in hand together, she and this boy had always gone. She knew that, she knew that, how could she have forgotten? "But what—" she began.

"Tonight," he said. "For greater talk we'll meet tonight, in the in-between. Tonight I'll begin to tell you all your mother should have told, except she died. You're home, ah, you're home at last. Clare, come tonight."

"Wait, in between what? Where do I go?" Clare asked.

"You know. Come just as you always did." He was somehow back in the center of the mushroom circle now. The flute hung from one hand. "I thought you'd come the day you came, and you almost did, until you didn't."

In the center of a wheel of ravishing color, he was a shadow or a rain cloud, and then he was gone.

Clare sat down hard on the forest floor. Meet him in between? "You almost did the day you came"—she ran over yesterday in her mind: how she brought her suitcase in, saw the stars on the ceiling, touched the spiral on the wall, and wrote, and slept, and slipped downstairs to put her hand in the—oh.

"Is it the tree?" she called into the empty air. But she knew it was. As she asked the question aloud, her mind was flooded by memory.

When I was a baby, he was.

When they were babies, their fists closed together. Her head against his head. Their comfortable sighs in the night, breathing together the smell of living wood, and earth, and herbs. Their small, square, bare feet, tangled together, dark and pale.

And didn't she miss him when they were apart, and cry?

And didn't she cry and cry, and then stop and go silent, once they left for good?

They had lain inside that tree as babies, then as tiny children, tangled, playing. She remembered the taste of the wood in her mouth, chewing it for comfort as her small hard teeth came through.

(*But that wood is poison*, came the passing thought, though she didn't stay to question it.)

Red hair, black hair, pale hand, dark hand, brown eye, gray eye.

Inside the tree.

Inside the tree is full of lights, she remembered: a Christmas tree inside out.

Inside the tree it smells of resin and licorice herbs, and wood under it all, she remembered: the smell of living wood and stone.

Clare sat on the forest floor, slowly fastening the chain around her neck. The trees towered and breathed above her, coiled and knotted beneath her, a speaking tangle of water and stone and life.

She stood, turned, ran home. As she jumped across the brook, she thought it sang to her.

The brook did sing. It sang its warning song. But Clare does not yet have ears to hear when the world sings to her through brook or wind or bird.

This was the brook's song: *He comes closer, he comes closer, the destroyer comes closer to your nest.*

"I met a boy today," Clare told her father when she got home.

He seemed distracted, fiddling with the phone in his hand. "Oh, good," he said. "And what's his name?"

Clare felt she should know this. *He knew mine.* Clare felt around her heart, looking for the name. She looked up to see if her father was waiting for her answer. But he was already ducking down the passage toward the door, frowning at his phone, going outside for better reception.

"Finn," she said into the empty room. Now she remembered. "His name is Finn."

Late that night, Clare slipped from her high bed, bare feet on the whitened wood. Her flannel pajamas were too thin for the cold, so she pulled the comforter around her and held it close with one hand as she climbed down the ladder. What she had been wild to do this afternoon now seemed a terrible idea.

I don't have to go all the way in tonight, she told herself. *I could just look and be sure this is safe.*

But she knew she'd go in. She was as curious as a cat—and as tense as a cat.

The blanket rasped softly along the floor, so she gathered it up. Her father's low, slow breaths behind the screen calmed her. She found the tree in the dark and knelt down beside it. Blind, feeling with her hands, she found the place where the tree split. Was it one tree that tore itself in two? Or two trees that grew together?

In went her arm, and her arm felt a change. The comforter slipped to the floor. She turned sideways. It was tight—she was no toddler now. But piece by piece, wriggling and stretching, Clare pulled herself inside the tree. The more of her made it in, the more her blood swirled with joy; all her body's cells hummed, *yes, yes, yes.*

She was in. Her knee was pressed into her chest, her arm squeezed up above her. She felt like the drawing of Alice grown too big for the house.

But soon the tree relaxed around her; it allowed her in. Or was she shaping herself to fit the space? They shaped themselves to fit each other, the tree and Clare. This is called making a home.

Sitting comfortably now, arms around her knees, Clare waited in the dark. Her blood vibrated like plucked strings. Where were the colored lights she remembered? For a moment she doubted, in the tunnel again: would the dark never end?

But at the end of the tunnel, as with all tunnels, a tiny light appeared. The light was warm and white, and hovered near. Other tiny, hovering lights joined it, swarmed beside it. The lights blinked off and on.

Fireflies.

Lovely: but Clare felt a clutch of fear, remembering the glowing horror-mask in the sky. The lights she remembered from the tree were *fireflies*? Did they even have those in Ireland?

But these fireflies danced around her head with tender attention, blinking a silent, delicate song. The skin of her arms and knees glowed in their creamy light.

Now at her feet came a wave of glimmering green, tiny green pinpricks of light that washed in and out, in and out, like a wave on the shore.

Now over her head a translucent scarf of indigo and spring green folded, unfolded, refolded. "Northern lights," whispered Clare.

And still the blinking fireflies danced lightly around her, as the northern lights and the luminous green waves kept their own slow rhythms. These were the Christmas lights she remembered; the tree was full of living lights.

How could something so Strange feel so strong and sure and home?

Slowly, by the faint and many-colored lights, she began to make out details of the old tree: its skinned-knee pinkness, its hard and curling roots.

Wait: she looked more closely at the roots. Nestled in the crook of the roots was something—she leaned in closer—was . . . the world? She laughed out loud. It couldn't be. But more than the world—the universe, a tiny doll universe, starry and fiery, green and stone, curled inside a root's curling arm. A forest rose up and died in one slow breath, out and in. A mountain range heaved up like a jagged wave, then softened, lost its shape, and melted away beneath the wind and rain. At her feet, a distant star blossomed from a burning bud, shone full and yellow-white, swelled up red, withered into darkness.

"Good girl yourself," said a voice in her ear. "You came."

Finn was beside her. *How is there room for him in this tree?* But this was Clare's home now, fitted to her, she fitted to it. This was always her home, only she'd forgotten. And Finn and Clare had always fit here together.

"You can see the whole world and sky in here," Clare said. "You see them so slow, though. Or maybe I mean so fast."

"Because this tree stands between our worlds, yours and mine, and has roots deep, deep into both," he said.

"Your world," Clare repeated. This was the question that had haunted her all day. "Are you . . . ?" No. Not that word. "Do you come from . . . the Strange?"

He laughed, a startling sound in the firefly-lit silence. "I call *your* world the Strange one. We call our world Timeless. Timeless, for it is great with beauty, my world. And the beauty is perfect, and never changes. Nothing changes there." Something odd in his voice there, but Clare pushed on.

"But so, all my life, those fairy-makings—wait, do you know what I mean by fairy-makings?"

"I do indeed." A fish threaded with light passed between their faces, so that his gray-blue eyes were bright for a moment, then shadowed again.

"Was that you? Was it you making them?"

He smiled, and turned his face away as if to hide it. "Some I did," he said.

A sudden, troubling thought. "But did you make—did you make the one from a couple nights ago, with the fireflies and stars, that made the terrible sort of . . . face?"

"I did not," said Finn. "But not only I make them. We all make those makings, in your world. We make more than that, much more. We made your home, my girl."

Clare forgot the firefly face, turning this thought in her mind. *My house was built by fairies?*

Clare didn't believe in fairies. But it is hard not to believe in someone sitting beside you, arm in rough wool coat pressed against your own, while fireflies and glowing fish swim in the air between you. It is hard not to believe the memories that come tumbling back every hour you're here.

"I don't really believe in fairies," she said aloud, doubtfully, as if testing the sound.

He laughed, a sharp and husky sound. His breath was like the breath of wild herbs after a rain. "Do not call us fairies, then," he said, "if it's only the word in the way."

They were quiet a long time, arm touching arm, as the lights of the universe breathed and pulsed, arose and died away around them.

Clare, who had had no real friends, had of course no boy friends, either. A featherless fledgling who hides herself doesn't talk much with anyone, let alone boys. She knew, or she thought she knew, that boys came in three kinds: the ones raucous as a pack of dogs, all vulgar jokes and savagery; the mute ones, their faces shuttered up, as stubbornly unproddable as a pile of wet towels; and then the third kind, the boys with intelligent eyes and bitter jokes, and a sadness at the edges that she thought might match her own.

There was one boy like that, a year older, who worked in her favorite coffee shop in Midland. She liked his floppy dark hair and sad, skeptical brown eyes. They exchanged a few words now and then, and shared ironic glances at overheard conversations.

She saw him once or twice a month for a year; had said maybe a hundred words to him; did not know his name. He was the closest thing she had to a boy friend.

Now she sat pressed arm to arm with a dark boy, a Strange boy, an intelligent boy with sadness around the edges. And to sit pressed arm to arm with this boy seemed like coming home, and how, how could that be?

"You and me were friends," she tried softly. "When we were babies, when we were small." The words were wrong and not enough for all she felt.

"We were," said Finn. "We slept and played together, here in the in-between. The two worlds, human and Timeless, like two eggs inside one nest, this nest, our nest."

She held up her hand, and watched the fireflies bob and dance around it. "Do other people come here? To this place, I mean, to the in-between. Do other . . . people of Timeless, or whatever?"

"Ah," said Finn. He held his own hand up, and the fireflies wove a glowing thread between them. "No. This place is our place, only ours. Well: and the lights. Whatever makes light may pass through our yew. But people, mine or yours, no. No one can visit the in-between, but Clare and Finn."

This was the most beautiful answer in the world. Clare's heart rang like church bells.

"It is a great joy to me you've returned," said Finn, and the bells rang higher still. "Because this tree has much missed its guardian."

The bells clanked a bit. "Its *guardian*?"

Finn paused, pulled back. "Do you not know about yourself and this tree?" said Finn. He seemed incredulous. "Your mother must have taught you *something*?"

Clare stiffened. "My mother's dead, and if she taught me stuff when I was *five*, I've forgotten it." (Not all, though, not all: *We leave it open so the fairies can come through.*) "I heard this tree was one of the landmarks of the fairy road, if that's what you mean."

Finn smiled, and fireflies bobbed around his face, blinking him dark and light. "Oh—the *fairy* road is it, after all?" he asked. Clare made a face—all *right*—and he continued. "You may call them landmarks, but we call them gates, which is what they are, gates between our worlds. Long ago, the two worlds were one. At least, that is what we say, or how we say it.

"But when the spine of the world was split in two, spots of connection were left. These are called gates. And this tree is the living heart of all the gates between the worlds. It roots into the earth with a thousand fingers, and it sends those roots in all directions. This tree's roots run even beneath the sea, where every road begins or ends."

Who said something like that before? thought Clare—but Finn was still talking. "When a series of gates falls in a straight line, that makes a fairy road whereby the fairies may travel as a host, leaping from gate to gate, as at certain times of year, fairies must."

Clare's face looked as if she were tasting something bad. Finn cried, exasperated, "Oh, girl, if you don't like 'fairy roads,' then you might call them 'the dreaming roads' or 'the gates of making.' The name is not important. But each gate, each gate the world over, has a guardian, who must keep it open and flowing. The job is passed down through the generations. Your family has guarded this gate, the most important gate of all, this yew tree, for long, oh, long."

Every generation, one girl is born into this house.

"My mother guarded it?"

"She did. And your grandmother, and great-gran, they all did, back and back."

"So, but," said Clare, something opening in her chest, "so how do I guard it? What do I actually do?" A small fish swam between them, swam as if the air were water, its bones glowing pale blue within translucent skin.

"You *use* it, girl," said Finn. "You use the gate. With neglect and disuse the gates become rusty and stiff and ruined. You keep it open with use."

"You mean I go visit . . . go visit your world?" A mixture of disbelief and anxiety. "I don't know about that."

Finn put his head between his knees and made an unreadable noise. Then he laid his face on his knees and looked at her through one gray eye. "Clare," he said. "You go there every night, or nearly. Did you not know? You come to my world every night, to dream."

Clare opened her mouth to scoff, to say no, to say—but she remembered now, oh, she *remembered* now, why his accent was familiar, and his smile.

Her dreams. The smiling people in her dreams, growing bird beaks, elephant trunks, to make her laugh.

The *fairies.*

"But—"

"Dreaming, passing back and forth, to and from our world, keeps the gate well and alive. That's one way. The other way is making—writing, music, dance, invention, anything you create."

"Why making? Why does that help?"

"Because making and dreaming are the same. Or say: making is a higher form of dreaming. In dreams, most of you wander blind and deaf as babies—making, but blind and deaf. To make awake is a higher thing. *My* people do not sleep," he added, as if this were a virtue of theirs.

Clare wanted to ask: but if I am making, when I dream, why do my dreams surprise me so much? But Finn was going on. "Making and dreaming tie your world to ours, for we are great makers. Great makers, indeed." For a moment he looked curiously wistful and silence fell between them. The green sea at their feet washed silently in and out.

Clare sat awhile digesting this. She felt herself growing sleepy, in the silence. She yawned. Finn laughed.

"So can I ask another question?" she said.

"Oh, ask away and welcome."

"So if there are all these gates around—"

"Not so 'all these' nowadays."

"Still. Why aren't people falling into your world all the time? I mean there are some old stories about it, but you don't hear now about people . . . I mean like that old castle, people must go in there all the time!"

"Oh, ah. But they are gates, you see, and gates lock. And each lock has a key. For the gate's own guardian, it will open. You might say, Clare, that you yourself are the key to this gate, this yew. But it will be locked to any other. The person who wishes to pass through a gate must find it out, the key. Must hear each gate's requirement."

"So, like a password," said Clare.

"And each gate has its own. You must find it out, by luck or by thinking." Finn sat up straighter. "Idea," he said. "We'll try you tomorrow. Your mother would have done the same, it's time you learned. We'll meet at the castle, for you to try if you can learn its key. I believe you will be good at key-finding," he added confidently. "It is much like making, and you were ever a maker-girl."

Clare felt a chill. "People keep saying that. I'm not really some big maker now, since I'm not, you know, four years old."

Finn looked surprised. "Never at all? You?"

Clare blushed. "Not never. Sometimes I write, I have little notes about . . . I mean it isn't anything."

"Bring some tomorrow to show me."

"I'm not going to *show* you," said Clare, shocked.

"But why?" He seemed genuinely puzzled.

"Because . . . well, everyone is afraid to show private stuff like that."

"Everyone," said Finn, once again closing one eye as if he were sighting her, or drawing her, "is not a maker." A sudden, slightly dazzling smile. "Tomorrow, then."

And he was gone.

Back in her room, though dawn was coming on, Clare was too electrified to sleep. First she ran to the tree and kissed one green frond and said, "I will protect you, I always will." Then she felt silly; then she didn't care. She thought of the old song that went, "I could have danced all night." She wished she could play music and dance.

Instead, she sat down at the yellow desk and found the

beginnings of her poem, the one about the girl running down the moonlight.

She held two thoughts in her mind, both at once, and both lightly, one in each of her mind's hands: fairies aren't real; and this boy, this earth-rainbow-making boy, this boy of her memories, Timeless boy—he is, he is real. Then, quite easily, she let the first thought spill away into the air. She had been wrong; almost her whole life, she had been wrong about fairies (still, that word, though, *ergh*), had been wrong about what to believe in. It felt hilarious now, to have been so wrong.

With her poem before her, she thought of how her small makings had a big reason: to keep the tree alive, to keep her *connection* alive: to the other world, and to making, and to dreaming.

And to Finn. She remembered sitting with him in their in-between, that was only theirs: how new but how familiar it was, to be in private with such a friend, a friend of her heart, the loveliness of it. The pressure of his arm against hers, the woody scent of him. A secret jewel.

Along the sea, the moonlight spills

A kind of path

For one with feet, not fins.

Bare feet and cold

Splash this radiant road.

On water and light she runs

Toward stone and tree,

Toward home.

After some thought, she added two lines:

The finless girl flies to her Finn

Tucked deep in the roots of the in-between.

Later, she lay in bed, one hand against the bark of her tree. She tried to feel how the yew sent green tendrils up through the ceiling and roots down to the sea. The wind howled outside, howled, howled, first one side of the hill-home, then the other. Then it took a breath and howled its howling, fearful song again. It sang with its mouth pressed against the walls, it shivered its voice through the tree.

But it never came in Clare's little stone window to shake her. So she felt safe under her comforter, and she fell asleep. She dreamed she sat in the lap of the moon, cool and soft, her legs dangling over a luminous green sea that washed up to shore and back, up and back. Above was a constellation she had never seen before, a horned thing, half man, half beast, and she felt afraid. Far below, a wolf stood on the shore and howled up at the moon, and where one of the wolf's eyes should be was a swirl of sparks like fireflies.

5

Her of the Cliffs

The next morning, breakfast hardly touched, Clare half ran to the castle, carrying an umbrella her father had thrust into her hands as she dashed out. The sky was cloudy and the air was moist and kind. This time she did push through the doorway of vines, abandoning the umbrella outside. "Finn?" she called. But there was no answer.

The old castle was roofless, open to the somber sky, its gray stone overrun with flowering vines and sweet-smelling grasses. A few inner walls and stairs remained as well, roughly marking the shapes of rooms and courtyards where people had worked and cooked and slept.

A delicate Strangeness ran through the space. It felt so old and so innocent, both at once, that Clare pulled out her commonplace book and wrote: *children playing on their grandfather's grave.*

In one crumbling, sun-warmed corner, Clare found a sprawling patch of wild strawberries, and made them her happy second breakfast, staining her mouth and hands. She trailed her hand in a creek that ran through the center of the castle, touched careful tongue to a wet finger. The taste was sweet.

Idea (as Finn would say): she'd see if she could guess the key before he even got here. Pleased to get a jump on him, she walked around peering at the crumbling walls, the soft-edged stones, looking for cracks or holes or something in-between-ish. No luck; but nothing could weigh on her light heart. She felt her way up narrow, edgeless stairs to the top of a rampart and looked around. Still no likely crack.

Instead of going down, she walked the edge of the wall, arms out for balance, a small figure making her way through vast ruins: a girl pretending to be a queen. Moving along the uncertain stone, she glanced around quickly for Finn, saw no one, then called, "I'm your queen! I command you!" to the cows and sheep. Her laughter floated over the wandering flowers, through the empty air.

She played on, alone, as she so often had when she was a much smaller girl, as she thought she had forgotten how to do. She balanced on the high stone wall with no idea of the danger she was in, and not only from the crumbling stone beneath her feet.

"Unfair, to start without me," said a voice behind her. She turned, almost lost her balance, laughed. He was sitting astride the wall, flute dangling from one hand. "Ready for your lesson?"

Clare straddled the wall facing him, a few feet away, and folded her hands in a parody of a good student. "I am indeed," she said. "Or no, but wait, a question. How do we do it in dreams, though? I keep thinking that. How do people go through gates in their dreams, if it's so hard, and you have to figure out the key?"

Finn swung a leg over and kicked at the stones with his heels. "Oh, in dreams, it's different. You people are all but fairies in your dreams—like fairy babies, if fairies had babies. Blind and deaf and dumb you wander, not knowing your powers, opening gates, making and unmaking recklessly, at the mercy of every emotion. You make cities rise and fall, monsters and murderers, much else. It's mad, watching what you do in dreams. You are a strange people," he added, "making with your eyes closed."

Clare wondered what she knew how to do in dreams, that she did not know she knew. But Finn had moved on to the lesson.

"To open a gate that is not your own, first you must know that gates exist, and that this is one. You are ahead of most humans in that, for you sense the drifting fairy-magic—"

"Oh my god. Can we just call it Strange?"

Finn half closed his eyes as if to restrain himself. "Strange, then. The drifting Strange around it. All humans can sense the Strange, but most pretend they don't. Why is that?"

So other people don't make fun of them. Or send them to a psychiatrist. "Because we don't think it's real, I guess. Same with magic, I mean, *fairy*-magic."

"Which for us is making," said Finn, "that looks like magic in your world. We make using the stuff of your world for our material."

"Still. I don't know if I believe in magic," said stubborn Clare. "I mean—yeah, it would be so cool. It would be amazing, if it were true. But it's not. Is it?"

Finn smiled his curious half-human, half-Strange smile. "That is exactly what the fairies say about love," he said. "And yet you call us the Strange." On his flute he blew three delicate notes and one mocking squeak. "But no matter magic now, for this is a lesson, and what have you learned? You gather that it is a gate, then you gather the *spirit* of the gate. Yes?"

Clare hesitated. "Maybe?" *Children playing on their grandfather's grave*, was that the spirit of this place?

"And then you make!" said Finn, pleased. "You make the key."

"Make . . . with, like, my hands?"

"Make in any way the key wants to be made. *Make*. Dream awake. Make a making to please the gate."

As she thought about this, Clare stood up on the wall again, stepping one foot in front of the other, careful with the balancing. She tried to turn to face Finn again without moving her feet, just turning on the balls. As she completed the turn, with a bit of arm-waving to balance, Finn's amused expression provoked a flash of memory. She saw another grinning Finn, smaller and softer, swinging his legs on that wall. "Finn! We played here once. Did we? When we were little? I think we did."

He looked unutterably pleased.

Another thought. "But you said there were no fairy babies."

A half smile.

"And you said there was no *change* where you're from, everything stays the same."

A nod, smile fading.

"But what about you? You were a baby, with me. And you changed, since then, you've grown up, like me."

His face closed up. "I'm different," he said. "I'm not—Clare, that's a tale too long for telling now. No, don't make such a face, it is no matter." Finn swung himself off the wall, hung precariously by his fingers, dropped to his feet. She couldn't see his face till he turned, but then it was clear again. "Let's do what we came for. Are you ready to begin?"

Surprisingly, Clare thought she was. "Though if I'm supposed to . . . I mean I didn't bring anything—drawing pencils or paints or anything."

"Not necessary," he said. He sat on a low stone and looked at her expectantly. "Make, my girl."

Clare flushed. "Uh, right. Not in front of you."

Finn opened his hands. "But, Clare, that's madness, don't you know I've seen—"

"Don't care what you've seen. Go to another part of the castle, go behind some walls until I call you. And *don't listen.* Say you won't."

He threw his hands in the air and walked through a crumbling aperture in the wall.

"SAY YOU WON'T!" called Clare.

"As you wish, mad Clare," said a faint voice, followed by a little flute trill.

Clare stood for a moment, as if listening—perhaps to see that Finn was really gone, perhaps for something else. *Children playing.* Well, it had been a while, but she would try.

She put out one leg, long and straight, drawing a toe in the dirt, then dropped lightly onto that foot; did the same with the other, then again: point-step; point-step. In this idle, half-dancing way she progressed around the perimeter of this large castle room. She stopped to pick a strawberry, but made the rule that she had to continue her point-step dance while balancing the strawberry on her tongue.

Part of her watched in astonishment, that she could remember so well, after all these years, how to play. Perhaps that fresh memory of small Clare playing here with small Finn had brought childhood close again. Or perhaps it was part of the magic of this place, to make it easy.

She made it halfway around the walls before the strawberry tipped so dangerously that she had to eat it. At that place, following her rule, she stopped and sat down. She was within arm's length of a crumbling gray wall with a low, shallow indentation, as if a small statue had once stood there.

Cross-legged Clare thought for a moment, and then began.

"The other day, day, day," she began. As she chanted, she lightly slapped her knees, then clapped her hands, then pressed her hands against the wall.

"The other day, day, day

I met a fae, fae, fae" (she *thought* you could call them that)

"It ran away, way, way

I cried all day, day, day."

Now she speeded up, and added some tricky every-other-time crossed-arm movements.

"But it came back back back back back,

And brought a sack sack sack sack sack—"

(Clare had no idea where this rhyme was going. And wait, was it a trick of her eye—it was hard to look closely and keep up the movements—or was the nook she sat before beginning to shimmer? She sped up.)

"And from inside side side side side,

It pulled its bride bride bride bride bride"

(The stone definitely seemed to be thinning and softening, becoming more mist than stone, and beyond the mist, Clare could almost see . . .)

"We danced a ring ring ring ring ring ring

Till we could—"

Clare stopped. In a blink, the stone had become stone again, and the air had gone ice-cold, and the Strange of the place had turned dark and poisonous. She spun around, rising to her knees.

Just inside the vine-curtained doorway stood a man in a black suit. To Clare on her knees, he seemed enormously tall—tall and broad, with shaggy black eyebrows and eyes beneath them like wet black ink. He was smiling, but not a nice smile: it was the smile of a cat who sees a bird with a broken wing. Or it was a smile painted on like a mask, like a clown's face, and if you peeled it off, the sight would be hideous and unbearable.

One of his deep black eyes was staring and fixed, and that eye gleamed with something like fire.

Her umbrella dangled from his curled finger.

Clare screamed.

Finn came running, of course, flute put away in his pocket now. But by the time he arrived, the man had vanished. Clare, furious with herself, kept saying, "It's nothing, only he startled me, I'm being an idiot, whatever, he's gone." But "Describe him," said Finn, and when Clare got to the part about the fixed, unmoving eye, he looked distressed.

"I fear a thing," he said, "and I must go home to say. Ah, it is a shame, I was going to show you a beautiful making I made in your changing world, I did want you to see it. Another day, soon, we will."

"I think I almost had it," said Clare. "The key, I mean. I could see a sort of door opening, it went all misty and . . . anyway I think I found the key, I really do."

"This surprises me not at all," said Finn. "I only wish I could have seen the making, Clare." He hesitated. "Listen: this needs not, I am sure, but I want to give you something."

He held her hand, palm up, and Clare felt herself go perfectly still at the touch. Into her palm he placed a flat black rock, square and glossy as a mirror. His hand was cool, and the rock was cool. "Keep this by you," he said. "It's a bit of shield. Not a big bit, but a bit enough. You may need it."

"Why—"

"Meet me in-between, just before twilight. I will take you to meet one you must meet."

It had been difficult to get into the tree unnoticed after dinner. But Clare announced with awkward untruthfulness that she was going to bed early. "Jet lag," her father had said, and then: "Clare—I thought perhaps tomorrow morning, we'd decide about your mother's ashes. What do you think?" She had nodded yes.

She had watched from her loft till her father stepped outside to get something from the car, then slipped down and into the tree. Now she sat in the in-between, watching blue foxfire throb along a vein of the tree, until she felt the familiar arm against her arm. Finn's voice in her ear said, "Come with me, to meet someone."

"Who?" she said, to stall. She liked it here, the only-Finn-and-Clare place.

"Her of the Cliffs."

Clare was not sure that sounded like a person she wanted to meet. "Is she one of your people? Is she nice?"

Finn snorted. "One of my people, yes. She is our Hunter—our leader, you would say. Nice, howsomever: no. But I believe you must meet with her, and she agrees."

Clare did not want to go. The air of the tree felt familiar and comforting already, so starry and still, faintly scented with wood and herbs. "But is she—"

"Wait and see for yourself what she is," said Finn. "Now watch. You should know how to do this, too." He placed his hand onto a knot in one of the yew roots at their feet. "Here, here, here," he crooned, stroking it gently. Whispered, to Clare: "I am thinking and asking and feeling only of where in the two worlds I want to go."

And just that moment the space around them got larger; or perhaps they got smaller. And the wood grew less solid—Clare could see again the many veins, twisted together, veins and shoots where the thick sap moved slow. And the tree got larger still, or they got smaller still, and she followed Finn as he stepped inside one of the roots.

Now they were in a new and dangerous place. The wind was angry, where they were; the wind was mad.

Clare sat astride a high rock pinnacle, thrusting out of a wild ocean at the base of an enormous cliff. Clare's own home stood on a cliff above the sea, but that cliff was doll-sized compared to these dark, towering crags. It was as if the edge of a continent had been ripped way by a raging hand.

Clare bent low over the rock like a rider on a runaway horse, clinging to the sides so as not to be blown off. It was a wind like anger, raging and changeable, a hand that slapped your hair against your face, snatched the sock from your foot and blew it—where? Clare watched her gray sock sail out over the vast ocean. How slow the sea moved under the angry wind, until it reached the rocks and rose up to slap them hard.

"Where are we?" she said, her voice shaking only a little, so little she hoped he couldn't hear, though she hoped he could, as well. She didn't like it here. She put her hand to the silver star at her throat to slow her pounding heart.

Cool Finn, cold-fishy Finn, straddled the narrow rock ahead of her, legs dangling, looking out to sea. He said, not turning, "That is the Cliffs of Moher behind us, a great spot of ours, great with beauty, I mean, but also great with my people."

"I don't like it here," said trembling Clare. "The wind doesn't want us here. If I fell, I would die."

The wind whipped his long black hair up and around and down again. He said, "Clare. You are here to know that you are in danger."

"From the wind?"

He pointed up. "See that bird," he said.

Clare saw a white seabird riding the wind, up, down, its wings still, serene.

Finn said, "You feel the wind is a bully, beating you. But that is your seeing. That is your story, not the wind's. To a bird who rides it, that wind is only a kind hand. Because the bird rides the wind's power. Do you understand?"

Clare, bitter, cold, and wind-battered, frowned stubbornly. "But a bird can fly. I can't fly."

He turned to look at her, and his face was troubled. "If you cling to the safety of the rock, indeed you can't. To fly, you open your arms and fall, heart first, trusting the wind to bear you up. That's what the birds do."

"Like you know how to fly!" said Clare, then wondered—well,

after all, maybe he did. She watched through the tangle of red hair across her face, the tangle of dark hair across his.

He looked abashed. "Well," he said. "Once I did. I trusted, and I leaped, and I flew. It is hard, though, the trusting. It's hard, hard—and hard every time, the trusting, or so I've heard. I was a boy then, and it was easier. I never could again."

"Well, I'm not a fairy, so I'm not going to try. Also because I'm not *insane*."

Finn smiled, but the smile faded. "You should not make Her wait," he said. He turned his back again. "Climb down."

So Clare climbed down the side of the rock ledge, one bare foot and one socked foot, clinging with cold hands to the salty-wet rock, finding small painful edges for her feet. Just above the slapping, frothing waves, the rock flattened, creating a place to stand, half sheltered from the wind.

A woman stood with her back to Clare, facing the sea as Finn had done. She had reddish hair pulled back and roughly clipped behind, wore knee boots and a fawn jacket. A quiver of copper-tipped arrows hung just below her coppery hair, and a bow was slung over one shoulder. She didn't turn around.

Clare's teeth chattered as she waited, and not only from the cold wind. She was overwhelmed by the wild and fierce Strange of this place, of this woman. Through every vein, down to her smallest bones, she felt magnetized by the woman's power. It was hard to catch her breath. She wanted to weep or kneel.

The woman turned. Her face was long and unsmiling, with strong bones and a fierce, straight nose. She seemed about her father's age, Clare guessed. Her eyes were dark brown—dark and kind? dark and cruel? Clare could only see that this woman was far more powerful than the wild cliff wind, that the wind was this woman's smallest sigh.

Clare held tight to the face of the rock beside her. She looked away, because she couldn't look at her.

The woman did not raise her voice, but it pierced the raging wind and crashing waves. "Clare who guards the tree," she said. "I asked Finn to bring you here, to tell you what is at stake. Listen.

"A thousand years or more ago, the human and Timeless worlds split apart."

I know that. But Clare was too shy to speak.

"That split left the two worlds with fragments of each other in their hearts. Humans—caught inside the churning changes of growth and decay, loss and love—humans long toward the perfect, Timeless world of art and dreams. But we who live in that austere, unvarying world, we long toward transformation and love." She paused and smiled a Finnishly half smile. "Although we do not always admit it."

She continued. "Finn told you that the connections between your world and ours are breaking down. When the world split, both our people were so lonely for the other; now they begin to forget, even, what they are lonely for. When you showed your people fairy-makings, what did they see?"

"They didn't see," said Clare, soft.

"And do they seem happy, not seeing?"

"No. They seem angry and lost."

"My people as well. I point them to love, and they shrug. This is why we must keep the gates open. When you protect that tree you protect the connection between human and"—(was that a tiny smile?)—"the Strange. If those gates close up entirely, it is the end of dreaming and making in your world. Your world will turn gray and colorless. And ours will grow colder and colder, our makings perfect, and loveless, and meaningless. Do you understand?"

Clare nodded. Her stomach hurt. Proud as she was to be a guardian, it seemed like a great weight to carry alone.

"Now I have a warning for you, Clare," said the woman. "I also have a gift. And I will answer one question."

Clare thought she had nothing to ask. She was afraid of this power and this wild wind, and she wanted only to be done and home.

"If you don't yet know your question," said the woman, "then I will begin with the gift. Open your hand."

Still clinging to the rock with her right hand, still looking away, still unable to look the woman in the face, Clare stretched her left hand out toward the woman. She felt the electrifying touch of the woman's dry hand, and the soft something placed in her palm. It felt like an olive or a small, smooth fruit.

"When the wolf's jaws are closing on you—and I fear they soon may be—eat this, and come under my protection."

Clare held it tight. Behind her the ocean slammed the side of the big cliffs in rage, and she was splattered by salty foam.

"Now your question," said the woman. "Ask."

Clare opened her mouth, with no idea what she would ask, and what came out was this: "Why is Finn the only one of you who changes?"

In answer, the woman told Clare this story. Afterward, when Clare remembered this moment, she remembered it as a kind of fairy tale, for that was how she heard it that day.

Long, long ago, just before the spine of the world was split, when my people and yours shared the one world, when the fairies had change and birth and death, and your people had magic and making—this story goes back to that time.

There was a dark man, then—I mean all kinds of dark, you

understand?—a fairy man, named Balor. A prophecy was made about this Balor, that his grandson would be his undoing.

Balor had but one child, a daughter. To prevent her from ever bearing a child, he locked this unfortunate girl in a high tower in a deep forest. She was there in the tower when the world split, and felt the tremble of the earth, felt the splitting in two of her own heart, as all did that day.

Soon after that terrible time, a human man wandering his own world found and unlocked a fairy gate. This gate led him to Balor's tower, where he found the lonely girl. He could not get her out, but he visited her often, and of course they fell in love. His name was Finnegan, this human man. You might know Finn's Cap, which is the gate he used. It is named for him.

The daughter became pregnant. Balor, furious, hid himself within the tower, caught Finnegan, and hung him on a tree outside, just where his daughter could see her lover's death struggle. Her heart and mind both broke at the sight. She went into labor at that moment—too soon, do you understand? Far too soon. She gave birth to a son who was not ready to be born. And as she gave birth, she died, because her half-human baby's blood had mixed with her blood, which made it possible for her to die.

Balor seized the tiny, half-made infant, already an orphan, and made to throw him off the tower. But the screams of the girl in labor had attracted others, including I myself. I saw Balor at the tower window, holding the child above his head. With a flaming arrow, I shot out Balor's eye. And I caught the child as he dropped.

The fairies banished Balor to the human world and locked all their gates against him. Meanwhile, I took up the child, wrapped carefully in warm cloths. I packed him into the crook of a yew tree that stood with roots in both the fairy and human worlds—just as the baby had roots in both those worlds. The fairies built a mound of stone and earth all around the tree, and they chose a wise and kind human woman—human, but with more than a little fairy blood—to be guardian of the tree and what it protected. Her daughter was its guardian afterward, and every daughter after continued to be its guardian.

And one day, centuries later—because a changeling creature made of earth and fairy takes its own time to be born—the baby boy opened his eyes inside the tree.

And that same day, that very day, a girl was born in the home, and opened her eyes. And so they grew together.

"Finn is that boy," said Clare. "He's half human. That's why he was a baby, and grew up."

"Yes."

"And I am the girl," said Clare, wondering to find her own story coming in at the end of such a long, strange one. "And my house was built to hide and protect him."

"Yes," said Her of the Cliffs. "But the story is not over. Now I must give you your warning."

Clare straightened as well as she could against the raging wind.

"Did Finn tell you that in the past year, the destruction of the gates has increased? All over your world, gates have been demolished, chopped down, poisoned."

"He did say something like that, but that you don't know why?"

"Now we know," said Her of the Cliffs. "Balor has come to suspect that the baby, the grandson prophesied to destroy him, did not die that day. He has been destroying the gates to preserve his own safety, as he believes—in order to keep the boy from entering the human world to destroy him. He will separate our two worlds entirely and forever, to keep that from happening."

"Is Finn going to destroy him?"

Her of the Cliffs shrugged. "It is the prophecy. Prophecies come true in their own ways. Balor knows for certain that Finn survived. But he must sense something of the importance of the yew tree and the home we built around it, and now he sniffs about it like a wild dog."

Her of the Cliffs paused, and a swell of her Strange power swept through Clare like a wave. "Clare the guardian," she said, with something like gentleness: "that was Balor of the Evil Eye who found you at the castle. Understand: the wolf comes for you now—not just for the roads, but for you, because you are the guardian of the tree. He comes to your door. At all costs, Clare—at all costs—protect the tree. Do not let him in. And keep my gift and Finn's gift with you at all times, especially outside your home. In your home, there is some protection. Out of your home, there is none, except those gifts."

Clare closed her fingers more securely around the fruit, or whatever it was, in her left hand.

"And not only you are in danger," the woman continued. The wind had tugged strands of hair from its clip, so that threads of red-gold danced around her head like little flames. "So is anyone who loves or helps you. So is your own father, who in hazard soon will leave you."

"He would never do that!" Clare shouted into the wind.

But he did, he did, he did.

6

Deep Voice and Dark Eye

That night, Clare sat with ankles locked around her chair, writing in her notebook. Notes for a new one. After many crossed-out words and lines, she had

In a belly of earth and stone, two eggs—

The color of winter,

The color of autumn—

Held in the root-claw nest

Of a brooding tree.

It was not satisfying. *Brooding* was good because it meant two things, but she didn't know if the tree actually *was* very brooding. It felt happier than that. Also, she liked a poem to do something or other with rhythm or rhyme, and this one just sort of sat there.

So what: just a note for a poem. She went to bed, thinking: *Making is hard. I hope it gets easier.*

As she slept, Clare dreamed she was deep underground, in a black, hot place. Across from her lay a great round dish or pool, but the pool was full of fire, not water. Above the pool, hung on the wall by a looping black thread, was a mask, like a comedy mask, a laughing mask. In one of the eyeholes sat a perfect white egg.

Behind her, an animal groaned. Clare whirled, somehow certain that someone had fallen in the fire. And yes: the flames roared higher now, as if they had been fed. But she could see nothing inside them.

When she turned back, the mask's face had become tragedy, and its mouth was open in grief or horror. Its eye-egg had broken, and was a scramble of blood and yellow flesh and light.

Clare woke up sweating, her heart drumming hard. Thin gray light filtered through the quartz. Her left hand was closed tight around something—the woman's gift. She saw that it *was* a fruit of some kind, she had been right about that: oval and dark red.

"Clare?" her father called. It sounded like he'd been calling for a while. "I know it's early, but I need you down here."

"Coming!" she called back. The previous evening flooded back: the woman of the cliffs (the woman, whom she had been so eager to leave, but whom she now somehow longed to return to); the warning about Balor, and about the wolf (did they have wolves in Ireland?); the story of Finn.

As she dressed, she put the fruit in her pocket next to the obsidian. It was strangely silent below.

"Dad!" she called. No answer.

She climbed quickly down—nothing—and out the door, where with weird relief, she found him. He was looking at his phone with a worried expression, holding his hair up with one hand. So she returned inside and sat near the yew, pushing at the trunk with her feet. She was thinking hard. She wondered if she could talk to her father about any of this, which seemed like a crazy idea, but sometimes he surprised her.

But when he came back in and sat down at the edge of the couch with an absent, worried look, all those thoughts dropped away.

"I'd hoped to put this off while we settled in, but I've dawdled too long—there's been a second cave-in at the mine, and now some men are trapped. If I don't go, they could die." He ran his hand through his hair unhappily. "They could die anyway. So we have to leave this morning, right away. Get dressed, my girl, and pop some breakfast in you?"

Clare hesitated, and glanced at the yew. It didn't feel right to leave it after what she'd heard yesterday. "Do I have to go?" she asked. "How long will you be gone?"

Her father looked surprised. "I hadn't thought of leaving you here," he said. "But it's true: Ireland not being Texas, the mine is only a two-hour drive from here. I could be back after dinner tonight. Still, we're so new here . . ." He paused.

Clare saw his indecision. "I'll stay. It's no big deal. If anything goes wrong, which it won't, I can find Jo, right?"

"Oh!" he said, jumping up. "I'd completely forgotten this." He dug through a nest of shopping bags, then triumphantly held up a phone—just a small flip phone, but still, Clare was glad to see it.

"I meant to give you this after dinner, only you had an early night." Clare nodded, self-conscious and a bit guilty. "It's only temporary until I can get you a proper one with data and so forth that works here. Look, I've put in my number, and Jo's as well."

"So really, if I have a phone, there's no reason to worry, right?"

"Well," he said. "Still I hate to leave you alone a whole day in a new country."

"I was born here," said Clare.

Her father smiled. "So you were."

A few minutes later—minutes crammed with paternal admonitions about staying safe, eating sensibly, and not hesitating to call—her father had packed up his laptop and they were standing by the car. "Ach, I almost forgot—take the key, so you're not trapped inside all day. Don't lose it, as it's the only one I know of."

He gave her a quick kiss and a long hug and climbed in the car. Just as he was turning the key, Clare had a thought. She ran to the car window. "Mom's ashes," she said. "We were going to decide this morning."

Her father put his hand on her face. His eyes were sad. "I know, sweet," he said. "But they have waited, and they will wait a little longer. I promise it won't be long. At least you're here with those lovely ashes now." He pulled back to look at her. "I'm sorry to leave you, Clare," he said. "But I will come back tonight. Tell me now: is it okay? Do you feel all right, staying alone?"

All the worry in his voice.

"Sure, of course," Clare said, though her heart said suddenly: *I don't know.*

Her father kissed her face and smiled. "Stay safe," he said. The tires crunched the rocks, and he was gone.

Who in hazard soon will leave you.

She felt in her pocket for the black stone Finn had given her and held it so tight her hand warmed around it.

Clare slipped through the small passageway and into the empty house, trailing fingers on the stone. She made toast and washed the plate. She sat for a while in the in-between, and felt safe there, and a little lonely. She and Finn had not spoken much after the cliffs yesterday. She wondered what it was like, to grow up with such a prophecy around you. It must feel a little heavy, and a little sad.

She wondered what it was like in Timeless and thought of trying the way Finn had shown her, holding the root and imagining.

But after what she had heard from Her of the Cliffs, she didn't want to go so far from her tree.

Idea: the gate at the castle. She had almost had its key, almost learned to unlock it. She would go back to see if she could finish the job. From the castle, she could keep her hill always in sight.

She ran upstairs to get her commonplace book and pen, in case that made it easier. She felt in her bones that she could not simply repeat the game from yesterday—it would have to be some new kind of playing. Carefully she locked the old door behind her and slipped the long iron key into her pocket.

~

But at the castle Clare found it was hard to get in the mood to play, for what Her of the Cliffs had said haunted her. She took her notebook up to the top of the castle wall, in order to keep an eye on her tree, though she knew it was silly. Straddling the wall, she opened the notebook to the frustrating poem from last night. After a dozen scratches out and false starts, she finally jotted a note underneath it:

I was born the same day as the prophesied boy. Am I part of the prophecy?

Adding, after some thought:

The one-eyed man.

Unable even to pretend these were notes for poems, she shut the notebook and lay back along the wall, watching the clouds gather and darken. "Rain, rain," she sang idly. "Rain, rain, go away, come again some other day, I think this gate wants me to play, rain, rain, go away." She laughed to herself and swung down inside the castle, began her point-step walk again, arms out like a ballet dancer, notebook still in one elegantly cocked hand. "Rain, rain, go away," she sang, point-stepping beside the wall, "come again some other day," stepping balletically past the vine-covered door; "I think this gate wants me to—"

And the notebook was snatched from her hand. As she whirled around, her angry thought was *Finn, DON'T.*

But it wasn't Finn, and her anger turned to terror, and she backed away. Her mother's green, cloth-covered notebook looked small in the large hand of black-haired, one-eyed Balor.

To make it worse, he was smiling his masklike smile, as if nothing were wrong at all. "I thought I might find you here again," he said. "I have your umbrella. And it would seem that we share an interest in ancient history." Clare must have looked blank, because he gestured around the castle. "I'm so sorry to have interrupted your . . . performance." The smile became a smirk.

Clare flushed as red as she ever had. "Give me that, please," she said, holding out her hand. "It's mine." Her stupid voice was shaking.

"Oh, it's yours, then, is it?" said Balor. His voice was deep as a lake, and every word a rippling black wave. "Are you"—he squinted at the notebook with his right eye, while his left remained open and staring—"'Áine Quinn, Fifth, no, *Sixth* Class'?" He glanced at her. "You look a bit old for it."

"It was my mother's," said Clare. "And now it's mine." Panicky anguish rose in her chest as he continued to thumb through it.

"Ah, I see. Yes, the handwriting changes, from good schoolgirl to sloppy mess. And the taste in poetry goes from simperingly pretentious to merely bad." He snapped the book shut and put it in his pocket.

"It's mine," Clare repeated. Her voice sounded absurdly small and petulant. Or worse, as if she might cry. The fruit and the stone in her pocket felt small.

Suddenly Balor was standing quite close to her, too close. "Clare," he said, low and near her ear, "give me the key."

She stumbled back several steps and did not reply. He neither followed nor took his eye from her. "Give me the key to your house," he repeated. "I have tried to get in without it, but that house has deep and very old protections around its lock. So give me the key."

"I don't have it," Clare lied. It was cold in her pocket. "My father took it with him."

Balor said, "Leaving you locked out of the house all day and into the night. An unusual decision."

Clare tried again. "It's hidden, and I won't tell you where, I never will."

Balor walked toward her. "Possibly it's hidden," he said. "Or, much more possibly, you have it with you." She backed up until she was pressed against a wall. He stood close. "Clare, stubborn Clare," he said, soft and cold. "Do not disobey me. I don't like disobedient girls." He towered above her, a black mountain she couldn't see around.

"Let me explain something, Clare," he continued. His coat was actually touching her arms, which were crossed against her torso. "I intend to protect myself. That means I must get into your house, to destroy something there. And I know that you have the key. It's tiresome, but one of the protections of that house is that only the guardian can let me in, and no one else. And I cannot take the key from you by force. So give me the key, which is in—this?—pocket." He touched the pocket, lightly.

Clare slid away into the open space and took big breaths of air, as if she had been holding her breath. "Well, I never will give it to you," she said. "And you can never make me." She felt a wild bravery, like a bird caught in a room, smashing against walls, intent on getting out.

"Can't I, though?" said Balor. His fixed eye bored into her shifting, frightened ones. "That's an interesting question. Let's test it. Do you know where your father is?"

"Yes, I do," said Clare. "And I'm not telling you." If she could make a run for it, get a little farther away, she could pull out her cell phone and call . . . who? Her father? Too far away to help. Did 911 work in Ireland? Wasn't it some other number? She glanced at the vine-draped doorway.

Balor, seeing that glance, walked toward the doorway, setting himself between Clare and it. He was smiling. "You should know there is no help for you," he said. "I have friends everywhere that matters, powerful friends, who owe me a great deal, in the guard—the police, you would say—in the schools, in hospitals. Everywhere. No safety for you, there is none, understand that. There is no stranger you can trust."

The hard little rectangle of cell phone in her back pocket.

"No safety for your father, either. I know where he is, Clare. I know, because I put him there. I own that mine. I bought it. And I buried those men alive, because I knew it would bring him to me. If I've already done all that, Clare, what do you think I will do to your father to get you to give me the key?"

How that made her feel: he might as well have sliced open one of her veins and let her blood drain to the ground. "You're lying," she whispered. But she knew he was not. *Not only you are in danger. So is anyone who loves or helps you. So is your own father, who in hazard soon will leave you.*

Balor stared at her, as if waiting for her to say more. "All right," he said finally. "Let's try another way." He turned toward the castle entrance, then paused. "I'm just fetching something from my car. Don't go anywhere."

That false and sickening smile.

The moment he left, Clare pulled out her phone, fumbling at the unfamiliarity of it, her heart pounding. She pressed 9, stopped. *You should know there is no help for you.* Instead, hands shaking, she found the contact labeled "Dad" and pressed call.

But the phone just zweed and beeped until a woman's voice said something about "out of range." It wouldn't even let her leave a message.

Grief swelled up in her throat. *There is no stranger you can trust.*

But there was Jo. She found the entry, called. It rang into voice mail. In wild agitation, Clare walked toward the castle wall and bent low to block her voice.

"I'm at the castle, Jo," she whispered. "It's Clare, at the castle, and there's a man here, he—" She hesitated, knowing she might be cut off at any moment. "Please come fast," she said. "I'm afraid."

A brutally strong hand wrenched hers from her ear, slapped the phone to the ground, where it was ground to pieces under a large, shiny black shoe. A growl in her ear: "I have something just for you, something I've been waiting to show you."

With the loping, purposeful gait of a hungry dog, Balor returned to the castle entrance. Watching him, Clare felt more and more like a small animal in a large trap. He picked up something he'd left leaning near the door—something tall and wrapped up in brown paper, shaped like a broom or a shovel, only Balor held it carefully, as if it might break or escape. As he unwrapped it, his big body in his black suit blocked it, so that Clare couldn't see it until he moved away.

When she did see it, she almost laughed. Almost laughed, but almost screamed. Her mouth stayed open, not knowing which to do.

The thing—the creature, she almost thought—was just a painted board on a stick: an ancient-looking rectangular board, maybe one foot wide and three feet tall, on a weathered three-foot stick. On the board was a face—at least, a sort of face, painted in faded reds and yellows and blacks, the colors of blood and infection and nightmares. It had one eye, as black as Balor's. But where the other eye should have been was a sort of explosion, a chaos. Above the eye and the explosion were two frowning brows. The thing, the creature, had a mouth, too: an angular mouth, open wide, as if to scream.

Or to swallow.

It's just a stupid painted board, painted to scare you, Clare thought. And it did scare her; it scared every nerve, scared her to the ground. It was the firefly face made real. It felt ugly, and bad, and strong.

"So what is that thing?" Clare said. She meant her voice to sound tough and unimpressed, but it sounded very small.

"It is a totem," said the man. His voice resonated against the crumbling stone. "The way that quartz pulls the sun down into your house—yes, I know about that, I know quite a lot—this totem pulls down a great power to me." His smile bared yellow teeth. "A power you won't like, not at all."

"I don't want to be near that thing, and I won't stay if it's here." The words came out fast, all on their own. Without planning it, she tried to run past him, then angled sharply to dart past him on the other side.

With one arm, Balor knocked her to the ground. She lay there gasping in pain and shock.

"I'm afraid I can't let you go," he said. "There is nowhere for you to go, anyway. Where are you safe? Nowhere at all."

Clare's hand slipped down to feel the outline of the fruit and the stone in her pocket: her protections. They felt small and still and useless.

At dawn the next morning, Clare sat in a far corner of the castle, as far as she could get from the totem, which was not far enough. The sky to the east was red as a rash. Measles red, inflamed red. A-wound-that-isn't-healing red. The sky around the sunrise glowed its usual radiant blue, but this morning the sunrise was an inflammation running along the edge of the world.

It had been a long and terrible night. Balor left her alone, but the totem hovered near, and Clare slept almost not at all. The few times a car came down the road she stood up, knowing it was her father, it had to be.

But her father, who had said he'd be home after dinner, still hadn't come, and neither had Jo.

Clare watched some birds a few feet from her, pecking at the June grass. They hopped from spot to spot, their eyes like tiny black beads shifting and rolling to find the food. They looked like little aliens. She pulled at her mother's silver necklace, which felt too tight around her neck, as if it were choking her. "I *hate* this thing," she said out loud, and yanked it so hard that it snapped.

One hand over her mouth, the broken chain hanging limp in the other, Clare sat still and shocked. *It's that board, that horrible thing*, she thought. *It's making the sunrise ugly, it's making birds ugly, it's making me hate what I love.*

She put the chain in her pocket next to the flat black stone Finn had given her. Where was the protection it promised? She pulled the stone out, saw part of her face reflected in its glossy black. That eye—was it her eye? It was her face, it was, but the eye seemed not hers, although it seemed loving, and sad, and familiar. Clare looked into the eye, trying to remember.

Ah, she could not bear being near that hideous totem.

She remembered Her of the Cliffs saying: *In your house, there is some protection. Outside, there is none.* If she could just get back to her house, and turn the key before Balor could reach the door. Balor sat by the entrance, cleaning his nails, and the totem blocked that way. Was there another? Obsidian tight in her right hand, she stood and moved carefully, slowly, trying to see with her peripheral vision a wall low enough to climb and jump from.

A flash of dirty yellow and red. Clare jerked around.

It was the totem, leaning against the wall inches away, watching her.

Clare almost screamed; she tried to scream, but her breath was gone and she couldn't find it. Only the smallest sound came out, like the cry of a small, lost animal. How did he get the totem here so fast?

Drained, despairing, almost ready to throw up, she thought: This thing will always be here, now. I will never, ever be free of it. *Dad, don't go. I changed my mind.* But he was gone. Was he even—but if she thought that thought, everything was over.

She closed her fists till the nails bit in. A way out. After all, the castle was supposedly a gate.

As if she could find it in herself to feel *playful*, with this totem here, with Balor here.

And even if she could—the wild-strawberry, childlike Strange she had sensed the first day was gone. This totem had poisoned the gate, she was sure, warped and bent it past use, perhaps forever. She knelt on the ground and put her face to the grass in despair. A shadow fell over her.

"You might make it," he said. "I don't think you would, for I am quick, and the totem is quicker; but you might. And then you'd be safe inside your home, at least for a while. But your father, now—would he be safe? That's another question altogether. Life is very precarious in a mine."

God, how could she not have thought of that?

What was there, then, except to give up the tree? Was it worth her life? Maybe. But her father's life? Would she sacrifice—?

A hand seized her arm, jerked her up painfully. "Enough self-pity for now," said Balor. "Let's have some culture, shall we? Let's have some serious art, while we wait for you to understand your position. Because look what I've found!" He waved her mother's commonplace book, upside down. "I've found some very, very serious po-e-try."

"Ah, *don't*," mumbled Clare, and it was a cry from her heart. But Balor sat her down, and sat down beside her, the wool of his black pants brushing her leg, and began to read.

The wind picked up and changed, felt like rain. In a mock-stentorian tone, like an old Shakespearian actor, Balor began to read, raising his voice above the rising wind: "'In a belly of earth and stone, two eggs . . .' Why, that's poetic, Clare. Not poetry, of course. But poet-*ic.* Poet-*ish*, you might say." He continued in his mock-actor voice: "'The color of winter, / The color of autumn—' Is it 'white and brown' you're trying to say?"

Clare stared at the ground, fists tucked under her arms. She felt as if he were throwing rocks at her unprotected heart.

"'Held in the root-claw nest / Of a brooding tree.' 'The root-claw nest'—well, that's hopeless, root *and* claw *and* nest? That's a dog's breakfast. Ah, wait, and there's a note below: 'I was born the same day as the prophesied boy. . . .'"

Balor stopped reading. His good eye lifted, looked at Clare, who looked back with her jaw set and her face hot. Balor returned to the notebook, reading now in his own deep voice: "'Am I part of the prophecy?'" He began to leaf backward.

Stop it, stop it, stop TOUCHING it, thought Clare, frantically and uselessly.

"'Along the sea, the moonlight spills / A kind of path' . . . juvenile," Balor muttered. He was skimming through as if looking for something. "'For one with feet, not fins . . . Toward stone and tree, / Toward home. / The finless girl flies to her Finn . . .'"

His voice died away to almost nothing. "'Tucked deep in the roots . . .' I knew it," he said. He flung the book to the ground and began to pace in a strange fire, at once exultant and afraid. "I knew the boy was alive. I sensed him, I have done for years." He turned on Clare. "Where is he? No messing now. No more disobedience. Tell me where he is."

Clare shook her head, jaw still set, eyes on her mother's book splayed on the ground. A few fat drops of rain fell, spattering the notebook, dripping cold down her face. The wind rose and whined, lifting her hair.

Balor was close to her now. He leaned down, his breath hot and oily against her ear, and said low: "My totem is preparing. I could have it kill you, and then wait until your father comes home, and persuade him to let me in. Or I could simply wait and have it kill your father. Do not mistake me, Clare. You and I are not playing a game here. I have already won."

Blood throbbed in Clare's throat; she thought she might faint. The wind was high and wild now, and the rain was a storm. Water slid down her face and under her sweater.

Balor pulled away, but his black eyes held hers. "Or you can give me the key, now," he said. "You don't even have to hand it to me, you know. You could simply drop it on the ground and walk away, as simple as that."

Without warning, the wind and rain stopped. In the sudden silence, Clare heard an odd noise, a dry noise, like a rattle or a scratching. Something scratching in the silence, just above and behind her. She wanted to look, but she held her head steady.

Balor did not look, because he knew the sound; he knew it well.

The scratching came again, louder, followed by a rattle like a snake's. The dry sound echoed off the stone walls until it seemed to come from everywhere. Clare held the obsidian tighter in one fist.

Gray, anxious light filtered down through the looming clouds. By now Clare's heart pounded like a stampede. She didn't want to look up to see what made the rattling, scratching sound. She was afraid that she knew what it was.

She was right. Above them, hovering in the air, was the open-mouthed, mad-eyed totem. Clare couldn't see what was holding it up. *Something must be, it must be*, she said to herself, though she knew nothing was.

The totem dragged itself and its silent scream along the stone wall across from Clare, then back a little, then toward it again. That was the rattle—the stick dragging itself along the stones, back and forth. Its hideous face frowned down on her, its slashing, open mouth, painted with a hand of rage. The gray sky glowed around it.

Wind and rain had begun again, stirring the air like a frantic sea.

The totem's mouth yawned open. Clare was as frozen as a mouse watching a snake. Why not give up the key? Why protect the tree—to make sure people could have *dreams* at night, and make up stories, and draw stupid pictures? How was that worth her life, or her father's life? How could a rock and a piece of fruit protect her from that thing? As the rain and wind battered her from all sides, hopelessness and despair washed through her. What did it matter, what did anything? *Fairies*, god.

In her right hand she still held the obsidian tight. Her left hand slipped down to her pocket, where the key lay heavy and cold.

And at that moment, a low voice, warm and clear as a clarinet, cut through the rain and wind.

"Clare!" Jo called. "Clare, it's all right, I'm here."

7

Down the Fairy Road

Relief swept through Clare like a clean wind: it was Jo, it was Jo, everything would be all right now. Jo crossed to face Balor, who stood with his back to the totem. She murmured, "Move clear, child."

Defending me. I have a protector. She walked a few yards from Jo, but not too far.

Jo raised her voice. "I know you for what you are, old Balor."

Clare closed her hand around the obsidian.

"And you're not welcome here, or anywhere near here," she continued. "I've protected that house all my life, and I'll protect it now, and you'll never see the inside of it. And this girl is my girl, and I am taking her out of your wicked grasp." She pulled her phone out and dialed three quick numbers.

"Oh, Jo," he said. "Oh, Jo, we are enemies, then. But I have been expecting someone to come for this girl, and I am well prepared."

As the storm receded, the totem's ratcheting against the stone walls was loud, loud. Jo was talking into the phone, but Clare couldn't hear what she said.

Then the totem stopped.

"Clare, run," said Jo. Her voice was steady, but somehow Clare felt afraid.

"Yes, Clare," said the man, mocking. "Run, run, run, as fast as you can!"

Jo and Balor stood facing each other, only yards apart. He seemed twice Jo's size, though that couldn't be right.

"The summoning is complete." Balor's voice was intense, galvanized, but he stood relaxed beneath the totem and its widening jaws. He did not look up. He looked only at Jo.

Clare stayed.

A wind arose. Winds start from far away; but this one seemed to come from within the ruined castle itself. It started low and slow, but within a minute it howled and spun inside the castle walls, and the light grew grayer still, almost black. Clare could hardly see. The winds whipped so wildly it was hard to stay upright.

Jo stumbled, then straightened, her hair blown hard around her face. The phone dropped from her hand.

Balor stood still. The wind did not touch him at all. He opened his mouth, as if to scream, but he didn't scream. His mouth made the shape of the mouth of the totem hanging above him. Balor made his mouth as if to scream: but the scream itself, a shattering howl of rage, came not from him, but from the totem.

As the totem screamed, three things happened at once. The first was a realization: Clare said to herself, in astonishment, *Oh, it was my mother's eye, that was the eye in the stone.*

The second was that, as the scream began, Clare threw the obsidian in her hand to Jo. She threw as if her body had chosen for her—the stone was flying from her hand before she thought. And although Clare had always had a good eye and good aim, this time her arm and hand knew before her eye, and threw with speed and surety.

It's a bit of shield—not a big bit, but a bit enough.

But a third thing happened, too, as the totem screamed. It was as if that howl of rage were a taut line, pulling some dreadful fish from the depths of the totem. But this fish was a bolt of lightning. For a split second, the ruined castle lit up in a bright white light. The flash was so bright that Clare could see every crumbling detail, even on the highest stones. She threw her hand in front of her eyes.

But she had seen, she had already seen, that the bolt had come through the totem's mouth, as if it were part of the scream, or the same as the scream.

And she had seen that the bolt was headed straight for Jo.

An enormous cracking sound, as if the air itself had cracked in half, as if the thunder were in the castle with them. Clare stumbled to keep from falling backward.

In a moment, the light was rain-dim again, and Clare's eyes, still adjusting from the flash, couldn't find Jo at all. But in the crackling silence, she thought she had heard Balor give a bark of anger and pain.

As her eyes refocused, Clare saw Jo was stretched across the ground, too still, too still. *Is she dead?* Clare's feet flew toward her.

The top of Jo's shirt was burnt and blackened, and beneath it, on the skin above her heart, was a rough, wide triangle, boiling red, in the shape of the totem's open mouth.

But in the center of the red triangle was a square of healthy skin, untouched by the totem's electric scream—a square exactly the size of Finn's black stone.

Was she alive? Clare didn't know how to tell. As she reached a shaking hand toward Jo's face, she grew aware, suddenly, of the silence behind her. She turned.

Balor's good eye burned at her. On the flesh of his throat was a fresh brand, boiling red, in the shape of that same square stone. It must have reflected the lightning bolt back at Balor himself.

"I don't know where you got that stone," he rasped. "But you'll pay for that, little girl. And if there's anyone else you want to call, I'll do the same to them. Remember that, when you think of calling anyone else."

My father, he means.

"Unless, of course," said Balor, his living and his dead eye both fixed upon her now, "unless, Clare, you want to let all this go, stop the pain and death you're causing with your stubbornness, and simply hand me that key."

Clare looked into Balor's face, then into the totem's gasping, silent scream above him. She looked at Jo's limp hand in her own hand.

She felt her other hand move toward the key in her pocket.

Outside the castle, the alien whine of an Irish police car, the thumping of car wheels over the field. But *I have friends everywhere that matters, powerful friends, who owe me a great deal.*

She saw Finn's face. She smelled the licorice wood-scent of the in-between.

Shouting voices. The cool iron of the key. Balor's eye.

Clare saw what she had to do.

As the police poured into the castle, Clare slipped away, snatching her notebook off the ground as she left, because it was her mother's, and because she could not bear to leave it in Balor's disgusting hands.

Outside the castle, Clare hesitated. *Home* was her first impulse, but even if she could reach it before Balor ran her down, wouldn't that only draw him there, with his police friends?

She heard his furious voice from the castle: "Yes, yes—call your captain, he can explain—get out of my way." That decided her. She ran for the closest woods. In these woods she had once followed

Finn's flute, but this time she followed no path at all, but crashed through underbrush looking for a place to hide.

Under a mass of vines draped around a fallen log, she stopped, breathing hard. Through brush and branches she could just see the castle and yes, now, Balor emerged and spoke to a policeman loitering outside, who shrugged. He looked around sharply as if deciding—woods, field, road?—then strode decisively toward Clare's home.

Outside, there is no protection: but now there was no choice. She could not go home. She waited until Balor was out of sight; until the police and ambulance people were all inside the castle. Then she ran, not toward her home and tree, but away.

Running away meant abandoning the tree, but she could not trust herself. If she had stayed with Balor and his totem a minute longer, she might have handed him the key. She was that close to despair, at what had happened to Jo, at the danger to her father, at the sickening face of the totem.

Key safe in her pocket, she ran. But where?

No stranger you can trust. I have friends everywhere that matters.

Except one place. There was one place Balor had no friends, where she could find help to protect the tree, protect her father, protect herself. She had to get into Timeless, into the dreaming place.

She could trust no human stranger, but she could trust Finn and his people—anyway, she could trust Finn. She had to find another gate into Timeless, and where else but the fairy road itself?

Running, Clare kept the ruined castle and her own distant stone window in a line behind her. She hoped that Finn's Cap, whatever it was, would turn up before she lost sight of them. She felt exposed, a panicked fledgling again; and when she turned to look behind her, it was not only to keep the hill and tree in line. She was also watching for Balor, or worse, his terrible servant.

Black-faced sheep, pale wool marked with fluorescent stains of pink or green to show their owners, looked up as she stumbled past.

The thought that kept her moving, half running, half walking, through aching side and gasping breath, was that as long as she moved away from the tree, she kept the tree safe. Her father, too: it was safer for them to be apart. *If he is safe right now—but he is, he has to be. He must be so worried for me.*

She did not know that her father was at that moment buried a thousand feet beneath the earth, too deep for any seed.

And she didn't know that she herself ran not like a hunter, stealthy and light, but heedless, leaving a wide trail, like prey.

The wind rose and rushed through the grass around her. It felt portentous to Clare, like the part of a story when you know the climax has to come, and the knowing is almost unbearable. With the rising wind came a rising sense of Strange, and she knew she must be close.

Rain followed the wind, sweeping across the field behind her. And below a little rise, just as the rain was upon her, she saw Finn's Cap.

It was unmistakable: a huge stone, nearly the size of a small car, balanced on two smaller stones. And the top stone looked like a cap, high and rounded at one end, tapering gently down like an elongated bill at the other.

As she pelted toward it, shaking wet hair from her eyes, Clare almost laughed with relief. She had reached a gate into the Strange—where Finn lived, where Her of the Cliffs could offer her advice and protection, where the key would be safe. And they could help her make sure her father was all right.

But when she reached the Cap, she stopped, hands pressed against the wet rock. She'd almost forgotten that she still had to discover the key. With a deep breath, she tried to force her pounding heart to match the gentle patter of the rain.

There was Strange here, for sure. All the hairs on her arms were rising up. What was its flavor, though; what did it ask of those who would enter? Something light—a lightness? She tried, tentatively, laughing: *ha-ha-ha*. She pushed her diaphragm harder: *hahahahahaha*.

Stupid. She didn't feel like laughing. And it wasn't a jokey kind of lightness she was feeling, anyway—more daring, more free, some sort of complicated joy. It was something about . . . *letting go of control*? No, there was controlling, but then also . . . not controlling? Giving control to something else?

This didn't help. Her heart began to work faster again, not from running now but from rising panic. She didn't have time to feel through this problem in the dark, to listen like a safecracker for the lock's clicking combination. Balor might not wait at her house for long—he could be on his way looking for her now.

Or he might have found some other way in. He might be with her tree. Her throat closed up. *I have already won.*

All right. Try. If it's giving up control, then maybe if she just lay perfectly still . . . She scanned the field anxiously for watchers or walkers, then looked again at Finn's Cap. Of course: it seemed made for shelter. *Like to see Balor take this cap down*, she thought, as she slipped into the narrow space between the earth and the capstone, *after it's stood for five thousand years with no protection at all.*

Under the stone, the feeling of Strange was stronger. Clare looked out at the world through a frame of stones. *Like my window*, thought Clare, and the thought was calming. All right. *Try giving up control.* She lay on her back and closed her eyes.

Almost immediately, blood pounded in her head. Her fingers

twitched. The face of the totem rose up in her mind and her heart started up again, faster than ever. She lay still for a minute, nearly two. Then she noticed she was holding her breath and let it out in a rush of frustration.

She turned again on her side. This wasn't the key. Her body did not wish to lie still, which might have to do with the key—or might just be the totem rising again and again in her mind. How were you supposed to tell? How do you figure out a key when you're too desperate to take your time? She didn't have *time* for this.

Awkwardly, she pulled the commonplace book and pencil stub from her pocket and smoothed a page. Sometimes it helped to write her thoughts, to see what she was thinking. Her left cheek propped on her left arm, she wrote what she knew:

Finn's father's gate. He went through and found a woman and fell in love. They had a baby, which was . . .

Clare's face colored, and she closed up the notebook, pencil inside. *He found a woman and fell in love. They had a baby.* So maybe something about love, and kissing, and . . . all that.

Clare, a strange and solitary girl who knew little of boys, knew less of . . . all that, except the clear, clinical, and uninformative facts that everyone knew. Certainly she had never been, for example, kissed.

She opened the commonplace book again and flipped through it, nervously and absently.

"That Pygmean race / Beyond the Indian mount, or fairy elves, / Whose midnight revels by a forest side . . ." Whatever. "Her antique race and lineage ancient, / As I have found it register'd of old / In Faery Land 'mongst records permanent." Blah. She had never liked that one.

She turned the page, and stopped. This had been one of her favorites for years, but now she looked at it in a new way.

I went out to the hazel wood,
Because a fire was in my head,
And cut and peeled a hazel wand,
And hooked a berry to a thread;
And when white moths were on the wing,
And mothlike stars were flickering out,
I dropped the berry in a stream
And caught a little silver trout.

When I had laid it on the floor
I went to blow the fire aflame,
But something rustled on the floor,
And someone called me by my name:
It had become a glimmering girl
With apple blossom in her hair

Who called me by my name and ran
And faded through the brightening air.

Though I am old with wandering
Through hollow lands and hilly lands,
I will find out where she has gone,
And kiss her lips and take her hands;
And walk among long dappled grass,
And pluck till time and times are done
The silver apples of the moon,
The golden apples of the sun.

"I will find out where he has gone," said Clare softly to herself, not noticing that she had changed the pronoun, and why not? Pronouns are made for changing. "And kiss his lips and take his hands." In the room of her mind, she allowed herself, just for a moment, to look through the crack in a certain door at a vast night sky. In that cool and starry dark, she remembered the feel of his arm against hers. She remembered the private joy and laughter of their own impenetrable world, in between all other worlds.

Her heart billowed up like a sail. "'Who called me by my name and ran / And faded through the brightening air,'" said Clare, soft. Her body felt warm and glad, remembering Finn, in a way it had never felt for any other friend.

Could he be more than just a friend?

Was it this feeling? Was this the key? But what did it ask her to *do* with the feeling? She did not feel any sort of opening in the gate. Her legs twitched, wanting to move with the feeling, wanting to—what? There was something she had to give herself to, but she didn't know what it was.

A voice inside her—a lying voice, or maybe better to say a frightened voice, but Clare did not know—told her this was stupid. What if Finn knew her thoughts right now? At that she blushed hard and closed the notebook, shoved it back in her pocket. She should be thinking of the tree, and how to protect it. Balor could come any minute.

The rain, which had abated, came lashing down again. Like someone stepping off a cliff, Clare gave herself to the despair. It came over her like sleep: and then, quite oddly, it *was* sleep—a strange sleep, perhaps, in fact, a Strange sleep, a sleep that was a gift from Finn's Cap.

As she slept, rain swirled protectively around this gate, and the stones cradled her close to the earth. She never knew that the portentous wind had said "your enemy comes" or that the rushing rain had saved her. She never knew how less than a thousand yards away, Balor had stood in the muddy field, rain pouring down the back of his neck, cursing; how he had turned back. Clare was pursued, but the world bent itself to foil her pursuer.

In a dream, Clare wandered down a forest path, holding a Houston Astros baseball cap, dark blue with a bright orange star. The light was the half-light before dusk, when colors are rich and wet, and the air smells clean and cool. The trees were tall and shut out the light, and Clare felt as if she were in a dark tunnel, and no light to show the end of it. Behind her she heard the deep, soft groan of some beast, and she imagined it coming from the totem's mouth.

"Finn!" she called. "Are you here?" The feelings she had tidied away in waking life came rushing back. His arm. Their private place, the place that was only theirs. How after a whole long life alone, she was suddenly lonely without him.

From behind a screen of rough dark trunks came a familiar voice. "Girl, you're noisy as flock of birds," he replied.

"Where are you?" asked Clare. Relief made her warm; the groaning beast and the totem's face vanished from her thoughts. "Where *are* you? I've been looking and looking."

"I'm right here," said Finn, and his voice was smiling. "It's your looking that's not so good."

"I found this cap," said Clare. "I think it's yours?"

The voice laughed, a free, full laugh. "It is mine indeed, Clare Macleod," he said. "And it was my father's before me. You're a clever girl in your sleep."

Clare frowned. "I'm not *asleep*," she said with dignity—but as soon as she said it she was sleepy after all, so sleepy, and she sat on the ground, then laid her head on a carpet of pine needles.

"Listen," said the voice, and it was warm, it lulled her like a bedtime story. "Look for the mirror."

She turned and sighed.

"Look for the mirror," he repeated. "When you find the mirror, you've found the way. Now follow on, Clare. Now. Now. Now."

Clare woke up wrapped in love like a warm cloak. *Not love*, she thought confusedly. *Just liking a lot.* (Not poems, just notes for poems.) Her face was pressed against the dirt, and there was a taste of dirt in her mouth, and she was smiling. She wondered if, in the dream that was slipping just out of her memory, she had been flying.

When she opened her eyes, for a moment it seemed she was in her home, face right up to the stone window. How had she got so close to it? Then she remembered.

The rain had stopped, and through the stone frame Clare, blinking with sleep, watched mists rise up from the warm, wet fields in the gray cloud-light. And what was that coming, through the mists? She rubbed her eyes, the smile still on her face. But what was that, so tall and broad and dark, its heavy gait and wet, deep, wheezing breaths so familiar from nightmares?

The smile was gone, all her joy turned to terror in a moment. The creature stretched a hand out, a thick, enormous hand matted with black hair, as if it meant to seize her. As its head bent toward her through the mist, she saw two curving, sharp-pointed horns protruding from its head.

Like a terrified animal, which is what she was, Clare struggled and shoved her way backward, out the other side of the Cap, and ran, ran, ran. Her thoughts stumbled along with her frantic feet: Balor in some horrible new form? But how could it be, when she knew that thing from her worst dreams, had seen it so many times, skulking in dark basements, breaking through doors, facing her at the bottom of long staircases.

How had it escaped her dreams?

Over the sound of her own pelting feet and thundering heart, she listened for lumbering tread behind her. She heard nothing, and ran on.

She heard nothing because what she ran from did not pursue her. Instead, laboriously, with snuffling breath, it bent over the ancient stones. From the ground it lifted something that, in her scramble to escape, Clare had left behind: her mother's silver chain and star, which she had wrenched from her neck under the totem's hateful glare and shoved into her pocket.

A thick hand closed around the necklace. The star glinted in the sliver of sun.

Her lungs aching, her throat raw from panting breaths, Clare finally slowed to a walk. Looking over her shoulder, she saw nothing, but that did not ease her terror of that creature and of Balor—unless they were one and the same.

In another quarter mile, she saw ahead a small grove of trees, separated from the woods to her left, as if six or seven trees had slipped out of the forest to catch more sun. At their center was a small tree in full, white-flowered glory, its blossom-heavy branches curved down to the grass, giving it an Easter-egg shape.

Clare checked: yes, the tree stood in a direct line with Finn's Cap and the distant outline of the ruined castle. *Fully dressed in flowers still, even though we're past May*, just as Jo had said.

So this must be the hawthorn, the fairy thorn. And though she had reached her goal, the fourth gate in the fairy road, Clare felt a surge of angry despair. Now what? She did not have time for finding the way in.

She walked beneath the hawthorn boughs. Flowers brushed her face, and she brushed them away furiously. The flower-scent wrapped delicately around her—not a sweet scent, but an earthy one, rich and complicated. It turned her stomach.

Along with the scent, as if part of the scent, came the Strange. Clare tried to breathe it in, but her adrenaline was too high, and both the scent and the Strange were too rich, too muddled—something about blossoming, maybe? But how did that help her? And she was too afraid.

"I don't know," she said out loud to the white blossoms that swam and bowed around her. Her frowning face was flower-shadowed. "I don't KNOW what you WANT. Why can't you just *tell* me?" She felt herself close to tears, but fury dried them before they fell. "Why can't someone just tell me? Why is it all guessing games?" She pushed the branches roughly apart and thrust herself into the open air, away from the suffocating scent.

"I can't," she said, to someone, to no one, to the Strange themselves. She grabbed a fistful of flowers, crushing them in her hand, dashing them to the ground. "It's *your* stupid yew I'm trying to save. Why don't you just let me in?" She swatted at the tree in rage. "I have to get in! Let me in, let me in, *let me in*!"

The silence rang around her, and without warning Clare felt empty as a spilled glass.

"I'm sorry," she said. Seeing the hawthorn-flower massacre at her feet, she knelt on the ground, gathering crushed blossoms. "I'm sorry." She put a hand to a stripped bough, aware she was apologizing to a tree, not caring. "Really, I'm so sorry. I'm just—I'm new at this. And I don't know your key, and you're the last gate I know. And I don't know where Dad is and I think he's in danger. And so is my tree. And so am I. And I'm scared."

She pressed the torn flowers to her face. The totem's face rose up in her mind's eye, and she flinched.

In the air just above her was a stirring. Clare looked up.

A flock of birds was descending. They swirled around her, silent as the grass. For a moment they made a circling shape, like a swirl of fabric, wrapping her in a streaming cloak of feather and muscle and claw and air.

Then the wind lifted the bird cloak up into the sky. Silent as the air, the flock turned and wheeled like a single thing, a wide ribbon of living bird. Clare's heart leaped and fell with the flock as the birds leaped and fell, fell and wheeled, a bird-fabric folding and bending, flattening, curving. The rhythm was like a ride at a fair.

Clare had never seen a murmuration of birds before, but she knew, as anyone who sees one knows, that it was something miraculous and Strange.

Now the silent flock rippled out over the meadow ahead of her, like a sheet shaken over a bed. Many people have seen a murmuration, but few do what Clare did now: she followed it, she ran behind it. She trusted the Strange it sailed upon.

She had no idea where she was going. Jo had only said that the next gate was inside the forest. But the Strange was the only way Clare had now, and the only home she knew. She followed the birds as they swept up and fell, carrying her heart upward, dropping it down.

The birds led her into the forest beyond the pasture, down a narrow sheep track of a road, with grass growing down the center. Around them, the trees bent leaf-heavy, sunlight glowing through their many greens. Like the flock that led her, the track curved and swooped down a hill.

Clare saw no houses, no bicycles, no walkers on this road. It was as if everyone in the world had disappeared, and she was entirely alone. The birds were silent, and she was all alone in the silence, following them.

Clare did not know where these Strange birds were taking her. But because she did not know, she had no choice but to trust their rising and falling, so much like the rising and falling of her own heart.

8

The Heart of the Strange

After almost an hour, the sheep track rose steeply, then widened and spilled her into a stand of birches. Keeping the birds in sight, Clare ran through the trees until she found herself at the top of a silky green hill, overlooking an iron-colored lake, sinuous and many-curved, like a woman lying on her side. Just where the woman's heart would be stood a small island.

Clare's flock flew to the island. There it bent like one thing into a wild ball of birds, a spinning feathered sphere. The bird-sphere exploded like fireworks over the island, sending birds off in all directions. Some flew past her, making the birch leaves turn and tremble in the wind, this way, then that, like thin green coins in a magician's hands.

Clare knew, then, that the island was the end of her fairy road, and her heart jumped high with the knowledge. Then it fell, just as hard. Because it was one thing to know that the island was the end of the fairy road.

But how do you get to an island in the middle of an iron-colored lake?

"Tell me what to do," she whispered, as if she could command the world.

But the world is not commandable. Nothing happened, except that the sun came out, sudden and bright in her face. She squinted. The sun made jewels on the water, a whole shop-window-full, diamond and silver. She pulled out her commonplace book and wrote: *It's like everything is making, birds and sun and everything. The world is always making and unmaking around us.*

As she put the notebook back in her pocket, the clouds passed. It was that kind of sun, going in, coming out, going in again. And with that shift of the slanting light, the lake's color changed for a moment, from dazzling diamond to paler silver, revealing what lay beneath.

Clare said, "Oh!" and began to slip, tumble, and slide down the grassy hill toward what she had just seen: a snaking line of stones that ran just below the surface of the water, like a vein beneath skin, from the shore all the way to the island.

In a story it sounds perfectly easy: if a snaking line of stones arises in a lake—well, a girl in a fairy tale would just run across the water, stone to stone, until she reached the enchanted isle. Easy: just like that.

But this is not a fairy tale, although it has fairies in it. This is a real story in the real world. The water was real water, cold and gray and muttering. Clare was a real girl, with real fears, and short legs. These stones weren't high and dry: they ran just beneath the lapping, iron-cold water. They were hard to see, and they were far apart. If they had been made as a bridge, it was for someone with legs far longer than Clare's.

She waded a few feet out into the cold water, pebbles grinding and sliding beneath her boots, cold water soaking through her jeans up to her knees. She scrambled unsteadily onto the first stone.

Now what?

She tried to make her leg long, so that she could keep one foot on the first stone and place the other on the next. But the stones were too far apart, and she slipped and fell knee-deep.

Next, holding the commonplace book between her teeth, she tried wading to the slippery second rock. But the water was waist-deep by the time she got there. Even as she pulled herself up to stand uneasily and barely two-footed atop it, she knew that beyond this, the water would be chest deep, then over her head. No more wading. The water was too cold for it, anyway—she was already gasping and numb.

She waded back, half soaked, to stand shivering on the shore, and put the notebook back in her damp pocket. One thing was clear. The only way to cross this bridge would be to run, to leap from stone to stone. It would be like running hurdles in track, she told herself. You just have to get the right rhythm going.

Clare looked at the curving line that would take her to the distant island. She would be out very far on the lake, all alone. She pushed the memory of many knocked-over hurdles, bruised shins, and skinned knees out of her mind.

Clammy jeans sticking to her legs, she walked a hundred yards back from shore. Then she faced the lake and, for no reason at all, gave an echoing, wordless war cry. She began to run. Her stride lengthened with each step. At the edge of the shore, she aimed her flying foot only at that first stone, not thinking about the others. She caught that stone, and only as she was pushing off did her eyes find the next one.

Sometimes, you can't skitter along like a mouse along a wall. Sometimes you have to run, right out in the open, and trust that your foot will fall in the right place every time. If you doubt yourself, you'll slip, and the cold water will swallow you. But Clare flew, eyes always on the stone ahead of her. All she heard was the up-splash of water when her foot hit wet stone, and the silence as she sailed between.

If you were watching from above, you would have seen a girl flying across the lake, from stone to unseen stone. It would look so easy, just like in a fairy tale.

Breathless, Clare stood on the island shore. Her guess had been right: this was the heart of the lake, and the heart of the Strange. Many Strange currents swirled through this air.

She was cold, she was shivering. *But he can't follow me here.* The lake would never show Balor those stones, she felt sure.

A sudden clamor: lake birds beating the water with their wings and their calls. *Woo-HOW-hoh-yee-yee,* the vowel-only language of the birds. Then the island returned to a lake-lapped silence. The lake cradled the island, rocked it, lapped its edges, sang to it with water sounds.

A late afternoon sun came out, and the air warmed—it was the warmest she'd felt in Ireland. It might even have been too warm for her, if she hadn't been so damp and cold. Her clothes and hair began to dry. Sometimes the world is cold; and sometimes kind.

She headed deeper in.

In the forest it was cool. In the forest there were many paths. Everything was rounder and softer; even the roots of the trees were rounded and softened by the green, green moss that crept over it all. Sharp slices of gray rock pushed through the earth, only to be wrapped up and softened by moss. *Green grows out of stone here,* Clare thought; *stone and leaf are that friendly.* This was an old place.

The Strange began to weave around her.

First, Clare heard singing off to her right—a high, humming, tuneful song that dissolved back into sounds of wind and birds and water. Then something flashed through the grass, silver on black, too fast for an animal. But all she caught was a tail or mane of silky white hair, low to the ground, as it flew behind a tree.

Though she felt no drop, rain rattled in the trees, like the ghost of rain.

An entry from the commonplace book came to her: "*'Be not afeard. The isle is full of noises, / Sounds and sweet airs that give delight and hurt not.' Shakespeare was there.*"

Not just Shakespeare. *My mother was here.*

She caught a scent, or layers of scents, on the breeze—black tea sweetened with some dark fruit, spiced with pepper and ginger. Her nose lifted and turned to follow the scents as they wafted and wove around her, then faded and were gone.

Oh, it was a magic island, all right, and the heart of the Strange. Strange ran in currents around her, warm and cool, sound and scent, unsettling and enticing. She walked on, eye and ear and nose alive to the changing air and light around her.

Another song rose up out of the water and bird sounds. She felt drunk or drugged. She felt she was in a dream. Her goals and plans, her fears and regrets—what she ran from, and what she ran toward—all of these slipped away. She wanted nothing but to drown in this Strange.

Her mulchy, leaf-shaded path led up, then stopped at the edge of the water. On this high point she knelt in the dirt behind a barbed stand of holly, watching the slow pulse of the lake.

I'll write something, she thought dreamily, pulling out her notebook, admiring the creamy pages. *I'll make a making.* She thought for a moment, then wrote a title:

Delight and Hurt Not

Afraid to watch my feet, I ran

Here. And then

Muttering birds' wings,

And other voices, sweet and rough

As when in bed you stir

And moan, crushed by sleep,

Struggling from nightmare's grasp—

Clare stopped, frowned at "nightmare." She hadn't meant *nightmare*—had she? She crossed it out and paused, pencil hesitating.

A wrong sound rose up: an angry buzz. Screened behind the holly, Clare looked up. A motorboat raced along the far bank, digging a deep crease in the lake. The startled water rose up again and again, a series of small mountain ranges, rising and subsiding and rising.

Clare sat frozen, yanked from her dreamlike, Strange-drugged trance, back into the world. The world in which a tall, broad, black-haired man stood in the prow of a boat, searching the banks of the lake with a long telescope.

Clare bent low, leaned forward, watching. Long after the boat passed, the waves against the island shore grew higher and more agitated. Something behind her reached out a hand; she spun around.

It was only the shadow of a branch. But Clare was already on her feet and running.

Path to path, stumbling along, Clare pushed deeper into the heart of the island. The gate. There was a gate on this island somewhere. But she felt no faith she could sniff it out in a place so thick with Strange, let alone find its key before that buzzing boat arrived.

Just as she was thinking, *And I'm so thirsty*, the sun fell on a spot off the path, a small clearing, where a tall bush like the fairy thorn spread flower-laden arms over a still pool. The pool made a perfect mirror of the trees and sky above: a pattern of black branches, green leaf, white cloud, and robin's-egg sky, rippled at the edge by the bubbles of the spring that fed it.

Breathless, Clare leaned down to sip water from the pool. When she raised her face, the world in the pool distorted, twisted, composed itself again. The face in the water was her own face, but older and fiercer (and to be honest, dirtier) than the face she remembered from the mirror at home.

When you find the mirror, you've found the way. Who said that? Was it from an old story, or an old song?

The angry buzz grew louder now, a wasp returning for the sting. The motorboat coming closer. Coming back.

Clare was a girl visited by the Strange. She was a girl who followed silver music to an earth rainbow, who saw a monstrous beast through a frame of stones. She was a girl led to a secret lake by a crowd of birds, a girl to whom the lake itself revealed a path of stones. She should have seen what was right in front of her.

But all she could hear was a motorboat that forced itself against the water's wishes.

Clare leaned over again, to look at herself in the water. Her face seemed to fill the sky, as full as a sun, watching the world below. She drank for a second time, dipping her face full in the water, eyes to eyes, nose to nose, lips to lips. The water was cool and sweet, a clean, stony taste on her tongue.

The wind swelled and breathed. The angry noise of the boat came closer.

A third time Clare dipped into the water to drink, then knelt back on the ground, wiping her dripping face with her sleeve.

And just then, as a thought began to dawn—*Oh, "when you find the mirror," so this is the gate, this pool is the gate, but then what is the key*—just then the motorboat sound grew louder, then stopped.

Footsteps.

Clare looked around in desperation. Up a tree? Out into the lake? But he would find her, she knew that he would. She had not the least protection, not even her black stone; all she had was—

She still had the red fruit.

When the wolf's jaws are closing on you.

He was a wolf, and she needed Her of the Cliffs's protection now.

Now came men's voices, one deep and dark, arguing over the sound of tramping, tearing boots in the brush.

Standing, ready to run if it didn't work, Clare closed her eyes and popped the fruit in her mouth.

Instantly, running was just what she couldn't do. She was as pinned to the spot as if she had roots there. In terror, she managed to raise her arms, but then she stood, arms flung above her head, her trunk unprotected and vulnerable to the enemy as he approached.

Rooted to the ground, arms flung up into the sky, fear roared and raged and ran in Clare's mind. *A trick. It was a trick. That terrible woman gave me a paralyzing poison, she must work for Balor, did Finn know?*

The tramping feet came closer.

Now Clare's eyes clouded over; now her skin began to stiffen; now the flesh beneath her skin stiffened, too. Soon, she knew, when her tender lungs were stiff and hard, when her throbbing heart was still as a carving—then she would die. Wouldn't she? Wasn't she about to die? The questions roared and screamed within her: but on the outside, she stood still and blind as stone. The stiffening crept into her ears, and there was silence.

And somehow, with the silence came a peculiar peace. Clare stood, arms raised to the sky, stiff as wood, blind and deaf, as the waves of rage and fear crashed over her for the last time, swept across the ground, receded.

It was not a poison; it was something much Stranger than poison. Her feet had grown long, much longer, and her toes more numerous. Her long feet, her many toes, plunged into the dirt beneath her. Her arms and hands had grown longer, too; her long and numerous fingers reached up into the air—yes, they *reached* up, so she was moving after all.

Was she moving? Or was she growing?

Or when you stand so perfectly still, is growing a kind of moving?

Her many toes dug through the earth, seeking water and food; her fingers grew long and delicate, seeking air and light. The air found and swayed her fingers, those tender shoots, and her fingers drank the light like water. The sunlight ran down every nerve and down into her toes. She stole the sun's fire to make green.

Clare's toes—Clare's roots, let's call them, because that's what they were, now—her roots like veins branched into capillaries, and found other reaching, questioning tree-roots, the circulatory system of the earth. Each thrill or pain that ran through one ran through all the trees of the island, all the feet of this forest tangled together.

She felt the devastation of a nearby sapling who was mutilated and dying (slashed, though she did not know this, by the machetes of Balor and his man). That sapling's death was felt by every tree as its own death; just as the birth of a new tree, a green shoot somewhere deep in the island, was felt by every tree as its own birth.

She knew now, because her roots knew, the key to the pool-of-water gate, and knowing it, if Clare could have laughed, she would have laughed out loud at how easy it was.

Clare's blood was sap, slow and rich. She became part of the unending, wordless, subterranean conversation of the trees, the ceaseless story they tell. For the first time in her life, she did not feel lonely. For the first time, she knew that she was not alone and never could be.

And perhaps because she stood in the heart of the Strange, Clare's roots spread even under the lake, to the field, to the fairy thorn (*oh*, she thought, *I see, of course, the tree said* blossoming *but for us that's* singing, *that's how we blossom, that was the key*), and finally to the yew tree itself.

And touching her yew—even her slenderest, farthest finger of root, touching the yew's own far and slender finger—even that bare touch split her heart with love and tenderness. The soul of her yew, at once ancient and innocent, broke through the shell around her heart. She wanted to stay with the yew, hand in hand with it, fingers knotted from tree to tree, underground, forever.

Deaf and blind, lost in that slow, slow dance of communion, Clare never thought of her enemy: who stood beneath her reaching arms; who put his hand on her bark, breathing hard; who cursed his luck, finding no cowering girl on this island.

Who in anger turned his back on the tree and, returning to his angry boat, sailed angrily away.

In time, Clare's arms began to shrink and lower; her roots withdrew from the earth, shrunk back from the tangled communion of trees. *Oh no, no*, said her still, woody heart, as her root-fingers pulled away from the touch of the yew.

But the hawfruit spell had finished its work. Clare softened, and shrank back, and pulled back into her lonely, only self. She was alone on a silent island, looking into a pool like a mirror—the paler blue of the sky in late afternoon, and the blacker tangle of branches. But she had not forgotten the tree-knowledge of this pool's, this gate's, true nature: it was not a mirror after all; it was a window. Perhaps a window in the sky, or a window in the water, but certainly a window into the Strange.

And what she saw through it—the sky, the branches, the girl with dirty hair and stubborn eyes—that was what lay on the other side.

She put her face closer. Even for Clare, to dive through a window that may be in the sky or may be in the water, a window on an island that floats at the heart of the Strange, was not an easy thing to do. Where would it take her? Would she ever come back? All the stories she had heard of fairy seemed to end with "And she thought she was there one short night—but when she returned, seven years had passed." Or "She ate just one bite of the fairy cake—but because of that, she was never able to return again."

Clare thought, *In the Strange place, I can protect the tree.* Her heart ached with love, remembering the sweetness of the touch from the yew's small finger. She straightened. She told herself that maybe the Strange people would know about her father, why he hadn't come home last night, how she could protect him. And she told herself Finn would be there. *So it will be a little bit home.*

She took a breath. She looked at the face in the window at her feet. "So, hi," she said softly.

She did not so much dive in, as let herself fall.

Clare climbed into a window in the water, but she climbed out of a window in the earth.

At first, as she stood brushing dirt from her clothes and hair, it seemed as if she had never left the island. Only back there, the afternoon sun had been high. Here, a curious luminosity hung in the air that seemed to have no particular source. When the light was like that, Clare's father used to say, "This is the magic hour," and pull out his camera. But he only meant the light just after dawn or before dusk, the long, slanting light that makes ordinary colors look miraculous. He didn't mean real magic.

But wherever she was, it was the magic hour here. The world glistened as if it were wet.

Damp and dirt smeared, Clare walked through the forest that hovered between day and night, light and dark, down a wide path, among dark trees. It was terribly quiet, no sound of water or insect. Every color vibrated. This place was dense with Strange, so much denser than even the island. It was as if she had walked into the kitchen where the Strange was made.

So I guess I'm where I meant to go, Clare thought. But where exactly was she going?

And then she heard the singing: high voices, like singing in church, but not any church she knew. The voices wreathed together in many parts and harmonies, just down the path . . . no, just a little farther down . . . and then just a *bit* farther, they must be down around that bend . . .

It was something Clare would learn one day—that when the people of Timeless were together, even their conversation felt like a song, a symphony, a *making*, since making was breath and life to them. But she did not know that yet. Now, she was only song-led again, tugged along until the singing transformed into a high, crowded weaving of voices that seemed half song, half conversation.

9

Magic Hour

Song-led, Clare found herself in a clearing where the trees bent toward one another to make a sort of roof, like the rib cage of a whale, if a whale's bones were tree boughs. Beneath this leafy shelter was a long table, crowded with elegant people in brilliant colors, in clothes trimmed with feathers and fur. Candles ran up and down the table, and candles hung from branches of the trees, so that the foliage and the silver and crystal of the table flickered in insubstantial red and orange. The table was so long that its other end disappeared into flickering shadow.

For what felt like a long time, Clare stood near the table, muddy and disheveled, vulnerable and yew-touched. But no one seemed to notice her. Uncertain, exhausted, and a little annoyed—*am I invisible?*—in the end Clare took the empty chair at her end of the table, which was the only empty chair she saw. She scanned in the dim, shifting light for Finn's face, or for Hers.

But the table was a confusion of beautiful, smiling men and women, leaning in toward one another, or leaning back to laugh. The flames flickered and shadowed their faces, so that they seemed as substantial-insubstantial as flames themselves. None of them looked familiar.

In front of each person, as in front of Clare, sat a dish covered in a silver dome. The silver domes reflected the flames, and reflected the faces of the handsome, smiling people, then reflected those reflections again, doubling and doubling each flickering presence. Their clothes, like Finn's, and Hers of the Cliffs, were a little old-fashioned.

Exclamations of surprise and laughter ran up and down the table. "Well made! Well made," several voices cried. Clare looked down: the silver cover over each plate had vanished, and before each diner sat a different meal.

One diner's silver dish bore a glass bowl in which a pale gold fish, about the size of Clare's palm, flicked its tail in nervous circles. Another held a small, perfect cherry tree, covered in tiny ripe fruit. One man dug into a little garden of leaves and herbs, still rooted in black dirt. A woman trailed one delicate, hungry finger down the back of a trembling gray bird.

On her own silver plate was food far more appetizing: a loaf of hot, steaming brown bread, split down the middle, with a fat plop of butter melting into it. Next to the loaf was creamy milk in a blue china cup. Clare had never wanted any food more than she wanted that loaf, that butter, that milk. She was famished—had not eaten since breakfast the morning her father left, a day and a half ago—and yet she hesitated. She remembered a line of poetry from her mother's commonplace book: "The bread and the wine had a doom, / For these were the host of the air." In the margin, her mother had written "??"

Still, she felt like crying from hunger at the scent of fresh-baked bread. To distract herself, she looked at those around her.

The man to her right, with the fishbowl on his plate, now held that pale fish lightly between his teeth. The fish waved its tail in slow, languorous fear, once, twice; was still for a few seconds; waved its tail again, slow, hopeless. The man waited patiently, the fish between his precise teeth. At first, Clare could not tear her eyes away; then she couldn't watch.

The silver dish to the man's right held an entire honeycomb, white-gold and dripping. The diner dipped one small, furry paw into the comb, brought it out dripping, licked it with long tongue from smiling lips.

Furry *paw*?

Clare looked up and down the table. Was it the shifting, flickering light, was it the distorted reflections in silver? But some of the diners no longer looked like human beings. To Clare's left, a woman whose hair had been piled high on her head was, for a moment, a tall-eared brown rabbit in a ruby silk dress. Then she turned her face against the light, and was a woman again.

With rising panic, Clare looked around the table: A pale green hand—a green hand?—hovered over a plate that bore only a round, glowing yellow mass, like a small sun. A man's fingers, pulling something like a long worm from the pile of dirt on his plate, were no longer fingers but a lizard's scaly, five-toed claw emerging from the black sleeve of a suit. A candle flickered, and it was after all only the thin, crooked fingers of a thin, handsome man. A woman's face was thrown back in laughter, her small, curving nose suddenly more than finchlike, but an actual finch's beak, a baby finch with its mouth open to be fed. A wide sleeve, stretched toward a dish of trumpeting pink flowers, became the wings of a butterfly. And at the far end of the table, a shadowy figure bent his head, and Clare saw, was sure she saw, long, twining white horns on his head.

The man who had held the fish in his mouth was now dabbing at his lips with a napkin. When he dropped the cloth to his plate, his teeth looked as spiked as a shark's.

Clare looked down, and her own left hand was large and thick and ink-black, just beginning to sprout coarse black hair. She jumped back from the table, knocking her chair over backward. The room went silent, and everyone sitting along the table—only men and women again—stared at her. Her hand was only her hand again.

She felt Finn beside her before she saw the gray and black clothes, the long, tangled hair, the questioning eyes. Comfort warmed her bones like a bath.

"Finn." Her relief poured out in a flood of words. "He came back, and he wanted the key, and he had this terrible, this thing with him. And he hurt a woman I know, he might have even killed her. And I ran away, so that he couldn't . . ." She hesitated. "Take the key" wasn't right, or even "make me give it to him." *So that I didn't hand it over.*

"I was afraid something was wrong," he said. "When I saw your dream, I wanted to—but Her of the Cliffs forbade me."

"And he's going to hurt my dad," Clare continued. It was pouring out faster now. "I'm afraid he is, so that I'll give him the key. Or maybe he already has. Dad didn't come home last night when he was supposed to." She heard her voice growing more agitated, couldn't stop. "So we have to go to the in-between, to see if Dad's home, so I can warn him about Balor. Or find him where he is and tell him. We have to hurry!"

She had not realized until she let that fear out of its cage how powerful it was, how afraid she was for her father.

Finn, brows pulled together, was just opening his mouth to reply when Her of the Cliffs appeared beside him, her hair flickering in the candlelight like fire. "Your father will not return to your home this night or the next," she said.

Relief ran through her like warm water. "So he's still at the mine site?"

"Yes," said Her of the Cliffs.

"He must be really worried about me, is there some way—"

Her of the Cliffs interrupted her. "Balor deceived him. Said the woman Jo was caring for you."

A comfort to set that worry aside for now. But something in her tone made Clare ask, "He's safe there, though, right?"

"There is no safety," said Her of the Cliffs. Heat seemed to come off her: she was copper and gold with cold-hot blue at the core. "Not here. Not anywhere. And—listen to me, girl: *looking for safety is wrong looking*. You should not have left the tree undefended."

Incredulous, Clare saw: *she is angry with me*. Her face flushed as she thought of her yew, of that delicate, unbearably sweet root-to-root connection. "I did not leave it undefended," she said in a voice both shaking and stubborn. "I ran to keep the key away from Balor, because he had this thing that made me feel . . . that made me feel like nothing was any good and everything was dirty, and nothing mattered, and I was afraid I'd—but anyway I didn't. So the key is safe!"

"The key is safe, you see!" said Finn. To Clare: "Where did you hide it?"

"I didn't hide it," said Clare. "He could have found it, if I'd hid it. I kept it with me the whole—"

But the hand in her empty pocket told a different story. Frantically, Clare tried her other pockets, but the key was gone.

Her of the Cliffs swelled like a bonfire with new fuel. "The key was iron," she said. "Iron cannot pass through into fairy, and you should have known that, how could you not? I tell you, this Balor knows iron cannot enter. He knows that wherever you entered Timeless is where the key will be. Does he know which gate you used?"

Clare had covered her open mouth with one dirty-nailed hand.

Her of the Cliffs blazed up as if about to speak or shout. Then she turned and strode out of the hall, straight into the relative dark of the twilight forest, her red-gold hair all but crackling.

Clare looked at Finn. He, too, turned stiffly away. There was a terrible pause. Then he knocked her chair to the ground and rounded on her. "What are you doing here?" His voice was high with anger and fear. "You left the key for anyone to find, for Balor to find! You left the tree unprotected!"

"I was, I was, I almost got *killed.* I was in danger in that castle, I spent the whole night there with him and his totem, it was the most disgusting—"

"I gave you the stone. You had the stone for protection." His eyebrows bending furiously.

"I *used* the stone. I used it to protect someone else, and it might have—"

"That is not what the stone was for. It was to protect you, so that you could protect the tree."

It was a hornet sting to her heart, and the cold poison spread. *So that you could protect the tree.* So that was her only reason for existence, to him, to these people. Guardian of the tree. It had made her feel so proud; and now it made her feel small and used.

She said, with all the hornet's poison in her voice: "I would never let a *friend die* just to save the stone for your stupid tree" (her yew-touched heart turned over to hear her own ugly words) "and your stupid road. My friend might be dead anyway"—her voice cracked, which was infuriating—"or she might not, I don't know. But at least I tried."

A look crossed Finn's face that might have been shame; or it might have just been pain. "If only you had stayed in the house," he said, "there were protections for you there. With you gone, and with the key perhaps in his hand, or soon to be—ah, the yew is in terrible danger."

"He's your enemy, not mine," said Clare. "He's your *grandfather*, not mine." Finn's face went blank with pain, and Clare felt a rush of shame, and raised her voice to drown it out. "So why don't you go *get* him? Why was it all on me? I'm just *one person*, and I don't have all your . . . *magic* or whatever. Why don't you all go STOP him?"

"At Midsummer, we will," said Finn, struggling to recover his aloofness. "At Midsummer, we ride. Her will allow me to lead the Hunt. We ride as a host, at Midsummer and Yule, and we cannot ride before. We must hope the tree can withstand Balor until then."

"Midsummer is FOUR DAYS away. What do you mean you can't ride?" asked Clare (thinking: *my birthdays are that close. Dad, come home*). Now her voice was high and fearful. "Is it some stupid RULE or something? Just get on your, on your horses or whatever and RIDE, and KILL him." She felt light-headed with anger.

"You're a fool." Finn made no pretense of cool now. "You know so much less than you should know. He cannot be killed, for one, only caught and shackled where he can do no harm. And no, we cannot ride before the time, because of the way the sunlight travels on the . . . ach, it doesn't matter why! It's how it is!"

Silence rang between them, and Clare realized that the table was silent, too. Everyone had been listening. A cold voice rose up from somewhere along the mirroring, flickering table. "Why hunt this year, after all?" it said. "Why hunt ever again?"

The question dropped into the silence like a stone in a pool. A babble of voices arose around it. The conversation that had been sweet music was now a dissonant symphony.

"We hunt!" Finn's voice rose above the crowd. "We hunt, or Balor fells the fairy roads, wrecks every gate."

"And so?" responded the first voice. Scattered laughter. "Leave the human world to suffer alone, without making or dreams. *We* will still have making."

"But we will not have love," said Finn, so softly that Clare thought perhaps the table had not heard him. But their silence said they had.

"Love is a child's fantasy," said a different voice. "It is foolish play. We do not need love."

"We do—" Finn began, with a note of desperation, then broke off.

Her of the Cliffs had emerged from the forest. Against the dark trees, she was made of light, snakes of gold and coppery fire writhing about her. As she walked back to the head of the table, she paused for a word in Finn's ear, and his whole body tensed. But when she reached her place and turned to face them all, Her of the Cliffs was calm. "I, too, wonder why we ride, when Clare cares so little as to leave her key lying on the ground unguarded, for anyone to find." She cast a hard look down the table to Clare, who dropped her head. "But no matter the work of a witless girl. We are the host of the air. At Midsummer, we hunt."

The power of her command was like a wave rocking the room. And yet the silence that followed felt uneasy.

"If Balor has the key," ventured a voice, "if he blocks the yew gate, then, what then?"

"The key is already—" Finn cut himself off. He began again: "If Balor blocks the tree, well, Clare is its guardian. She will find a way to open it."

Clare stared at him, shocked. The table's silence seemed equally skeptical.

"You say she will find a way," said a new voice, low and gruff, "but she is no maker."

"She is," said Finn, hotly. "And I was teaching her our making ways, only—"

"To open a gate, you must be a true maker, as we are makers. And you're no true maker till you know your beast," said the gruff voice.

Clare felt a chill. "What does that mean?" she murmured.

Something like fear crossed Finn's face. "No matter," he said. "He is wrong, I'm sure he is. A human maker need never confront the beast. Still. I have much to teach you in the next four days, and—"

"I can't wait here *four days*," she protested. "My dad would go *nuts*." A thought surfaced. "He's not home, but can I go to him where he is, at the mine or wherever he is?" She thought of the roots of the yew tree and how Finn knew how to follow those paths all over the world. Hope colored her heart.

"No," said Finn. "That is far too dangerous." Clare opened her mouth to argue. "Dangerous for him," he added. "It is playing into Balor's hand, do you see?"

Her of the Cliffs nodded. "Balor means to use your father to lure you out so he can kill you both. To keep your father alive, you must stay away. That is nothing like safety, but it is all your father has."

Clare flushed with frustration and anger, from the top of her head down to her feet. "All right," she said bitterly. "I didn't think of that." Her voice rose as the heat rose. "But I'm not staying here, where no one cares about my tree or my dad but me. I don't care." She surveyed the table, not sure whom to address, so raising her voice to address them all. "I'll protect them on my own. I don't know what I'll do, but I'll do *something*, and I won't need your help to do it. I'll go back through the island gate and find the key before Balor does. I will."

And as if that heat were all she had had inside her, and now that it was expelled, she had nothing left, Clare fainted.

When Clare swam up from the dark water of unconsciousness, the noise of the banquet had resumed around her. But all she could see was Finn's dark face and worried eyes above hers, his long black elflocks making a curtain around his face and hers. Inside that dark curtain, just her face and his, all her anger and hurt disappeared. She felt secret and alone with him, as in the in-between, their breath tangling together like roots.

"Finn," she whispered. Perhaps because she was only half conscious, all her heart was in his name, and what she most wanted to say was ready to be said. "Finn. I'm really sorry I said about him being your grandfather."

His eyes clouded up like a wet morning, but the cloud passed. "You're right and well," he said. "It's all of it right as rain, and there's nothing more right than rain. I myself am sorry for my harsh words. I was only afraid." He smiled. "And I'm sorry, mad Clare, not to have shown you yet my making, my making I want you to see. But soon we will and soon enough." It was the soothing tone you use with a sick child.

"Oh, but the key!" Clare cried. She struggled to sit, pushing her hair from her face. "Will you show me how to go back to the island so I can find the key and—"

Finn's smile faded. "Ah, no," he said softly. "She has been to the island already and back, Her of the Cliffs has. The gate's been poisoned, by Balor no doubt, and the key is gone."

Clare put a hand to the floor to keep herself sitting upright. "Then there was no point?" she asked. She felt shaken. "Everything I did, all the running, the keys I found, no point at all? I might as well have handed him the key as soon as he asked."

"Every point, every point in the world," said Finn. He took her hands and pulled her to her feet. "By coming here you've helped protect your father, is that no point? And you've kept yourself alive as well. And we don't know that Balor has the key, although . . ." He paused, and Clare felt the hot flush of despair. Finn must have seen, because he tried to smile. "But even if it's the worst, girl, your yew has protections craftier than an iron lock. Some we've given it, some of its own. There's hope he cannot use it yet."

A little comforted, Clare couldn't bear Finn's kind gaze. Her eyes drifted around the room until she frowned, remembering. "The people here," she said. "Is it just a trick of the light? I see, I keep almost seeing—"

"Maybe something of a trick of the flames," he interrupted her, as if he knew the question. "And a bit of something else as well. As we breathe, we make, and so . . . But, ah, don't worry about that now. You need to eat, I think."

Clare felt her face go anxious and tight.

"It must be the stories again," Finn said, now truly smiling his old sly smile. "Oh, the *fairy stories.* Have they ever been better than half wrong? Forget the stories; you've forgotten greater things. Here."

He held out a goblet made of a gray metal and a silvery metal, woven together in long lines like the high horns of her white stag.

Finn's smile grew dryer. "Fear to drink from my own cup? Clare, listen: you're a changeling, and our food has fed you many times before. It will change nothing. Or perhaps," he said, considering: "perhaps truer to say that any way it would change you, changeling, it changed you long ago."

It was all she needed to hear. She drank a sweet and herby liquid from the cup, and it ran warmth through her veins. Finn helped her back to her chair and leaned against the table beside her. Chatter ran up and down the flickering forest-room, no one looking her way at all. Clare pulled apart the still-steaming bread, smeared it with butter, ate, drank the cool milk. From beside her, Finn laughed. She looked up. "No, then, hungry, don't stop for me. Eat."

Clare scooped up puddles of butter with the fast-diminishing bread. The woman who sat beside her said to Finn, "You are taller, Finn, than when I saw you last. And is that a gray hair?"

Finn grunted—amused? annoyed?—and the people around them laughed. "Because I change," he said—as if to Clare, but clearly for all to hear—"they fear me most, and love me best." Those near them laughed again, and there were a few claps. Finn stood. "I hope you will excuse me as I return to my own meal," he said.

"Oh, but wait," said Clare, swallowing hastily. "Could you just tell me really quickly, just a very short explanation, of this thing about making and . . . beasts?" At that word, she thought of the creature at Finn's Cap, and the bread dried in her mouth. "Also, I need to figure out if Dad is okay, and just . . . I need to talk to you."

He hesitated. "I must return now, else offend Her of the Cliffs, which is easy to do and ever a mistake. But after this meal, we will talk." He smiled. "And I will be glad to talk, Clare Macleod."

Still rather hungry, Clare looked regretfully at her empty plate—and found it piled up with strawberries, blueberries, raspberries, and several other berries she didn't recognize, all of it swirled with something like honey, but not honey, something sweet and tasting of flowers.

"Change-poisoned," murmured a throaty voice beside her.

"I'm sorry?" said Clare, startled away from her fruit. It was the woman in the ruby dress, with the high-piled dark-and-silver hair, who had looked almost like a rabbit in the weaving flames. She looked human now, though—a little older than her father, Clare guessed, with large, wide-set eyes that were the dark blue of a mountain lake threaded with ice. Her mouth was wide and smiling.

"What is 'change-poisoned'?" Clare asked politely.

"He has change in him, Finn," the woman said. "He is made of human and Timeless both, and he can age. And he will die one day. He killed his mother, with his change-poison," she added, selecting a long fragment of greenery from her plate. "She was my friend."

"That wasn't his fault," said Clare.

"He is Finn the Change-Poisoned," the woman continued, "despite which, and because of which, he leads our Hunt to ruin Balor. That is the prophecy."

"Will I go on the Hunt, too?" This had been weighing on Clare's mind. She wasn't sure what she wanted the answer to be. "I'm the guardian of the yew tree," she added.

Those mountain-lake eyes turned down in amusement. "I know. But that question is foolish. How hunt, with no beast to ride?"

Chastened, Clare ate a spoonful of nectar-drizzled fruit in silence. Then she cleared her throat. "May I ask you something?"

The woman turned her ice-threaded eyes to Clare. Clare cleared her throat again. "Can they . . . can you . . ." She stopped, shy. Then she tried again. "I don't know if it's just a trick of the light, but sometimes tonight, some of you looked, looked different than you look now. You looked like"—she took a deep breath—"like animals. Or maybe beasts?"

"Ah," said the woman softly. Her eyes seemed to change shape, a little, in the changing light. "Ah, well, we make. Making is what we are. We make with water and earth and air. The way a dancer lifts and drops a hand, we make; as we breathe, we make."

"What does that have to do with beasts, though?"

The woman lifted a single shoulder in a shrug of liquid grace. "In the same way that you can only ride, when you ride your beast—in that same way, you can only make, *truly* make, fairy-make, when you make with the help of your beast. My people . . ." She hesitated. "My people have grown so close to our beasts, the difference between us . . ." She rubbed thumb and forefinger together, a gesture that said "a tissue's worth of difference," or perhaps: "no difference at all."

"And my people don't have beasts," said Clare. She popped another berry in her mouth, feeling both relieved and sad.

The woman laughed like tumbling water, like tiny bells. "Of course you have beasts. And you make with your beasts, when you truly make. In your dreams, or in your better art: then you make with your beasts. Only you do not *know* that you make with your beasts. When you meet them in your dreams, you flee." She laughed again. "I have so often seen it in your dreams: blind and terrified riders, fleeing their own horses. You are blind to your beasts, you leave them lonely. Which is why you will never make as we do."

Ideas bubbled up in Clare's mind as this information sank in. "Has any human ever met her own beast?"

"And survived?" asked the woman. "Oh, surely not. I think not." She licked up one last bit of lettuce from her closed bud of a hand, then watched the candlelight flicker in her flame-confused silver plate. "But I do not know, to tell the truth," she said, still gazing down. "I know it would be dangerous to try. Some here believe that Balor was somehow defeated by his beast, and that is why he . . ." She trailed off. There was silence.

"If a human wanted to," said Clare, knowing she sounded awkward and obvious, but feeling stubborn, "if someone, some human wanted to get to know, or understand, or whatever, their beast, how would you start?"

The woman looked up. Her mountain-lake eyes had deepened to near black. "You would listen, Clare the Guardian," she said. "Listen carefully. And know a beast can only speak in pain, or in pleasure, or in making."

Clare scooped up the last bit of sweetness with the last spoonful of berries, feeling full and thoughtful. She leaned back in her chair and closed her eyes. A sweet, soft exhaustion swept through her. She gave a huge, unexpectedly noisy yawn.

In an instant, the room went silent. Clare blinked, sleepy, and looked around.

The tableful of smilers were staring, unsmiling.

"She's falling asleep," said a high, complaining voice from one end of the table.

"She mustn't fall asleep," said the man whose once-pointed, sharky teeth were normal now.

Clare was frozen in confusion. Eating was all right, but she mustn't *sleep* while she was in this place?

"Send her back," said a soft, papery voice. "If she falls asleep, she could destroy us all."

"Finn, if she falls asleep . . ." began a whole chorus of voices, high and low, rough and clear. But Finn's own voice, deep for a boy, interrupted them.

“She won’t fall asleep,” Finn said, sharp and even. He was striding toward her end of the table. “She won’t before I’ve taught her how to dream. Come, Clare.”

She felt a hand on her arm. She was standing now; the table and chairs were gone.

10

The Work of Dreaming

Clare thought, *There are no transitions in this place.* In my world, we have This, and then we have That. But here, they have no "and then"; it's just ThisThatThisThatThisThat, everything happening shoulder to shoulder, with no space between, like the slats of a wooden fence.

They were alone now—no leafy hall, no table—on a sandy beach, more like a California beach than an Irish one. Beside them stood a tall pile of broken branches, driftwood, and twigs of all sizes.

The light still hung between, it was still the magic hour, the blue hour, the slanting light when you can no longer see the sun, only what light scatters back to us from the sky. *Why doesn't it get darker?* wondered Clare.

The light would never change, as long as she stayed in this world. The magic hour, just before dusk—the time when the world is loveliest and strangest—is the only light the people of Timeless have. And living in an eternal magic hour, they long for midnight and noon.

But Clare did not know that yet. She only knew the breeze was salt-damp, and the low waves ran back and forth across the sand. There was something odd about the water's peaceful back-and-forth, though she couldn't quite think what it was.

"This reminds me of a beach where we went on vacation once," she said, and then immediately yawned. She turned to hide the yawn, but not before she saw Finn's pleased expression.

"I got the idea from you," he said, "from one of your dreams."

"How did you . . ." She realized what he'd said. "Wait. Wait a second. You've seen my dreams?" She didn't even want people to see her poem-things, let alone her dreams. Memories of certain dreams in particular made her face go red with embarrassment, then anger. "That's, I mean, that's an *incredible* invasion of privacy."

Finn's face fell. "I saw only those I was in, of course, I was no sneak. You've forgotten our visitings, in your dreams?"

Clare opened her mouth, closed it again. Under Finn's Cap, her brief sleep—wasn't Finn in that dream? Or his voice, at least? And not just then: in little flashes of dreams all her life, she saw a dark boy her age, who knew curious games and . . . "Was that really you? How?"

"It was," said Finn, looking relieved. "And you will see how, soon. I brought you here that we might be safe as I teach you dreaming. Clare"—she was yawning again—"do not sleep yet. Watch."

"Wait, but . . ." Yawn. "What's the big deal? If I fall asleep, what? What happens?"

Finn walked around his pile of branches and twigs, adjusting them, not looking at her. "Do you understand, girl, that in dreams, you come here to my world to make?"

"Yep," said Clare. She was so glad to be out of that hall, and she felt so relaxed. She ran her hands through hair growing fat with salt air.

He shoved a thick piece of driftwood low in the pile. "And what you make here is real—real *here*. But it can't hurt you. Because in your normal life, when you dream, your body stays safe in the human world, tucked under blankets. Say in a dream you make a bridge, and you make a murderer; and the murderer chases you over the bridge, and you're well afraid, you're terrified. But when you wake, you say, 'Oh, it was only a dream,' is that right? Because your body was safe at home, nowhere near the dream."

"Yes," agreed Clare, still almost-yawning.

"But if you dream while your body is here in Timeless, as yours is now, then what happens? It is not 'only a dream,' then. It is real. The bridge you made, real. The murderer you made, real. And if you have made a knife in that murderer's coat, and he puts the knife to you—you will die a real death."

Clare's sleepiness fled, and she stared at Finn, appalled. "I can't control what I dream. Half the time I can't even *remember* my dreams." She thought of her dream of the theater mask, and its eye-hole of broken, bloody egg, and felt a sick horror: *if that thing were real.* "Finn," she said.

"No, no," he said. "I will teach you. I will teach you how to open your eyes in a dream, and know that you are the maker, and make only what you like. It will be like when you make awake in your own world, pictures and stories and such. That is a kind of dreaming-awake, and you can do that, yes?"

Clare thought of her hidden, Balor-ruined poems, and said nothing. Finn seemed not to notice.

"And so now you will learn to walk awake in dreams. Some humans can, even without teaching. With my teaching, all will be well. Now watch, then. I wish we had more time but—but I can teach you. Watch."

He touched one branch in the pile of wood, and a little thrill of blue fire ran across it. The fire ran through the pile, and soon a blaze flickered between them.

"Watch," said Finn a third time. And the fire between them rose up, shaped itself into a fountain of fire, like a fountain of water—in fact it did seem to be water, Clare felt she could almost reach out and touch the water—only it was red, and the spray was sparks, not droplets. The red faded—oh, she had *thought* that it was fire, but that must have been a light from underneath, of course—and now the light was blue, and it was water, it surely was, it must have always been. The clear, blue-edged water surged up high, and Clare laughed as the spray spattered her face and hair.

But the light under the fountain must have turned green, because now it almost seemed to be an enormous plant of some kind—oh, a tree! It was a fir tree, how strange, growing straight up from the sandy beach. How could she have ever thought it was a fountain, or fire—it must have been a trick of the light. The tree towered and swayed in the wind, and she could hear the rush of the wind in the branches.

But the tree must have caught fire! Because now it was all flames, a huge, angry pillar of fluttering orange and red, towering over the beach.

(And through the flames, on the other side of the fire-tree, the fire-fountain, she saw a boy staring steady at her, sometimes; and other times, she saw a young white stag, watching her with the boy's gray eyes.)

The fire sank down, and was once again no higher than her own head.

"What happened?" said Finn, flickering from across the fire. "What happened? What did you see?"

Clare felt startled, felt confused, as if she had just been waked from a dream. "I saw, I saw that you made a fire, you lit this fire," she began. "And then, and then I thought it was—I think it was a fountain—Finn, it *was* a fountain, look, I'm still wet."

"And?" he said.

"And, but then it was a tree somehow, a fir tree on a beach! I could smell it, and . . ." She paused. "Did you do all that?"

"I did," he replied. "And so must you, to practice, to know you can. Fire is easy to practice with, because fire is change, one of the few pieces of change we have in Timeless. Try."

She stood looking into the fire. She felt absurd. "I don't even know how to start. I don't understand what you did."

Finn's voice was anxiety wrapped in impatience. "You do know, Clare. You do it in every dream; you come here every night. You just have to know what you want, what you wish for, and use that desire to make. That's the material you make with."

But Clare did not understand, and would not say she did.

"Try," Finn persisted. "This is where you dream. You know how, Clare."

Clare remembered dreaming. She remembered mornings, half awake and half still in the dream, when she felt a choice, for a moment, of whether to stay in the dream or join the day. That luxurious feeling: will I keep dreaming? what would I like to dream?

What would I like to dream? The fire formed and re-formed, wavered, grew, shrank. She watched its colors. She looked for what she wanted there.

"Dad," she said softly. He knelt behind the fire's billowing orange curtain. He was smiling with relief, his arms were opening to her—

"Stop," said Finn. He grabbed her arms, shook her. "Stop. Not that. It's not safe for you yet. Where your feeling is too deep, you are laid open. The feeling makes you foolable. Do you understand? That's the trick of it. You must make what you desire. But if you are unpracticed, the desire may blind you, and you will lose control of the dream."

Clare looked with longing as her father faded like the dream he was. She turned her face from Finn and said, "I'm sleepy now. You have to let me sleep." The fire swelled and sank beside them.

"Not yet," said Finn. "Here: I will fetch you a drink that will help you keep awake. Stay awake till I come back."

Easy for someone who has never slept to say "stay awake." But Finn thought sleeping was like eating—you might be hungry, but you could still refuse to eat. He did not understand sleep's sneak-thief ways. *I'm only closing my eyes one second*, thought Clare as Finn disappeared behind the dunes.

But it had been a long, exhausting day, after a long, sleepless night. And maybe, too, part of Clare wanted to practice dream-making alone, in private, the only way she had ever dreamed or made. So in that split second when she still had a choice, she let the river of sleep carry her away.

In her dream, Clare walked through a bombed city at dusk, amid its rubble and blackened, smoking walls. In the distance, sirens wailed and wailed, around and around and around.

Picking her way through smoldering debris, she almost stepped on a small hand thrust out from beneath a concrete block—a child's hand, blue and motionless. She bent to touch the hand. But the wreckage was so recent, the building so freshly fallen, that the concrete burned her wrist, and she pulled back with a cry.

Across the street, from the skeleton of an office building, came a hollow animal groan, followed by the snuffling breath familiar to her from nightmares. Clare hurried on. A distant, piercing scream met the still-wailing siren and made a kind of harmony with it.

Clare began to run. She remembered now: she was looking for someone, someone lost, her father? Not her father, but someone, she would know when she found them, and she had to find them, make sure they were all right.

She rounded the corner of a half-fallen building and stopped. A half block away stood a tall, thin man in a tall black hat, face obscured by the dusk. In his cupped hands, he held a red bird, a cardinal. As you can in dreams, Clare saw the bird far away and close up at the same time. It trembled in the man's yellowish hands.

Somehow, of all the terrible things Clare had seen and heard in this city, this man holding a red bird was the worst, the most unbearable. She screamed a scream of pure terror, straight from her bowels—thinking, as she did: *oh yes, I see now, that was* me *screaming, my scream that made a harmony with the siren, just like it's doing now.*

The dark figure looked up and smiled an unnaturally wide and wolfish smile. A red eye patch creased his jaundiced skin. He held the red bird out toward Clare, as if urging her to look closer.

She saw that his fingers were as red as the bird, were dripping with a dark red that fell in long thick liquid strands and pooled on the ground at his feet.

What he held was not a bird at all, but a bloody and beating heart.

Clare's hand flew to her chest. Her heart, her heart. Was it there? She couldn't feel it—could she? Was that a *hollow* sound, inside her ribs? She pounded her own chest frantically, but it was no good, there was nothing there, and she fell to her knees, feeling something desperately important ebb away from her.

But somehow the siren was forming words now, drowning out everything else. The wailing, circling siren song said one thing: *Clare! This is a dream! You have control! Take control!*

She caught her breath. *I have control.* She spoke. "It's my dream, and I say . . . I say it's a bird. It's a bird, I make it a bird. It has to be a bird. Drop that bird!" she shouted, as she had once heard a woman shout to a dog. "Put it down! Now! Drop it!"

The tall figure shrank and bent. Now it was a shambling mongrel with one cataract-covered eye. Growling, the dog opened its jaws.

A little red bird fell to the ground, shook its wings, and flew away.

As relief flooded Clare, and the siren whined her name—*Clare! Clare!*—hands seized her arms, and she woke up.

It was Finn holding her arms, and the smoking ruins beneath her were dissolving back into cool sand, and the ocean's rush covered the fading siren.

They were kneeling on the sand, and Finn was out of breath with running. "Say, Clare, how you are! Are you all right?"

"How would I know?" said still-half-dreaming Clare. "How would I know if I'm all right or not? Let me go."

Her legs and hands were filthy with soot and ash, and she had a painful burn on her wrist. "Well, I'm okay," said Clare, as she brushed the dirt from her jeans. "It ended up all right."

"Glad for that," said Finn, gruff. "But you should have waited. Take this drink, now, to stay awake, at least for a while. Keep you safe, in this next bit."

He sat on the sand beside her, his legs stretched out, eyes closed.

Clare drank the bitter drink, which tasted like strong, unsugared tea. She felt tired, shaken, and ashamed, and her wrist hurt a lot, but she wasn't going to say that to Finn. "I need to wait a minute, okay? Just give me a minute, before we try again. That was . . . that was a lot."

He nodded. She looked up, searching for a first star, something to wish on, or just to see. But stars never come where no night comes.

"I don't even know why we dream," she said. "It's such a weird thing to do. Do you know?"

"Ah, well," said Finn. The light around him was so clear, each dark hair outlined against the silvery sky, and Clare's heart ached toward him, just a little. "I believe you come to converse with your true selves. I believe it's the only place you can. You converse with yourself. You choose who you are."

"'True self,' though," Clare said, doubtful. "What is my *true self*, exactly, if it's not me, if I can talk with it."

Finn frowned into the silver-gray sea. "I did not say 'talk,'" he said. After a silence, he added, "Your true self is the part of you that loves. The part that sees and makes beauty."

"All my dreams aren't beautiful. At *all*," said Clare, thinking of the blasted city.

"You mean all your dreams are not pretty or nice or sweet. But beauty is in what's true."

Clare thought about her dreams of clogged bathrooms, of tests she didn't study for, and still felt doubt. "I don't know," said Clare. "I still don't know about 'true self.'"

"Ah, you care so much what things are called," said Finn, with sudden emotion. "Choose what you want to call it, the part that sees, the part that loves."

"I guess I would call it my mind," said Clare.

"Your mind! Oh, well then," said Finn. He was silent for a moment, hunched in like a coiled rope, the sea-sound a steady wash behind him. "Then what do you call the part of you that's ever planning a meal or a revenge, or nursing a grudge or a fantasy?" He turned to her now, frank and incredulous. "What do you call the part that frightens you away from making, except when it's sound asleep and you can slip away to Timeless? The part that chatters away in your ear, when with just one moment of silence, the whole ceaseless beauty of your changing world would open itself to you?"

"I call that my mind, too," said Clare stiffly.

"Well, then," said sardonic Finn, "'mind' is not the most useful word you have."

They were quiet awhile, in the unchanging light, whose unchangingness was beginning to make Clare feel a little ill. "So but then, if the roads were closed, and we couldn't dream, how would the human world change?"

Finn stared at something in the sand. He said, "Your world wouldn't change. But you would no longer have eyes to see it. Even your scientists know that when people cannot dream, they go mad.

All of you would go mad. The world would look like dust to you, and you would love no one, not mother or father, not husband or friend."

Clare tried to imagine a world without dreams and without the Strange fairy-makings, the flowerings of Timeless. She tried to imagine all the people walking around in it, unable to love.

Clare stood, brushed herself off. The leg she had been sitting on was stiff and painful. "I'm going to try now," she said. She felt stubborn. Sometimes she thought her stubbornness—which her father would tease her about, *bullheaded child*, and which had so enraged Balor—was the only thing that kept her going.

"Aye, then," said Finn, not looking at her. "I'll be here."

"Will you be *watching*?"

He looked up with a tired expression. "I can't leave, how can I? I'm your teacher. I don't understand why you fear for anyone to see your dreams and makings."

"Because dreams and makings are my private self, not for just anyone to see."

"It's mad, to me," he said, "but you are mad Clare. But—another but—I am Finn the Sane, and I am not just anyone to see."

Clare smiled to herself. He was not just anyone, though perhaps that made the seeing worse. The ocean rushed and rushed behind their comfortable silence.

Suddenly, Clare realized what was strange about that sound.

"Finn," she said. "This is weird. Does the ocean sound never change? Does it always go back and forth in the same pattern, like that, and never change its speed, or get louder or softer, or—"

He stood up abruptly. "Just dream then," he said coldly. "And be careful with it this time, and stay awake inside it. The danger you make won't be only to you. If you fall asleep or lose control, the murderer's knife could just as well go into me."

Bewildered and embarrassed, Clare said, matching his coldness: "Don't worry, I'm awake." She thought, *I've hurt his feelings*, but could not imagine how.

Everything I do goes wrong.

"I think I need to be farther away from the fire to begin this," she said, not adding, but thinking, *and farther away from you.*

"Well enough," said Finn.

Clare pointed toward the dunes. "I'm going to climb up there," she said. "Maybe you'll be *safer.*"

"Good," said Finn shortly. But when he turned toward her, his face was unexpectedly warm and worried. "Only remember, Clare. In a dream, what you want will come out, one way or the other."

"So . . . So I should be careful about what I want, then, right?"

"No, you can't be careful with what you want. Wanting isn't a pet who stays at your heels; it's a wild animal. You must become friendly with it. It will make an offer, and you will respond. Converse with what you want that way."

"So what should I try to want? What should I look for?"

"Never look for what you *should* want and desire, but what you *do* want and desire. You should know that from your poetry. It is the only way to make true. What you desire will appear, no matter how you try to erase or recolor it."

"All right," said Clare. She turned her back on the ocean and the fire, and began to walk toward the dunes.

Clare nodded. She walked a few hundred yards from the fire, took the dunes in a few dozen long, sinking steps, and sat at the top, looking down at the fire. Then she stretched her throat, looking up at the pale, transparent blue sky. She missed stars.

Clare thought of the story from *The Little Prince*, where the fox taught the prince how they could tame each other, by sitting together every day, each day a little closer. *I'll tame my wants*, she thought. *Or I guess we'll tame each other.*

The fire flickered on the beach, pulsing colors of sun and orange. *What is it?* she asked herself. *What is that flame? It's what I want*, she thought. *Or no, not what* I *want. It's just: wanting.*

And what did Clare want? What did she want to see there? She followed the thread of her desire to find out.

The flame became a tall statue of a grieving face.

The flame became a curtain of dark, tangled hair, the face obscured.

The hair became red hair, and the head turning toward her, and the face she almost saw—but *no*, she thought, *I can never tame that.* "No, no, I'm sorry, I can't," she said, soft but aloud. And the red hair shifted, became red flame again. The flame became a tall black man, old and thin but strong, tough, with a hard face.

The man grew immensely tall, and his legs became a gate. Clare thought, *Yes. I want to see what is inside the gate.* And as she felt that, beyond the gate a stairway appeared. Clare walked down the dune, entered the gate, and descended the stair.

Clare dreamed she was in a tunnel. She dreamed it awake, although she could not remember making the tunnel, and feared it, a little.

She feared the tunnel because it was alive. It throbbed delicately around her.

But I don't have to feel afraid. It's my dream. A little surge of wicked freedom, in that feeling.

She touched a hand to the wall of the tunnel. The wall was wood, but living wood, not carved and dry. Immediately, with a flood of pleasure, she knew where she was: inside the root of a tree, the same tree she had become on the island.

In that case, if she ran all the way to the end of the root, she would find her yew again.

Now her feet flew down the wooden path, her fingers brushing the sides of the root, sometimes brushing empty darkness where the root branched off in new directions. She did not remember the way, but her body and blood recalled her hours as a tree, and they flew on. In this crazy maze of passages, her body knew each twist and turn as if she had ridden them on her bike to school every morning. Heart wide-open, almost laughing, she ran on, until she reached the branching she knew, that her feet and blood and heart knew, would take her to the yew.

But the darkness of this last passage felt very dark. She stopped.

Something was in there: something large, taking long, harsh breaths, grunting and snuffling to itself, as it waited for her.

A flush of fear. Then Clare remembered: *I decide.* "No monster," she said. "There is no monster there, the path is clear and easy, I can run through and be free."

But the low, hoarse breath continued, slow and deep.

It's my dream, thought stubborn Clare. She knotted up her fists and walked toward the grunting, monstrous sound. For a while she walked, blind in the blackness, her skin twitching at the most delicate caress of air. The wet, rasping breath seemed to come from all around her.

My dream, Clare thought. *And I want light.* But she wasn't sure she wanted to see what breathed like that. So she called up just a glimmer, just enough to see, far down the root-passage.

"Be my yew," she whispered to the light, putting into those three words all her longing, and sending them out like a message in a bottle to this dream-world. And yes, yes: now someone was walking toward her out of the darkness, as the breathing still echoed around her, someone no taller than she, someone whose fists were clenched, whose hair was red, whose face was pale and strained.

Clare came face-to-face with the mirror and stopped.

But the figure in the mirror kept walking toward her, closer and closer, until only a single eye filled the glass. Clare put her hand to the reflected eye, as gently as she could, in case it hurt. And at that touch, she was flooded once more with a thrill of joy and release and relief, the joy she'd felt when her roots touched the roots of the yew.

The joy washed through her; she closed her eyes; she let her head drop back and her throat open up; she laughed and laughed and laughed.

11

Digging

When Clare opened her eyes again, still laughing, a wooden tunnel and a tall mirror were draining away into the beach sand, leaving only beach sand, low, shining waves, and a crackling bonfire beside her.

Finn was a few feet away, kneeling on the sand and grinning. "Not so bad, student," he said. "Not so bad at all. I did not understand all your making, but"—adding hastily as she opened her mouth to answer—"I know it was not made for me to see."

"I didn't make the roots I ran through," she said, "but I could control what happened there. It was like partly I was controlling it, and partly it was happening on its own."

"That is the customary way of making," he replied. "Another part of you made the roots. That you can control what happens is all that matters."

"Wait, but"—Clare sat up, shook sand from her hair—"but if I made it and it was real, where is it? Where are the roots, and the mirror, and . . ." She thought of the snuffling, raspy breath, the heavy tread behind her. "And all that?" she finished awkwardly. The ocean crashed, gentle and regular, a slow, soft metronome. Clare had a sudden realization: "Oh, Finn, did you make this place? Is this one of your makings?"

"I did," he said, with a crooked smile. "As you made the dream. But what I make stays, as long as I wish, for the most part. What you make here dissolves when you awake." He regarded the ocean with a disapproving eye. "I know it's wrong, that changeless rhythm of the waves. Ah, making here is poor making," he added with sudden passion, "because nothing changes, nor will ever change, nothing changes but the moon."

No wonder I hurt his feelings. "It's beautiful here," Clare said, "and peaceful, and it reminds me of a place I loved."

No reply.

"You really love making, I guess," Clare ventured. *Boy, that came out stupid.* But Finn didn't seem to mind.

"I do," he said. "I know my task in life is to end my grandfather's evil. I've known since I could speak. But I will be greatly glad when the task is done, and I am let alone to make in your world, where the makings change and decay and die, and are so much richer for that."

They were quiet again. He was vivid against the gray waves, all shoulders and angles, dark hair and set jaw.

"I have a question," said Clare. Finn pulled in his long legs and rested his face on his knees. His eyes caught their color from the sea, a shining gray-blue. She cleared her throat. "There was something I couldn't control in the dream. Do you remember when I said NO MONSTER, but the monster-sound stayed? What was that? How come I could control everything else, but not that?" Her voice sounded high and strained, the joy of the dream beginning to drain away like the dream itself.

"Well, it may have been your beast," Finn said. He sat up straighter and looked out on the waves, whose regular, mechanical crashing was beginning to wear on Clare's nerves.

"A woman at the banquet said humans make with our beasts without knowing," she said, "but fairies have tamed theirs and can maybe almost become them."

Finn looked down, as if something in the sand had drawn his interest.

"Have you tamed yours? Even though you're only half?"

"I have," he said. He was drawing in the sand, crosses and curves and swirls. "I have." He looked up at her. "But it was not easy, Clare, though I was too young and foolish at the time to fear it as I should have. It was not easy, and very nearly I did not succeed. Do not trifle with your beast, I beg you."

He unfolded his legs, dragged a heel across his sand doodles, and smiled at her. "You did so well, Clare, making awake in your dream. You have your mother's fairy blood, I'll swear to that." He stood and brushed off his pants. "Let's return to the hall and proclaim your progress."

"It's not just my mother's blood," said Clare as she stood and brushed as well. "Not just Mam but Dad, too, he's a Macleod, have you heard of them? He even has a little piece of this fairy flag his family has, supposedly like a zillion years ago this . . ."

She stopped.

Finn was staring at her, mouth open. Then he smacked his own head. "Macleod, of course!" he said. "I never thought—and your father has a piece of the flag? But Clare, that's great luck, greater than any I thought to have. That flag has the power to rally the fair—the people of Timeless. They are bound to it, absolutely bound, even Her of the Cliffs is bound. Ah, my worst worry soothed then, you brilliant Clare!"

"I don't really understand," said Clare, though it was hard not to be delighted at his joy.

"You heard some grumble at the banquet, that we ought not make our Hunt. It was not the first, and many say worse than that. They say we should let Balor succeed, let the gates be closed." He was striding around now, kicking up gouts of sand with his energy. "But if I hold the flag, they have no choice. Ah, mad Clare," he said, and took one of her hands in both of his, "you are the mad savior of both our worlds. Is the flag in your home? If we went there now, could you find it?"

Clare, who was staring at her hand in his, looked up. "Oh! Well, I don't know exactly. I think Dad brought it, but it might also be in one of the boxes that hasn't come yet . . ." She felt him deflate. "Couldn't we go find him where he is and ask . . . Yeah, I know. Not safe for him. Well, then, but let's just go home, I can look. If it's there, I bet I can find it! I mean"—a second, terrible thought—"as long as Balor isn't there, so I have time to look. I'd need a lot of time."

Finn dropped her hand, clapped his together. "Better idea," he said. "We'll visit your father's dream and ask him where it is."

Clare was not sure she'd heard correctly. "Visit his . . . *what*?"

"He comes to Timeless, at night in his dreams, as you all do. We'll visit him there. It's night, now, in the human world. That's why you've been so sleepy."

"Let's go, then!" Why had no one mentioned she could see her father? "Let's go right now, let's not wait! Where is he?"

Finn looked surprised. "I don't know. Why would I know? Timeless is vast, as vast as your world, and great parts of it uninhabited, except by a once-in-the-while sleepwalker from Time."

Clare pretended a patience she did not feel. "But you came to *me* in my dream. How did you find me?"

"Oh," said Finn. "I described you to a bird."

That was why Clare now sat under a stand of birches, while Finn stood nearby among the turning leaves.

She thought: *I miss shadows. Stars and shadows.*

But where there is no night, there are no stars; and where there is no noon, there are no shadows. She felt a surge of impatience. "What are we waiting for?"

"We are waiting for a bird to come by," said Finn. "This is a good place for birds." Clare recalled that the Finn-made beach had had no gulls, and she felt a protective tenderness toward him for this error. Slouching against a white trunk, he plucked a birch leaf and twirled it in his hands. She watched the changeless, rushing wind excite the birch leaves; it was like seeing the sound of a thousand tiny silver bells. Glancing up to make sure Finn wasn't looking, she pulled out her commonplace book and made a quick note: *Even the birch leaf knows how to ride the wind that is. But I still don't.*

"Hey, Finn?" said Clare, tucking the book in her pocket.

"Hey, Clare?" said Finn.

"Was that you, was that your voice, when I dreamed under Finn's Cap?"

His slow, pleased smile. "It was indeed. You remember."

"If it was you, though," said Clare, "then why didn't you just tell me what the key to Finn's Cap was, so that I could get through?"

"Ah well," said Finn. "But it doesn't work like that, does it? You must make your own key. If the key was to draw a picture, I could not draw it for you, or tell you where to move the pencil, each line of it, could I?"

"I guess not."

"Also, and you should know this for your father's dream, dreams are not made for business-talking. Dreams are poems, are complicated and savory, like a stew. They are not efficient."

This made Clare feel both somewhat discouraged, but also more interested in dreams, if indeed they were like poems.

"How will the bird recognize your father, to know where to take us?" Finn asked. "You should think of how you will describe him. What is he like?"

Clare hesitated. Out of all the dreamers in the world, how could she describe her father so that a bird could pick him out? "Well, he's not very tall, and he has brown eyes that sort of turn down at the corners, and he—"

"No," said Finn. "What is he *like*. The bird is looking for his true self, not his body."

"Oh," said Clare. She wasn't sure how to begin. "Well," she said, "he's really nice, and funny . . ." Finn's frown made her stop.

"This poor bird. How many billions of you are *nice* or *funny*? Do you not know your own father, for who he is, for who only he in all the world is?"

Clare frowned back at him, because sticking out her tongue, which is what she would have preferred, would be too babyish. But she understood what he meant, and thought harder. She said, "Okay. I'm just going to close my eyes and talk. And you tell me if it will work—*afterward*," she added hastily. "Don't interrupt me *during*, just don't, Finn."

She closed her eyes without waiting for his assent. She thought about her father; tried to feel him sitting right next to her. She said:

"He strokes my hair when he's thinking, so his hand is on my hair, but his mind is not, and sometimes his hand just stops and rests on my head, because he forgets.

"He also strokes my hair when he's sad about my mom, and then his hand touches my hair like there is nothing more beautiful and nothing more sad. It's a totally different feeling.

"He likes to sing old songs from Skye that his mother sang, but he doesn't remember all the words, so he sings 'and so and so and *so*, and this and *that*' for the parts he forgets. He always uses those words.

"If a rock on the road catches his eye he will tell you the whole history of the place—not the person-history, but land-history, that starts with 'A hundred thousand years ago' and goes back from there. He can tell you everything from, like, one or two rocks. He gets really excited. It's kind of dorky, and also kind of cool.

"When we go out for ice cream, he always holds my cone up before he gives it to me, like he's giving it this big scientific examination, and he always says, 'Bit crooked on that *one* side, let me correct that for yer, miss.' Then he gives it a big lick. When I was little, it made me so mad, but now, even though it's still annoying, it's also sort of hilarious.

"When there's a part on a movie or TV when the people who love each other will never see each other again—married people, or a mom or dad and a kid, or a grandma and someone, or even like a girl and her dog—anytime they love each other and have to say good-bye—when a part like that comes on, he doesn't cry exactly, like make any noise or breathe, but the tears go down and down his face, like rain on a window. Every time. Even before Mam died, but even more after."

Clare was quiet then, but she did not open her eyes. Finally, she said, "Once, about a year ago, when we were driving in Texas, we saw a bird flapping on the ground in circles, really badly hurt, and he stopped to go look. Then he came back to the car and got the tire iron, and he killed it with one hard hit. He got back in the front seat, and he put his head on the steering wheel, and then he did cry, really hard, mostly totally quiet, but his shoulders shaking and shaking, and sometimes he made these loud gasps of breath, like he was drowning. It really scared me. And we never talked about it afterward. After a while he just started the car, and we kept driving."

When Clare opened her eyes, she saw Finn standing, watching her. There was a bird on his shoulder, a small brown one, but red-stained from the top of its head all the way down its front, like it had fallen into a glass of cranberry juice.

But Clare hardly saw the bird—she only saw Finn's face, which was looking at her in a new way, with a new interest, and new respect. "Well made, Clare Macleod," he said. "That was a fine making, a poem indeed."

The bird sang a long trill into Finn's ear, and flew away. "My thanks," called Finn, "to you and your flock"—then, looking at Clare, he called again: "Our thanks, that is: our thanks."

"How do we get there?" asked Clare, standing up. She jumped up to grab a low birch branch and pulled her feet up, hanging free for just a moment to stretch her back and arms. "I mean I know it will be that thing of, We're *here*, then we're suddenly we're *there*—but how does that work? Could I learn how?"

Finn laughed. "You know how. It's only the way you move in dreams every night of your life. It's easy—it's just . . . you see where you are, and then you see that you should be somewhere else: and then you are. I don't know why you can do it asleep and not awake. But come here, girl, and I'll take you."

And he did.

They were standing in a rainstorm, in a black night. The darkness was a shock to Clare after all those hours that hovered between light and dark. But the darkness was a relief, too: like switching off her bedroom lights after a long, anxious day.

The darkness was a relief. But the rainstorm was wild around them, and thunder rolled across the flickering sky, and that was dreadful. When the lightning came, it flashed against a wide black plain, where a lonely, mud-covered man dug frantically into the ground. His breath was coming in deep pants and sobs, and the wind around them seemed to gust and blow in tune.

Finn spoke. "When you visit the dream of one who dreams asleep, you have some power over their minds. You may feel you can control or divert him, make him feel this or desire that; and you may be right. But even if you only wish to help him, or ease his pain—don't use that power, Clare. You can help him with your hands, but do not try to change what he feels or thinks. Let him dream his own dream. Nothing else is right."

Clare nodded, but did not respond. The muddy man horrified her. She had never seen her father so undone. She was shocked, and embarrassed, and afraid. It was not what she had imagined at all. She wanted to run to him, and she wanted to run away.

Finn said—more gently than usual, and the gentleness frightened her—"He will likely not see you for what you are, Clare. He is dreaming. He may not be able to hear you at all. Some people, in a dream, they only listen to themselves, only see what they create in their minds. Don't be hurt if he does not know you. We can try again tomorrow night."

The rain was hard and cold against her face and throat, and her hair clung wetly around her face. As she walked, lightning lit up the roiling sky again and again, making the muddy man vivid against the wet black ground, as his shovel plunged and lifted, plunged again. At each crack of thunder, he startled as if struck.

Clare drew closer and, in the next flash of light, saw his face was wet with rain. Rain had drenched his hair and clothes, his face was spattered with wet mud, and his eyes were swollen and wild.

"Dad," she said.

He turned wildly in the black, roaring night, his eyes unfocused. "Áine?" he said.

Turning and turning in the rain, his face desperate, shouting, "Áine?"

Then he thrust his spade in the ground again and roared with fury and grief. Clare stumbled backward at the sound, for it contained more pain than she knew how to bear. She saw that in someone else's dream, their mind is clear as a picture book to you. *How much he misses her, so much more than I knew.*

But something else was also driving this grief—there was something in this picture she couldn't quite see.

He bent to the earth, knotted muscles in outline under his wet shirt; he dug and dug and dug. "I lost it," he cried, as his spade cut the earth, flung the dirt, cut again. "I lost the watch you gave me, I must have lost it out here, but I don't know where it is, I can't find it, I've been digging all night, I'm so sorry, Áine, I'm so sorry, love, I will find it, I will find it, I'm so sorry."

Clare thought: *It's me. He misses me, but also, he is afraid for me.*

(And yet still, something else as well—what was the part of the picture she was missing?)

Without warning, the ground collapsed beneath her father's feet. He was drowning in the muddy black ground, only his head and one arm visible as he struggled and writhed in the dirt. "Dad!" Clare screamed—*it's only a dream, Clare,* but she was in the dream herself now, and could not control it—and she was beside the hole, digging at the dirt with her fingers, freeing his other arm, pushing the mud off his face and mouth. Her father stared at her, bewildered, not seeing *her*, she could tell, but seeing *something*, as he choked and coughed. "Dad!" said Clare, sobbing. "Dad, please, Dad!" as she pulled the mud from his mouth. "Dad, look at me! It's me Clare, it's *Clare.*"

His face changed. "This isn't real," he said under his breath. "This is a dream." His eyes focused on her eyes, and in that moment, Clare knew, he saw. He saw her for who she was.

The rain had stopped somehow—the somehow of dreams; and the clouds had dissolved, somehow, and the moon made a murky light. Somehow, Clare was no longer kneeling over a muddy hole, but sitting on the ground before a campfire. On the other side of the flames she saw her father.

"Clare," he said. "How are you here? Are you—" His face twisted for a moment. "Please, are you—" He could not finish the sentence.

With a flash, Clare saw that he feared she was dead, a ghost-daughter visiting his dream. "I'm fine, I'm fine, Dad, I'm alive and—and I'm fine," she finished awkwardly.

The fire crackled in the silence. He gave a short laugh, and Clare wished she could see his face, to see if the laugh were real or sad; from the sound, she couldn't tell. Across the blue and yellow flames, he hummed a small fragment of song to himself, one she had never heard before. He looked smaller, younger, almost like a boy. She saw how private a dream is, what a secret place her presence violated.

"Dad," she said softly. "I came to ask you something."

Silence.

"Are you listening?"

"I am," said his dreamy, sleepy, boyish voice.

"Oh, okay. Good. So, well, one thing, I just wanted to tell you that I was all right, in case you were worried. I'm so sorry, but I had to leave the house. I'm really sorry. But this bad man came, Dad, and he wanted me to give him the key, and he hurt Jo, he might have—" She stopped. "And I was scared."

"I'm so sorry, sweet," he said. His voice was low and rough on the other side of the flames, and she could not make out the expression on his face.

"But, so," Clare said—she had not given much thought to how she would explain all this to her father, only knowing he must be worried, she had wanted to ease his mind—"but, so, I went down the fairy road, because . . ." Bad start: she took a deep breath. "Because, well . . ."

"The people of the tree," said her father. He seemed hazy, and smaller still, almost like a small boy.

"What?" she said.

"When you were a baby. The people of the tree," said a sleepy, distant boy.

"Wait," said Clare. "Do you mean—are you talking about . . ." But he interrupted her with a hoarse laugh, a man's laugh now. Although he was more the right size again, now he seemed old, an old man.

"You're like your mother," he said. "Your mother used to visit me in dreams."

My mother knew how to walk in dreams. A thought to turn over and look at carefully: but save it for later.

"Well, so—so now I'm with them," said Clare, "with . . . those people, and they're protecting me. And I'm safe. You keep changing in the flames," she added anxiously.

"Do I," said the voice of a drowsy old man.

"Dad. Listen, please. Here's what I wanted to ask. Where do you keep the fairy flag? I need it for something. I'll bring it back," she added, hoping this was true.

The old man with her father's eyes smiled. "That flag," he said. He was silent for a while.

"Yes, that flag," Clare prompted him. "The fairy flag. Where do you keep it?"

"I keep it in the sky," said her father.

"In the sky . . . ? But no, wait," said Clare, anxiety rising. "I don't know what you mean. Tell me in different words, please."

"It's one of the stories in the sky," said the old man, dreamily, soft, almost asleep. "So I keep it there."

"Dad, please." And at that moment the ground shook once, hard. Clare toppled over almost into the flames. When she righted herself, her father was himself again, and staring at her in horror.

"Clare, get out. It's not safe here. Get out. Get out. GET OUT."

Once again, Clare had that sense of the world draining away: the darkness drained, and the fire, and the mud, and her father. They became paler and grainier, blurred sketches of themselves. The world was gone; and her father was a dissolving ghost, a Polaroid going backward; and then he was gone.

"He's waked." Finn was pulling on her arm. "And so must we be gone."

Clare rose unsteadily. The vanishing of her father's dream had left nothing behind but ice. Clare and Finn stood in a blue-and-white, frozen world. Her breath came white. Her hands were frosting over. "Finn," she said into the white air. Her voice to her own ears sounded small and shocked. "What happened? Did you make this icy place?"

"No, I did not." Finn's hands were thrust deep in his pockets, his shoulders hunched, his face a misery.

"Can you change it back? I'm freezing." Clare took a lungful of spiky air. "I mean, I'm actually freezing, I think." The new ice-world was flat and blue-white and still, as far as she could see. In this landscape, the clear half-light of the eternal magic hour was blue and cold.

"Clare," said Finn, his words pushed out against the cold. "Listen to me."

"At least he knows I'm safe now," she said. "And I know he's safe."

"But you don't know that." Seeing Clare's uncomprehending look, Finn pulled his hands from his pockets in a gesture of despair. "Were you not paying attention? Did you not see all his dream was saying?"

"I saw that he misses my mother," said Clare. She shook her head to clear it. "I saw that he misses me, and was afraid for me, but I fixed that, I told him—Finn, please, would you change this place, it's so cold!"

"Why change it?" said Finn, all frost and thundering gray eyes. "Why change it, when this is truth, this is the ice that lies beneath our world. Did you not see in his dream what was plain to see? The mine where he was working has collapsed. He is alive, he dreams, but he is buried beneath twelve tons of earth. He dreams, but he is buried deep, deep."

"It's not true," shouted Clare. A wind arose, blowing Finn's hair forward and Clare's hair back; it stiffened, became a staggering gale. "Change it," she shouted, not knowing whether she meant this cold landscape or what Finn had read in her father's dream. "Please change it, please!"

The wind felt somehow hot and cold at once, a checkerboard wind, freezing and burning, until Clare could not tell freezing from burning, because they seemed to be one thing.

"Clare, you need to see this." Finn carved each word into the frozen air—and as he spoke, Clare did not know, still, whether he was talking about the cold or her father's peril. "This is what is real."

"It isn't," Clare insisted. Her ears hurt so badly, and pressure was building inside them. The thought of her father in danger—near death?—had punched her in the stomach, had cut away all the ground she stood upon.

"This is our world. This is our real world. This is Timeless, what lies beneath our makings," he said, adding, more gently, "and that is real, what your father's dream said."

"I will change it," she shouted. And now she knew exactly what she was talking about. "I will change it, Finn, I'll figure out a way!" She brushed furiously at stinging ice-drop tears. "I want to see Her of the Cliffs. Take me there."

At their departure, the ice sighed a long ghost sigh.

12

It Works Through Plumbing and Words

Clare and Finn stood in a wide clearing surrounded by evergreens on three sides, and on the fourth by a golden river. Her of the Cliffs stood with bow raised, as if aiming at the curving remnant of moon.

Clare ran toward her, stumbling and furious. "You knew."

Her of the Cliffs lowered her bow, but did not turn. "I did."

"You let me think my father was safe."

"I did not say that."

"You lied to keep me from leaving."

Her of the Cliffs was silent. Wind rushed soft through the tops of the trees, a steady, unchanging wind, like traffic. Not real wind, more fake-magic-making. "I *hate* this place," said Clare.

"Balor buried your father to blackmail you," said Her of the Cliffs. Finally, now, she turned. "He caused the collapse. Now he keeps your father and the miners caught with him like insects in a bottle, to kill when he likes."

When Her of the Cliffs said that, her voice was so cold that Clare thought she must have no heart at all. She had heard, but not really understood, that these people left their best and truest selves in their fairy-makings, which lie outside them, radiant and Strange all over our world, like abandoned shells, like exoskeletons. So to Clare, as to many other humans over the centuries, the Timeless ones themselves seemed soulless and frightening and cold.

But then, to the people of Timeless, humans seemed inward, self-obsessed, unlovely, and unseeing.

Her of the Cliffs continued. "Although the mountain hangs over your father's head, it is your head Balor heeds. It's you he would frighten. And if Balor wishes to frighten you, perhaps it means he has not found that key." Her bow beside her like a staff, arrow in the other hand, she rolled one shoulder back to loosen the muscle. "So in that sense, your father's peril is good news."

At this final callous sentence, a fury mounted in Clare that was also, as furies often are, a wild and climbing terror. "You people have to help him," she said. "We have to make sure he's all right."

"But we know he's well and right," said a miserable voice, a few yards away. Finn opened his hands as if pleading. "You just talked with him in his dream. He is good at dreaming, almost as good as a fairy."

"He is far away, and not our trouble to take in hand," said Her.

It was a slap to the heart. "My father is ALL I HAVE," Clare cried. "And I won't let him die for you. If you want my help, you'll save him."

That made Her of the Cliffs pause, but only for a moment. She slid the copper-tipped arrow back into her quiver. "Far more is at stake than your father," she said. "Dreaming is at stake. And making is at stake, yours and ours."

"As if making's all that matters," Clare snapped. "I have to go to him. Now. Not in dreams. In reality, my reality, in the human world. Now."

The sound of a boy kicking a fallen log in frustration. "That's what he wants, don't you see, you stupid girl!"

Clare flew around, her face hot. "Don't call me stupid. *Ever.*"

Finn blinked, and his voice changed. "I didn't mean—you're not stupid, but—Balor wants you to come out in the open. The mine collapse is his design to drive you out where he can see you and kill you."

"I don't care," said Clare, who didn't. "I have to go to the mine and tell someone so that they can protect him, until they get him out." Not *if they get him out. When, when, when.*

"And what will you tell them?" called Her of the Cliffs. She had walked to the wide, roaring river, was leaning her bow against a boulder.

That question stopped Clare. What *would* she say? She heard herself explaining to some tall, important, frantically busy person: *My dad left me alone, and a bad man came, the guy who owns this mine, he's a fairy really, and he's trying to close the fairy roads. And he made this mine collapse, to scare me into letting him in our house.*

Even if someone believed that, which no one ever, ever would, what were they supposed to do? Her hands were fists. She kicked the grass in frustration. She felt sick with the adrenaline spinning useless in her blood.

Finn walked down the riverbank. *Walking away from me and my stupidity*, thought Clare. He began picking up stones, turning them over, dropping some, keeping others.

"Clare, come here," called Her of the Cliffs. She was sitting, now, on the end of a fallen log that stretched out over the rushing river, wide and overfull, bronzy-gold in the fairy light. She raised her voice again. "I believe your father is protected. Even when you are not in it, your mother's house still offers you both some protection."

"You believe, but you don't know," said Clare. Reluctantly she moved toward the river. Finn was a dark figure against the half-light, skipping his stones, one at a time, with a low sidearm toss toward the water.

"I have to do something," Clare said to Her of the Cliffs. Her own voice sounded pleading and desperate to her ears. "There has to be a thing I can do." She felt the bitterness of it, that she had been so brave, had escaped Balor, had protected the tree, had found her way through the last gate, had even learned to dream awake—and it would all mean nothing, if her father was to die for it. *I won't ride this wind, not this one. I'll push against it as hard as I can.*

Finn tossed a stone. It hopped over the cascading water three, four, five times. Clare found herself counting as he tossed again. She had stood on the beach with him, learning to dream—when? Hours ago? Half a day ago? She had lost all sense of time here.

Finn tossed another stone. Three, four, five. Her father's face in the wild dream-rain, how she could see his grief and the source of his grief, and how Finn had said she could help him in the dream, if she wished.

Four, five, six. "Finn," she said. She held perfectly still, so that the thought she had caught by one delicate wing did not get away. "Ma'am," she added, shy, because she did not know what to call Her of the Cliffs, and because that was what she had been taught to call women in Texas. *In Texas*—it seemed like a stranger and more distant land than fairy now.

"There is a way to help my father without leaving Timeless," Clare said. "I could visit one of Balor's dreams."

Finn had flung the rest of his stones into the water in a furious splash. The word *stupid* had been used again, with even greater heat, on both sides. Finally, Finn had proclaimed, "Balor is a fairy, he does not dream." He turned to Her of the Cliffs. "Is not that right?"

She hesitated, and Clare leaped upon the hesitation. "He does dream, doesn't he?"

"This plan is out of the question," said Her of the Cliffs. She slipped off her log and walked closer to Clare. "You must not even consider it. But yes, he does sleep and dream," she added reluctantly. "His thousand years in your changing world have reshaped him."

Clare bulled ahead. "Finn said when you visit a dream you have power over their minds, you can make them feel certain things and want certain things. I could—"

"No. Out of the question. If you let your concentration lapse for a moment, he would see you for who you are. And that would be very bad for you, very bad indeed, and perhaps for us as well. It is far too dangerous, Clare, and if—"

"But my father . . . ," Clare began. She stopped. Her of the Cliffs seemed to swell, power surging out from her in a single, swamping wave, like a blow to the chest. Clare looked for Finn, but he still stood on the riverbank, arms wrapped around himself, frowning at the water.

"All right," said Clare, bitterly, looking at her boots on the grass. "Okay. I understand."

But Clare did not understand, not at all, and she did not agree. She kept a secret resolve in her heart to wait for her chance.

Turning her fierce disapproval now to Finn, Her of the Cliffs asked: "And why did you take her to visit her father's dream?"

As Finn explained his plan to use the Macleod fairy flag, Clare thought an odd expression flitted over Her of the Cliffs's face, something like tenderness. In any case, she subsided and softened. "It is a good plan," she said. "And, Clare, while I cannot promise this, perhaps we will be able to help your father, not now, but when the host rides at Midsummer. But you must know that we cannot help him, whether we will or no, until we have that flag. Did you learn where it is?"

"Not exactly," said Clare. She sat on the riverbank and dug at a smooth river rock. "Dad told me something, but it didn't make sense. The flag could be at home, or in some box on a boat on its way from Texas. I don't know." *In the sky*—could it be on a plane? How was she supposed to know?

"She doesn't know how to read a dream," said Finn. He was walking toward them, hands in his pockets. "She could not read her own father's dream-map, though knowing him as well as she does."

"Well, you were there, too," said Clare, ice in her voice, "and I guess you're this big expert on dream-talking, or reading dreams, or whatever. So where's the flag?"

"Clare," said Her of the Cliffs, surprisingly gently. "Do you know what a dream-map is?"

It was hard to wear a false face with Her of the Cliffs. "No," she admitted.

Unexpectedly, Her smiled a young and girlish smile. "Then I get to tell you," she said, settling down beside Clare. Her power now swirled around her as softly as a song. "When we dream—all of us, human or fairy, dreaming asleep or awake, which is making—when we dream, when we make, we make with ourselves. We make with what we are. We ourselves are the material. Do you understand?"

"Maybe I do," said Clare. "Sort of."

"Here is what that means: each piece of each dream or making is a version of ourselves. Each snapping dog, each scolding father; each new rose or blasted pine; each tumbled barn or dirty kitchen; each bicycle steering out of control down each steep hill—each of these things is some part of ourselves, or version of ourselves, some fear or joy or desire."

"So how do you know which thing in the dream is the real person?"

"Ah, but you see," said Her of the Cliffs with pleasure, "it's the *whole* dream, or the whole making, that is the person. The dream maps the person at that moment. Or you might say the dream is a sketch of the person, drawn on that night. The picture will change from night to night. A kitten will grow into a tiger; a dirty kitchen will become clean, or become a bathroom. If you go back to the same dreamer many nights, you can learn a great deal.

"But when you only see one dream, you must be a skilled map-reader to understand what you are seeing, even when you know the person well. Tell me about your father's dream, and let's talk about it."

So Clare described her father's dream in the wild rain, digging and digging for the lost watch her mother had given him, and being swallowed by the earth. "But he doesn't have a watch like that," she added. And then, shyly: "So I wonder if that might be me, the watch? But then," she said, "you said everything in the dream is *him*, so . . ."

"It could be his connection to you," Her of the Cliffs said. She was watching Clare closely. "The watch might stand for that. But why a watch, do you think?"

Clare thought, without success. She was feeling rather tired.

"What does a watch do?" the woman prompted her.

"Tells time," said Clare. "Oh: time? Is it something to do with Timeless?" She frowned. "But Dad doesn't know about that—I don't think he does anyway. Does he?"

Her of the Cliffs did not respond directly. "What else about the watch? What about the word itself? Dreams like to pile meanings one on top of another. They are not so fussy about spreading their meanings out in a clear line."

"Um, something about seeing? Like watching something? Like he couldn't see me?" Clare, rubbing her face in weary frustration, was stopped by a thought. "Or, oh—like he didn't leave anyone to watch me while he was gone? Or he's worried who's watching out for me now?"

"Perhaps. A nice beginning. What about the rain and wind?"

Clare yawned, then shook her head. That drink must be wearing off. She thought about how the wild wind echoed her father's wild sobs. "Like, his emotions?" she asked. "Maybe like—like wind for his worries swirling around, and rain for his sadness. Like rain for tears!"

"This seems a good reading to me. And now: what did he say about the flag? His precise words."

Clare thought. "He said it was in the sky. No, wait—he said, 'It's one of the stories in the sky,' so he 'keeps it in the sky.' I thought . . ." She hesitated.

"Say," said Her of the Cliffs.

"I thought of, like, constellations? How they're named after myths, which are like old stories? But I still don't see . . ." She trailed off, and was silent for a while. "It's hard to read a dream-map."

"It is not only hard." Her of the Cliffs selected a stone and threw it across the river. "It is impossible, in the end, for the meanings are that dense. That is what I best love about dreams, and about makings, good makings. They are folded-up buds of complications and mysteries, and if you stay with them patiently, they will unfold and unfold, and never stop unfolding. Dreams are flowers that never stop blooming."

"But then what's the point of trying?"

"I said it will continue to unfold and unfold," said Her of the Cliffs. "I did not say you could see nothing at all."

Clare sat in a frowning and frustrated silence.

Finn spoke up. "It's practice is all she needs. I will take her to the dreaming place, and we will practice reading dreams. After a few practice readings, she will know where to find the map."

Her of the Cliffs eyed Finn for a moment. She nodded. "Practice, then it shall be. But you will only watch the dreams, not enter them, as entering might be harmful, to the dreamer and to you. Agreed, Clare?"

"Agreed." Clare yawned hugely. "Oh! Sorry."

The red head cocked to the side. "Have you slept since coming to Timeless?"

"Uhhh." Clare thought. "Not really. Except when I practiced dreaming-awake, I guess. Was that a kind of sleep?"

Her of the Cliffs frowned. "A kind of sleep. But you need true sleep."

Clare thought she ought to be tired—the banquet, and learning to dream, and seeing her father. But the light hanging half bright around her told her it wasn't time. "I'm fine," she said. "I had that wake-you-up drink. And I did sleep some."

Her of the Cliffs stood, nodded. "Then Finn will take you to dreaming place." She strode off.

Clare and Finn stood together, alone and a little shy. "It's beautiful here," said Clare. "This place, this river."

"It is Her's making," said Finn.

"But even this, it's only ice under the surface, right?"

"Yes." A sadness in his assent, almost a shame.

"Is it really ice in my world, too?"

"No, no." Finn wouldn't quite look straight at her. "Where you live, the fire you call 'change,' turns the ice into water, and the water flows on and on, makes ponds and oceans and storms and rivers and snow that thaws and runs down the mountains. Ah, but I wish my home was there," he said with passion.

"But after a while," said Clare, "the fire of Time turns the water to steam, and the steam vanishes. Where does it go then? Where does what used to be water go?"

Where do we go, when we die and vanish, she thought, but didn't say.

"Maybe back to water," said Finn. "Or into air. Or maybe there is a third world we don't know about. Timeless, and Time, and something else."

They were quiet together, thinking. Then Finn tugged her sleeve. "Let's go," he said. "To the dreaming place."

Now they stood at the top of a path that wound down in switch-backs to a wide plain, a plain that stretched out to the horizon. Clare put a hand to her mouth and took a step back.

It was not a sweet, grassy plain; nor was it a vast, dirty city of tall black buildings; nor a rocky desert; nor a snow-carpeted plain; nor a valley full of little houses with chimneys that smoked.

It was all these things, and many, many more.

As far as Clare could see was a confusion, a chaos, of landscapes and objects. There were city streets; there were jungles; there were great white monuments; there were oceans and lakes.

She saw a gigantic statue, taller than a skyscraper, whose enormous stone head had fallen to the ground, where it lay, frowning, on its side.

She saw a merry-go-round spinning out of control, and an old man on it screaming.

She saw a white man and a black woman in red robes doing a slow, complicated, lovely dance down a dirt road.

She saw a tall sooty building, covered with graffiti, every window alight, a man dangling from one window ledge and laughing.

She saw a group of children standing still in a green field of rice, as if they were the rice plants themselves.

This was the tiniest patch of what she could see. The valley stretched beneath them much farther than her eye could follow. It was as if all the paintings of every museum in the world had been scrambled into one dish.

Clare found that she had sat down on the path, and pulled her knees up, and was peering over them. "Why is it like that?" she said in a small voice. "What is it?"

"The place your people come to dream," said Finn.

"This isn't what it looked like when you took me to my dad's dream," she said.

"I took you a different way. I took you straight into his dream. Once you are inside one of these dreams, you won't see the rest of them."

"Do *I* dream here?" she asked. She got back to her feet, her legs wobbling. She stamped one foot at a time to bring them back to her. "Do I?" It seemed so sad, so congested, so thick, all these screams and laughs, this heat and cold, all this misery and loveliness packed together like cells in a body, and each person unseeing, not seeing the others.

"Sometimes you come here," said Finn, glancing at her for the first time. "But you are one of the few who wanders out of this place, and into the rest of Timeless, to visit us."

"They don't see each other," said Clare. "I hate it."

"Usually they don't. You are an unseeing people." He added more kindly, "But all these dreamers are connected underneath what you can see, like mushrooms or trees. But mushrooms and trees feel how their fingers tangle beneath the earth, and you do not."

"We never feel it, not ever?"

"Some feel it always," said Finn. "And all feel it sometimes. That's why your dreams may cross the dreams of people you are close to."

"Close, like, people I'm in the same house with? Or people who are my friends?"

"People desiring what you desire. People whose hearts hum in harmony with your own. Sometimes you know them, sometimes not. Then you make the dream together."

Then without speaking, Finn took her hand and led her down. Clare was so shocked at this gesture, at the warm rough feel of his hand in hers, that she could neither speak nor think clearly. She just walked beside him, the world rushing around her, blood rushing in her ears.

At the top of the last switchback, Finn stopped. He did not look at her. He kept his gaze on the crazy-quilt dream landscape before them, a chaos of smells and sounds and strangely washed-out colors.

"I know what you're planning to do, Clare," he said.

Startled, Clare pulled her hand away from his; regretted it. "I'm not—" she began.

"It's a foolish idea," he said, still not turning toward her. "It is dangerous beyond what you understand. And the anger of Her of the Cliffs when she learns—" He closed his eyes.

Clare's mouth set, pulled down at the corners, waiting for the fight.

"I know what you plan," said Finn, "because if I had a father, and he were in danger, I would do the same. Which is the selfsame reason I will help."

Clare thought of the word *dumbfounded* and saw how well it fit this feeling. "You're going to *help* me?"

"But I cannot come with you," he continued, as if she hadn't spoken. He sounded anguished. "I thought it through a hundred times while you talked with Her of the Cliffs." (*He doesn't care, he's just skipping rocks*—she felt ashamed to have had that thought.) "He would know me, in a moment he would know, and all would be lost. Clare, I am downcast for it. We are too close, Balor and I."

"Too close in blood?"

"In blood and other ways." Finn smiled a crooked, painful smile. "My whole life has been dedicated to him, to knowing that I was meant to destroy him. His life since my birth has been dedicated to escaping me. Our two hearts are tied in one terrible knot."

"I never thought of it that way. That must be, it must not be . . ." She searched for words: ". . . very nice."

He laughed a brief, startled laugh. "No, mad Clare. Not nice indeed." He smiled. "But though I cannot go, I can help you, a little I can. We are meant only to watch the dreams, that you might learn to read them. But if you're willing, I'll take you right inside." He looked at her anxiously. "I'll teach you to stay safe inside another's dream, at least as safe may be. What say?"

"*Yes.*" Impulsively, Clare took up his hand again. They both looked down at their hands, as if surprised to see them there. Looking down, not in his eyes, she felt safe to say aloud the hope and fear she had been nursing: "Is there a way to be *invisible* in dreams? That's what I was wondering. So that he couldn't see me at all?"

"No," said Finn, his low voice so close to her own ear she could feel his breath. "No, I'm so sorry, Clare, you cannot *be unseen.* But"—as she slumped a little—"you can become part of the dream, blend into the dream. Make yourself a passing cat, make yourself a book on a shelf, make yourself a broken doll lying in a corner . . ."

"You can do that?" said Clare in astonishment, looking up.

"You can, of course you can. You just make, as you do in your dream, only using the stuff of their mind. You decide what to be, and you become that. It will be easier if I show you. Come."

And Finn led her into the dreams of the world.

They entered an old house, like a haunted house, many gabled, with broken windows. The door was off one hinge, and creaked as they pushed it open. The front room, empty of furniture, smelled musty and moldy, a rotting smell. They stood on a grubby wood floor in the dim, colorless light.

At first Clare didn't hear the sound, it was so soft, and came from all around them. But it was there: a high, whispering song. She could not make out the words.

A voice in the next room. Hand in hand, Clare and Finn walked to the doorway, and peered carefully through.

An extremely old man, his face all dusty wrinkles like a dying apple, was scrubbing the walls with a large, dirty rag. He wore jeans and a thin, faded plaid shirt.

"It works through plumbing and words," the old man said to himself under the soft hiss of the song. His voice was both reasonable and mad. "If you find the words written down, you must erase them. Fast as you can, erase them."

Words covered the walls. Urgently, carefully, the old man erased some words while leaving others. *The potter's cup unbroken*, said one line. *The cup with water fills.* Carefully, urgently, the old man erased the word *water.*

Clare suddenly understood that the strange song all around them was the sound of water running through pipes. *It works through plumbing and word*s, she thought and shuddered. The words the pipe sang were clearer now, like a dense poem.

Ourwordsmakeshapesandeveryshapeistrue, whispered the ghostly song of the pipes.

Her hand was empty. Finn had vanished. Clare looked around the bare front room, a little wildly, then once more put her head into the old man's room. High on the wall, in chalky blue-gray, she saw new words, in a new, spikier handwriting: *The fish that swims must flap its*, the new words read. Must flap its *what*? thought Clare, squinting to read the last scrawled word.

Fin. Must flap its fin. Clare pulled back, pressed her back against the wall, and put a hand over her mouth to keep from laughing. Such a grim situation, and yet such a good joke.

But how to join him? *Just think it*, Finn had said. *As if it were your own dream.*

Forwordswereallthemusicyoucouldhear, whispered the pipes.

Clare thought. She thought of a line to fit the watery words of this plumbing-haunted room, to complement, to fit in and not to spoil the old man's dream (if he was really an old man, or really a man, even—there was no way to know). She thought of an old poem she'd had to memorize in school, and smiled to herself.

Soon, high on the wall, too high to be erased, and just beside *the fish that swims*, were new words, in small, looping, orange-red script: *Neptune taming a sea horse, thought a rarity / does not disturb the water's clarity.*

~

After that, her worries about her father slipped to the back of her mind, from the joy of dream-walking. They visited an old farmhouse where a dog thrust its long nose through the screen door, farther in every time; Finn and Clare were the photographs, watching down from the wall, as a dark little boy beat the dog's nose with a broom and cried for his mother.

As they walked from one dream to another, they talked over the dream-maps, and guessed at meanings. "You're doing well," said Finn, "and it is so much harder with strangers. You'll get it, you'll find where the flag is, for sure."

"Yes!" said Clare, a little guiltily, because the flag and the yew had fallen so far from her mind at the pleasure of walking through this world of dreams with Finn. *This feeling*, she thought, *this feeling of moving through someone else's dream is strangely familiar.*

They joined a crowd at the edge of a cliff, dancing to a dread-locked band playing wooden flute and wild drums. Finn raised his arm in invitation, and when Clare took one hand, he rested the other on her waist and turned her expertly among the other dancers, so expertly that Clare, who was no dancer at all, felt herself light and easy with it. His hands felt so light and so firm against her, she thought she could lift into the sky. "You're good at this!" she said above the music.

He laughed. "I do love to dance. They say I get it from my father."

They visited the dining room of a great ship, where a motherly woman was tapping on a porthole. All at once a huge black sword-fish leaped through, then lay on her table, gasping and dying. Finn and Clare were among the doctors the weeping woman called to set the fish right.

Clare next found herself drawn to the dream of a woman hanging from a tree from dozens of ropes around her arms and chest. Finn tugged her shirt to pull her away, but Clare moved closer. The woman was short and thick, with dark, gray-spattered hair, just curling in at her jaw. When she spoke, in a long string of firm and cheerful curses, Clare recognized the voice. If she was dreaming, then Jo was alive, oh, Jo was alive. As Clare was slipping away, with a heart so light she thought she might float, the curses slowed, and Jo's eyes widened.

"It's Clare," said Jo. "Girl, are you away?"

"I don't know what you mean," said Clare, abashed. You weren't supposed to let them see you.

"Away, among them. You are, I see you are," said Jo. "Those that are away among them never return. Or if they do, they are not the same as they were before. If you come back at all, you will not be the same, Clare Macleod."

Clare must have gone rather pale, for Jo smiled, her black eyes crinkling, even tied to a tree as she was. "Your mother was never the same, when she returned from away. She came back with the power."

"What power?"

But then the dream faded away—Jo must have waked up—and Finn was pulling her away. Soon, at the site of a plane crash in a busy Indian city, they were among the passengers who walked laughing and unhurt from the wreckage.

In the midst of these dreams, Clare finally understood what it was that made them so familiar, why the sensation of strangers' dreams, which should have been alien and surreal, instead felt like home.

The dreams felt Strange. "Standing in someone else's dream" was exactly the feeling of a fairy-making.

And it came to her that fairy-makings were the dreams of fairies, the dreams of the Strange, because their makings were what they had for dreams. She saw that she had been walking through fairy dreams most of her life; that she was a dream-walking girl.

I can do it, she thought, *I can walk through Balor's dream, and fool him, and save my father, even though I'm so afraid.*

But perhaps she wasn't afraid enough.

13

The Teeth of the Wolf

When Clare and Finn reported back, Her of the Cliffs had said: "Before anything, she must sleep. After that we will see what she's learned, and whether she can make out where the flag might be."

And Clare had concurred, had even exaggerated her drowsiness, with an enormous yawn, and *Yes, I'm so tired, please take me where I can sleep, far from the fairies, just to be safe, in case I forget to dream-awake, and let my dreams carry me away.*

Finn had looked at her with pain in his eyes. She had all but winked back.

For Clare was clever, or so she thought. She planned to sleep, because she was tired indeed. But she meant to wake a little early, before Her of the Cliffs came for her, so that she could sneak off to enter Balor's dream. There she would trick him into leaving her father alone.

She was afraid, and she was brave, and she would not let her father be harmed.

In Her of the Cliffs's evergreen woods, under a fairy-made quilt colored in all of the thousand shades the sky can be, she slept. Sleeping, she dreamed she was in her California house, and a man had come to their door dressed in a pirate costume, a parrot on his shoulder whose eye patch matched his own. *Oh, that's right, it's Halloween,* she thought in the dream, *that's why everything feels so Strange.*

But in the dream the pirate forced his way into their house, and seized her father by the throat, and began to swing him around like a bat, smashing him against the furniture. She screamed, and her father cried out in pain, and from another room came a terrible, bestial bellow.

And she remembered: *This is only a dream, and it's your dream. Make it whatever you want.*

"It's only Halloween," she shouted at the pirate, "you're just a little kid."

Obediently, the pirate shrank into a five-year-old, squalling for his mother. His parrot flapped out the door into the night, and her father sat on the floor, laughing and laughing, his eyes crinkling down at the corners.

She woke wild and sweating and proud.

But she had waked early, earlier than she knew; much too early. How could she know, with the half-light that hung eternal and unchanging around her, that she had only slept a single hour. She thought she had slept nearly a full night.

That was her first mistake.

She awoke knowing herself as a dream-walking girl, proud of her making skills. She wanted to show Finn, and show Her of the Cliffs, what she could do. *Your mother was never the same, when she returned from away. She came back with the power*, Jo had said. What power? Was it this power? She felt that perhaps nothing was beyond her now.

That was her second mistake.

She woke and saw, above her quilt-nest, a solitary bird on a branch. She saw the bird as a sign: *Now is the time.*

And that was her third mistake.

"Bird," she breathed, from beneath the quilt. It was a little gray titmouse with a black crest and an intelligent eye. She wriggled out softly until she was sitting cross-legged on top of the blankets. For a moment, sleep swept across her again, and she felt herself drifting away, but she shook her head, made a face, and sat up straight.

"Bird," she said. "Please take me to Balor."

The bird cocked its head toward her, as if inclining an ear, and Clare felt a sinking dread: that's right, she would have to make Balor, make the poem of him, the way she had her father. The idea of lingering in the essence of Balor made her sick. But she set her jaw and pressed on.

"Bird, listen," she said. "I will tell you who he is."

And sitting cross-legged on her quilt, her eyes closed, trusting the bird to stay, Clare spoke.

"He doesn't like *disobedient girls*," she began. "When he leans in, he's a black mountain over you, and when his coat touches your arm you feel ashamed, and you want to scream.

"He wants to make sure he's safe from Finn, and he'll do anything to make sure he is, he doesn't care what worlds he ruins.

"He has black eyes, and one eye is dead, and it stares in one direction, never, ever moves from that one direction, just stares, like it's insane—like that one psycho eye is dragging the rest of him along with it. That's the feeling.

"His smile when he smiles is the opposite of a smile, it looks like a smile but it feels like a snarl, and that's such a weird feeling, that it looks like one thing and it feels like the opposite, it makes you want to throw up."

"And that's such a weird feeling, it makes you want to throw up"—very poetic, Clare Macleod, she thought bitterly: *glad Finn can't hear this.* And that reminded her.

"He makes you ashamed." She was whispering now, but not too low for a bird. "Of your making, or of—of yourself, really. He makes you see how embarrassing and worthless you are." Her voice was rising. "And he keeps a thing with him that *is* him—I saw it once made of fireflies and stars"—Who had sent that fairy-making? Had it been warning or threat?—"but really it's made of wood and paint, and it's *him*, somehow, this crazy eye, this open mouth, it's always him, it ruins sunsets and makes birds ugly and makes you think your poems are worse than dirt, and it makes you so *ashamed.*"

Clare stopped talking. Her eyes were still shut. Her heart felt too big for her chest; it was climbing up into her throat.

Tiny claws on her shoulder; feather brushing her cheek.

"Oh, bird," said Clare, "thank you." Then: "Can you take me to his dream the fairy way? Can birds do that? Because it will take too long to walk."

~

Balor's dream was hunger. His dream raged like an animal, cast around, tossed its head, looking for what to tear into. It was an angry, fearful hunger, a huge head swaying side to side, looking for what it will have in its belly, what it will eat, and crunch, and swallow. The oldest, most savage joy, the joy of *feeding*; and then, the different, sated, unregretting pleasure of *having fed.*

Inside Balor's dream was a wolf. It prowled a black and blasted ground, a ground that looked as if every living thing had been swept away by a wildfire. The wolf had eaten all, and was looking for more.

Clare stood, small and exposed, on this bleak landscape. The wolf was far from her, but not far enough; and if she felt terror, she also felt awe. A wolf is a creature of great beauty, although the beauty is not easy to see when you are prey.

The wolf raised its nose, sniffed, turned its nose in her direction, sniffed again.

So Clare ran. She ran past carcasses of half-devoured prey. In her terror, she knew with certainty that she could not do this, that it was too hard, and she should never have tried; that now she was trapped with a wolf on its way, and she would not survive.

With equal certainty, she knew: *maybe I can't do this, but I have to. I made the choice. I have to try.*

In the distance, she saw—did she see? or did she *make*? she and Balor, making this place together—a house, black and smoking, and she ran for it.

A ravening hunger loped behind her.

The dream-house was burning. Clare knew that she could be hurt in this dream, badly and permanently, or even killed; but having no choice, she ran inside. She flew through flames and smoke, coughing, trying to see what Balor's mind-house might tell her.

Her mind flew even faster than her feet. She had to find an *underneath*. Surely her buried father would be *underneath*. When she saw what Balor's mind had made of him, she would know what to do.

She opened a door—a wall of flames. She opened another and choked on black smoke.

A snarl behind her. The wolf at the door.

She opened the last door to find stairs leading down. *Underneath.* Slamming the door behind her, she half tumbled down.

The basement walls were thick black dirt, and the floor was dirt beneath her. No window, but from somewhere, a dim and dirty light.

Silence.

And then, from a corner, a small skittering sound.

Clare knelt down, put her face to the ground.

A skittering near the wall, and the flash of a long gray ear, disappearing.

A hole in the floor, a rabbit inside it, quivering nose, terrified eyes.

This is how he sees my father.

A wild howl at the door above, a heavy, muscled body flung against it.

She had only so long, only seconds, perhaps, to decide: what could she become that would put Balor off this rabbit's scent, without making him see his dream had been invaded?

She thought of impersonating the rabbit herself, a furious rabbit with sharp, vicious teeth; but she also knew she would never defeat Balor in a physical battle, for the wolf was his true self, and a rabbit would be a false one to her.

She thought of becoming iron bars around the rabbit's hole. But iron bars did not belong here, and would make Balor realize that someone else was in his dream: another mind, another maker.

She thought of becoming an escaping rabbit—*see, it's gone, too late, forget about it.* But that would incite the wolf into a chase, which it would likely win.

All these ideas had flashed through her mind, had been discarded, in the few seconds before the door above burst open. She heard the wet, slavering sniff of a wolf seeking its prey.

Sniffing. Smell.

She knew what she must become; and she became it.

The wolf made its way down the stairs, shoulders rolling, tongue hanging out, tasting the air. But as it walked toward the rabbit hole, the wolf stopped. It curled its lip and backed up as if struck.

Before the rabbit hole lay the rabbit, dead—quite dead, *already dead*—and not freshly dead, either, but long dead, putrid, rotten, and inedible.

The wolf whined in disappointment, tossing its head back and forth to rid itself of the smell. Then it wound its way slowly up the stairs.

The dead rabbit lay still and rotting on the floor. Inside the dead rabbit lay a very alive girl whose heart was beating wild and hard.

She knew she could not for long fool Balor into believing her father was dead, not with nothing but a dream. But she hoped that she could imprint on Balor's mind somehow a new story: that her father was *not for eating*; that he will *make you sick.* Leave him, leave him, forget him. *He is not prey.*

So maybe the next time Balor thought of her father, buried in the mine, and made a plan, or even just licked his lips—maybe something deep inside him would feel nauseated, would sicken, would think—not today. Forget him for today.

Clare waited to be sure Balor's prowling wolf-consciousness was gone. Her plan was to then slip out as something small and hard to see, an ant, a night-moth, something beneath attention. Her heart-beat slowed, inside the rotting rabbit. It would be all right. She had done it. It would be all right. Her father was safe—he was dead to Balor now. And she was safe. She had done it.

Drowsily, she remembered her father's face from his dream, old and young, and how he told her he kept the flag *in the sky, it's one of the stories in the sky*. And it came to her—she almost laughed out loud—oh, I see: not sky, *Skye*. And suddenly she knew the flag was in the house after all, and she even knew exactly where it was. She could find the flag, and save the fairy roads, just as she had saved her father. All the fighting was over now, everything was as right and well as ever could be.

Rocked on those lulling, beautiful words, the girl who had barely slept in days fell fast, fast asleep, and began to dream.

But she was not dreaming inside her own safe home, or under Finn's careful eye. And because she was so exhausted, she was not dreaming awake and aware.

She was dreaming asleep inside the mind of Balor of the Evil Eye, and when she arose from the floor in her true shape, still dreaming, and walked through the burning house, that eye fell hard upon her.

In her dream, she wandered through a burnt, black, and smoking house. It was the magic hour, and the clear half-light came through the ruined roof, making every corner sharp and clear. She remembered this house, she almost remembered, it was her house but it wasn't, and her father might be here somewhere, and she was looking for her father.

At the end of a charred and smoky hall, she opened a door to a smoke-filled bedroom, blue-flowered wallpaper peeling from the walls. Inside the room was a huge white horse. It stepped toward her, muscles sliding under its hot, damp skin. This was her horse, of course it was—how could she forget the horse she had left in this room? How thankful she felt that the horse was all right, had not starved from her neglect. She almost wept with relief to see it. Its mane was long and tangled, matted, and she picked it apart with her busy fingers.

Now they were outside, Clare and her horse, in a long pasture that ended in a dark evergreen woods. Still she picked and untangled the mane.

The horse's eye rolled in its head. Oh: it had been in the room too long, of course—it needed to run. She stood on a low, cap-shaped stone and mounted the horse bareback. In the dream, she knew she was good at riding. She straddled the broad back, her legs hugging muscle and bone. And the horse leaped forward, from a canter to a rolling, flying gallop. Together, Clare and her white horse flew into the forest.

Behind her—or beside her?—was a heavy, galloping tread, was a wet, hoarse, heavy breathing, and it was a terrible beast, she knew it was, had known that beast all her life. Clare and her horse were chasing the beast, that's right, of course it was ahead of them, and they had to catch that evil thing, the thing that threatened her mother—no, her father—yes, her father. Fear and rage rose up in her. She had to kill it. Of course, that was why she had a bow in her hands, and an arrow in a quiver slung over her shoulder. She had forgotten how good she was, how brilliant with bow and arrow. The horse moved from gallop to run, its spine from head to tail one long line. Clare held tight with her legs, at one with her mount, bow and arrow in her hand. Warrior, warrior. She will be the hero, she will kill the beast, she will save herself and her father. She rode through the clear, saturated twilight, every unreal color of it.

In the dream, Clare felt driven to hunt this monster. *Driven* is a good word. She believed she was in control, but she was only a passenger in this vehicle, no more driving herself than when as a toddler in her parents' car she turned her toy steering wheel this way and that, beeped her toy horn, and laughed.

Someone else was driving, someone not her friend.

Crouched over her leaping, flying horse, the beat of its heart beneath her calves, her breath panting with its breath, now Clare hears another breath. The breath of the beast, the running beast ahead of them. *In dreams, beware the beast.* They are almost there. She selects an arrow and fits it to the string. She sees the flash of white and flash of hooves ahead. Her fear and her rage twist together into a new, terrible power. The horse beneath her, the strength of her arm, her *righteousness*, her *certainty* that she can fly an arrow through a grove of trees and kill the beast within it.

She has become the teeth of the wolf.

She draws the bow. She closes her eyes, she is that sure. She lets the arrow fly. She strikes like lightning, like a bolt of lightning from a screaming mouth, she strikes like one for whom the kill is pleasure and righteous joy.

Clare awoke, standing in pine-scented woods, in the unreal colors of the magic hour.

The horse was gone.

But at her feet stretched a strange figure—man or beast?—oh, both: a boy, but with white horns twining complicated from his head, horns that were dissolving now, as his hooves transmuted to human hands and feet.

In one of his eyes, an arrow stood quivering.

In one of Finn's eyes.

In one of Finn's eyes.

It was Finn, it was Finn, it was Finn.

He wasn't dead. In the war between human and Strange that was Finn, the Strange won out this time, and the wound did not kill him. But his left eye was gone. He sat stiffly in the hall made of tall, bending trees where Clare had come that first night. Her of the Cliffs sat beside him, in a new, terrible form. Her hair was unbound now and wild, and her face was deep red, red as blood or flames, and her eyebrows black and pointed with fury.

And now the smiling people were gathering again, but they were not smiling, and looked at her hard.

Clare stood a yard or two away, unable to approach closer, fixed by the twin nails of grief and guilt. "I'm sorry, I'm so sorry," said Clare, a hundred times, two hundred times, to whoever was near. But the hard looks did not change, and the gathering continued, until fairies surrounded her on all sides, colors and feathers and fur and teeth and cold, hard eyes. *The Good Folk*, thought Clare, her heart hammering inside her. *Good dog, good dog.*

"You have become the teeth of the wolf," said a hoarse voice from the crowd.

"You *allowed yourself* to become teeth of the wolf," said another voice, high and dangerous.

"I didn't mean to," said Clare. She jammed her hands in her pockets, felt the commonplace book there, hard and useless. A line from the book she had read so many times came into her mind, something about your heart being "like a cup / That somebody had drunk dry." That was how her heart felt: drained dry as bone.

But drained dry or not, she was a coward not to face Finn. "Excuse me," she murmured, pushing through the crowd. "I'm sorry." She made her way closer to Finn and Her of the Cliffs. The fairies followed close; she felt the chill of their bodies at her back.

"I'm sorry," she said, and her voice was not much more than a whisper. She could not bear to look at Finn; even Her of the Cliffs's dreadful new face was better than that, so she turned toward her and said, "Please, I am so sorry. What can I do, is there some way I can help, or make it right?"

"What matters your *sorry, so sorry*," said Her of the Cliffs, lifting her terrible face, "when *sorry* comes only when it is too late?" Her low, hard voice was far more dreadful than a shout. "You lied to me, and disobeyed me, and thought too highly of your half-learned power. You may have saved your father—I say may, only—but at what cost? How can Finn shoot now? All his life he has trained for this time, to destroy Balor, to save the roads. How can he shoot with one eye?"

And now the voices came from all over, came so fast that Clare could never see where any voice was coming from, only heard the orchestra of anger.

"His eye, his eye."

"He cannot shoot with one eye."

"She is the teeth of the wolf."

Desperate, Clare said, "But some people shut one eye when they shoot." She still could not force herself to look at Finn's ruined face, although every nerve felt his presence a few feet away, felt it like fire.

Her of the Cliffs looked away, as if the contempt she felt for Clare were too much. "We are not like you. We look with one eye of our own, and one eye of our beast's. You have blinded his beast."

"I'm sorry. God, I'm so sorry," said Clare. "I did . . . I mean I know this doesn't make up for anything, but I did figure out where the flag is. I understand now what my father meant. That's something. I can go get the flag."

But now Her of the Cliffs rounded on her in a rage: "Ah—can you indeed? Can you, Clare? I doubt you can. For while you wasted time, Balor learned how to use the key you carelessly left. He has blocked the tree. It is cut off now, not its thinnest root can touch another root, nor touch the ocean it is rooted beside, nor anything at all. That gate is locked to us now."

Clare felt nailed to the ground. To think of her yew alone, caught in Balor's cage, unable to touch any other tree, its gorgeous, tender spirit caught in some hideous, totem-made trap—she almost fell to the ground at the force of it.

Her of the Cliffs was not finished. "I feel now what the other fairies feel. Look what your human *change* has done to me." She turned to Finn, and her hard face cracked into misery. "Look what your *love* has done to me. What good is it? What good is it? Ah, the human world brings us nothing but grief and ruin. Close the gates, for all I care! Destroy the roads! Cut the connection forever. I will not hunt at Midsummer." She strode out of the leafy hall, disappearing into the woods.

Finn stood unsteadily, stumbling after her, calling, "No, I beg you, wait!"

Clare saw that in one single day she had destroyed Finn, had lost the faith and help of Her of the Cliffs, and had failed her own lovely yew. It was not possible, it was too much, it could not be.

"No," she said.

The low chatter of the fairies ceased.

"No," said Clare again. She felt that the word was branded on her heart: NO. "There has to be something I can do."

No response.

"Someone tell me what I can do."

A long pause. Then a dry voice from the crowd said, "The tree's guardian can unblock it. Possibly, possibly."

"How? Tell me how!"

"By going underneath, of course," said the dry man, emerging from the crowd. His skin was dark, his cheekbones high, and his smile as dry as his voice. Although he looked young and strong, his hair was starry white. "Underneath into your own roots, where you and the tree are connected."

"But Balor . . ." a quavering voice called.

The young white-haired man overrode him. "Balor cannot block that connection, not that deep one, no matter his magic."

"I will do it," said Clare, without hesitation. "I will go now, just tell me how to begin." Adrenaline raged through her veins. *Just let me go, just let me act, just get me away from all this horror and failure.*

"But the beast," someone murmured, and the chorus took up the phrase, murmuring, "the beast, the beast."

"That's where your beast lives, too, they mean," the dry man said. "At your deepest root. You'll have to face your beast and conquer it, before you reach the tree." He said this as if he were giving her directions to a grocery store; then he turned his back and disappeared into the crowd.

Icy anxiety cooled the heat in Clare's blood. "Wait, though, but . . . what if it conquers me?"

A long whisper ran through the crowd of Strange, like wind through pines. Then a voice separated out: "I believe that's what happened to Balor."

Clare tightened her jaw to keep her teeth from chattering.

"She will fail," said another voice, louder.

"She will die. Humans who try, die."

"She is too young."

"Trying to keep her father safe, she destroyed our Finn."

"I thought I could keep both of them safe," cried Clare.

"There is no safety."

"She is stupid and spoiled, she is the teeth of the wolf."

Like a bear teased by a pack of dogs, Clare spun around. "So how do I find the beast?"

"Find the center of the labyrinth, from which no human has ever returned."

"Finn returned," called a voice from the back. Was it her white-haired friend?

"Far more fairy than human, Finn," said another. "Our child, raised by us. No *real* human has ever returned."

Clare felt ill, recalling the hoarse, snuffling breathing, the heavy tread, ever behind her, around the corner, in the next room of every dream. "I have a little fairy in me," she said. "I don't know how much. Will it be enough?"

Silk and color and fur around her shrugged. None of them knew; none of them cared. Again they spoke, in voices low and rough, high and soft.

"You may never find the beast."

"If you do, the beast will be angry indeed."

"If you fail or die, the roads will be closed forever."

"And that's no great loss." There was laughter at this.

"Even if you succeed, but succeed too late, the roads will close. Your people will never dream again, nor visit our world again."

"And good riddance to an unlovely race." More laughter.

"But we will never see the stars again," cried a low voice.

A brief, sad silence. Then the phrase was taken up by the whole crowd in a kind of mournful, heartbroken fugue: "The stars," they sang. "The stars, the stars, the stars."

Through the melancholy music, the dry voice came through clear: "We worship the stars, Clare, did you know? The stars are sacred to us. We cannot see them from our own world, because here the night never comes."

"The stars," the people of the Strange sang. "The stars, the stars, the stars."

"STOP IT," cried a voice.

It was Finn.

Clare turned at his voice and finally saw him full on. He stood straight in a loose white shirt stained with blood. A green cloth was tied over one eye, and his hairline near that eye was caked with blood. She made a small involuntary sound of pain.

Finn looked at her—and his one good eye did not, as she expected, express fury or contempt: it held only pain, which was so much worse. "She can't do it," he said. "It's too dangerous for her. We must find some other way."

Dumbfounded, again. He was a dumbfounding boy. Finn's whole life had been a readying to fight Balor, which was all his duty. And unless he won that fight, he could never make in the human world again, which was all his love.

How could her safety be more important to him than his greatest duty and greatest love? Especially after what she had done?

Did he like her that much?

And was the beast truly that dangerous?

As if in answer, Finn said, "Clare, don't go. It is as dangerous as they say, for you. You will likely never return."

Clare remembered what she had learned: that in dreams and in making, you choose what you are. But you do not choose only once. Over and over, at every turning you must choose. This felt like a turning, a time to choose what she was. Her heart beat high in her chest, and she tasted blood from a bitten lip. A whole life of dream-running from the hoarse breath of an enormous, unseen creature. And now to run toward it, and meet it, and fight it? How?

"I will do it," she said.

14

No Out to Find

Finn had asked the others for a moment alone with Clare, but to her surprise, he didn't argue against her decision. For a while, in fact, he said nothing at all. They stood beside each other, facing out, close enough for her to feel the warmth, the un-Strange warmth of his arm near hers.

They could still be silent together, anyway.

Finn spoke. "You found the flag, then? Or where the flag will be found? Her of the Cliffs says she will not hunt, will not, and will not be persuaded. Without her, the others will never come. If we have no flag, we are lost."

"I did figure it out," said Clare, watching her feet. "I finally realized he meant Skye, not sky. No, sorry, I mean—the island of Skye, where he's from. Not the sky above. We have an old book, it was my granddad's, called *SKYE: The Island and Its Legends*, that tells all these stories from there. Including about the flag. It's in the house. I know exactly where he will have put it, even the page."

She stopped, embarrassed by the pleased note that had crept into her voice. She made herself look up, and again, the sight of his face destroyed her. "Oh, Finn," she said. "I'm so sorry, I'm so sorry.

I could say it for a million years, and never say how bad I feel. I'm so sorry."

A Finnishly crooked smile, but still he did not look toward her. "You make me sound a monster—am I?"

"No! no, no. Only your eye . . . oh, Finn."

"Now, Clare, mad Clare. I know you never meant it."

"Finn." She wouldn't cry, would not, when he wasn't crying, and he was the one so hurt.

"Only," said Finn, and stopped. Now he too was looking down, at his feet and hers, beside each other, her boots blue and gray and narrow, his round and scuffed and brown. "Only," he said, almost too soft too hear, "what will I be, with a blinded beast? Can I make, will I still be a maker? And can I bear it, if I am not?"

Clare felt her heart sink, when she'd thought it could sink no more. The thought of Finn, unable to make.

"Also . . ." He hesitated. "Also: will it make me like my grandfather?" He turned his face to her, all naked anxiety. "Will it, do you think? That would be beyond bearing, oh, far beyond, Clare."

"*No*," said Clare. She knew her voice was cracking, did not care. "*No*, you never, that could *never* happen. And of *course* you'll still be able to make."

"It may be." Finn looked down again. "It may be." He did not seem to believe it. "If I can't make, though, Clare . . . ," he said, softly.

Clare felt vertigo-sick, seeing the plunging depths of her crime.

"Tree-guardian!" called a high, sharp voice. "You have little enough time."

Reluctantly, Clare pulled away from Finn, letting her arm brush against his coat as she did, and hoping he felt it, and knew what it was: a good-bye. He leaned in to whisper: "Remember, you must return before Midsummer's Eve, when we hunt. That is a day from now, and no more than a day, or all is lost: Your tree destroyed. The two worlds, forever apart. You and I, forever apart. Do you understand?"

"Yes," said Clare. She turned away, then turned back, impulsive. "And I'm going to make it up to you, Finn. I am somehow. I swear I am."

He smiled sadly. "You'll have to come back, to make it up. And that will be making it up enough for me."

Clare nodded, then walked into the crowd of fairies, who pulled back as she moved through. When she was entirely surrounded by feathers and fur, leather and bone, crimson and indigo and every peacock green of spring, she spoke.

"I'm ready," she said. "Except"—this was probably a stupid question, but Clare was beyond caring—"do you guys have, like, a weapon or something to give me? Like in stories? To conquer the beast?"

The fairies stared at her in silence.

"All right," said stubborn Clare. "But then once I conquer my beast"—once *I do, not if, not if*—"then how do I open the blocked tree?"

A rustle in the crowd; sprinkles of laughter. "How would *we* know?" said an airy voice. "You are the guardian. It is your gate. You contain the key."

Clare took a deep breath. "Can someone at least tell me how to *get* to this labyrinth?"

For a moment, there was silence. Then the crowd of fairies began to whisper. The whispering rose, like a field of insects rising, as the crowd parted for the woman with the ice-threaded eyes and the long, unsmiling mouth, the one Clare had sat beside that first night.

With an expression Clare could not read, the woman stretched out one skinny arm, one skinny finger, and with just the tip of one long, dark blue nail drew a light scratch on Clare's forehead, just between her eyes.

Then all the fairies withdrew, silently, back and back, until they mingled and vanished among the trees that lined the leafy hall.

Clare stood alone, facing into the dark forest.

A wind swirled. Dead leaves, grass, twigs, spiraled upward. The leaves on the trees at the edge of the forest fluttered in agitation as the wind whipped through them.

The whirlwind moved toward her. Clare backed up, away from the wind, until she was backed up against the table and could go no farther.

But you cannot hide from a fairy wind, which gathers up everything in its path. Clare turned away, covering her face against the whirling grit and stinging sticks; she opened her mouth to scream, but instead she gagged and coughed on a mouthful of dirt and dead leaves. More than dirt was in this wind: Clare heard, though she could not see, a clamor of excited voices, men shouting, women laughing, running feet and pounding hooves. Clare was lifted up, could not find the ground with her feet, was not sure if she was upright or sideways or upside down. The wind spun her around, and around, and around. She was sick, then sicker and sicker from the spinning, and when she could not bear it another moment, the whirlwind dropped her, and spun away.

Clare lay on the ground, eyes shut tight, coughing the dirt from her lungs. The whirlwind had spun her and spun her, then dropped her, but her stomach continued to spin, and she lay.

When she finally opened her eyes, the world was gray and hard and tilting. The half-light said she was still in fairy. But the fairy hall had vanished; or she had. She was in a narrow passage; gray stone walls pressed close around her, covered with curious carvings, like the walls of her own home. But above her was no comforting starry dome, only a pale, violet-blue sky. Was this the labyrinth? *From which no human has ever returned.*

Her head was still spinning in one direction while her stomach spun in another, but Clare stumbled to her feet and looked around.

The passage's stone walls were high, much higher than she could jump. She could just spread her arms and touch the walls on each side of her. Behind her was another high stone wall, blocking the way. Ahead, the passage branched off in two directions. Because Clare was still a little dizzy—or was that why?—the spirals and stars carved on the walls seemed to shift and move and slowly spin. They felt like eyes, watching her.

A day from now, and no more than a day, or all is lost. So she must begin, no time for dizziness or indecision. She strode forward, hesitated at the fork, then turned right. She had begun to walk the labyrinth.

At the next fork, she turned right again. At the third, biting her lip, she turned left. And so it went, fork after fork, soon she could no longer say for how long—an hour? Many hours? Uncertain, anxious, she moved through the maze making guesses, stopping herself, turning back, and turning back again.

Finally, paused before a three-way fork, she heard something. From down the right-hand path came a hollow, guttural growl that bent the way thunder bends in the air. Another, wilder howl followed, this one rising higher, more anguished, more raging. She could almost feel the hot breath behind it.

Good intentions and brave words in the fairy hall were one thing. But Clare was an animal like any other animal, and an animal who feels she is prey has only one choice. When a third half scream, half roar burst down the right-hand passage, Clare turned down the left-hand passage and ran.

Running, never slowing, she took left turns and right turns almost at random. She ran in no direction at all, turning and twisting away from herself, toward herself, into and away from more stone walls, more spirals, more dark walls carved with eyes that watched her, tender and stony cold. Soon she had lost all trace of the monster, and all trace of a way out, all trace of anything except her own fear and anxiety.

Hurry! No more than a day!

And yet *the beast will be angry, angry indeed.*

Finally, in exhaustion, she dropped to the ground and lay there, panting. She closed her eyes: enough. Enough spirals and labyrinths and endless magic hour. Curled up in a ball, she made no sound, but her chest convulsed.

In time, her breathing quieted. As it did, she heard a high, soft voice from the passage ahead. It was the voice of a young girl. "Don't cheat," said the girl. "No peeking. Don't cheat."

The girl said it again, and a third time: "Don't cheat!" The voice was closer each time. Perhaps she had been saying it for some time, and Clare could only now hear as her breathing slowed.

"All right," said Clare, soft. She was so tired. She kept her head pressed into the crook of one arm, eyes shut. "I won't cheat."

A cool hand touched her hot face. The scent of the girl's skin was a familiar, calming perfume of licorice and woody herbs.

"I've come to help," said the girl into Clare's ear, in an exaggerated whisper. "I'm not supposed to, but I am." A pleased pause. "So . . . what help do you need?"

Eyes tight, Clare thought hard. "I have to do something," she said, "but I'm so afraid. So I keep running one way and then the other way, and I don't know where I am."

"That last part's the right part," whispered the girl, each word a breath of sweet herbs against Clare's face. "That's the right way to start a labyrinth. Say: *I don't know where I am.* And here's the right way to keep going: Forget your eyes. Forget seeing. Smell instead. Feel instead. Put your fingers out and feel one tiny inch at a time. Be like a tree. That's how you find the center."

"And after that"—Clare was whispering now too—"how do I find my way out?"

"There is no out to find," said the girl. "Only in, to what lives in the center."

"I'm afraid of what lives there," said Clare. She could no longer whisper; her voice was trembling. "How can I not be afraid? Is it something nice?" But she knew it was not. Oh, the scent of this girl was where she wanted to live forever.

"No," breathed the girl. "Nice? No. A monster lives there. A beast lives there. But, Clare, a beast is what you need."

"I know," murmured Clare deep into the crook of her own arm. "I know I need it but . . . why is it so angry with me?"

The girl didn't answer, and her woody, herby, healing scent began to drift away.

"It's your birthday soon," said the singsong, licorice-herb voice, far down the passage. "Happy birthday, Clare. Don't be late."

"But wait, please, tell me why the beast is *angry*—" Clare began, eyes still tight closed, for she was not a cheater.

But the girl was gone.

Eyes closed, Clare turned over in her mind what the girl had said.

There is no out to find. All right. Clare had known that in her heart, and had proved it in her mad run.

To start a labyrinth, say "I don't know where I am."

"I don't know where I am," said Clare aloud, curled on the ground, holding herself tight.

Forget your eyes. Forget seeing. Be like me.

Clare stood up unsteadily, eyes still shut, and felt her way down the wall to the next intersection of passages. Time was short, but she understood that she had to let time go.

Which way to go?

Silence, except her own breathing, her own heart.

She smelled the dirt under the dead grass beneath her feet.

She smelled sweat, her own and—oh.

Her own sweat, and another's. And from the right, the other-scent was stronger, and the faintest trace of an animal heat touched her face. She took a few steps in that direction, eyes still closed. Blindness was like a thread that led her on.

From the distant end of the right-hand passage, she heard a long breath, like steam from a grate.

Keeping her hand on the wall, she turned to face the scent, the heat, the hissing breath. The air felt colder. *Oh*, she thought: *it's because I'm sweating.*

The stone wall was rough under her fingers; her fingers trailed through cracks and carvings. Eyes closed; no eye.

She stretched her hands out to touch both walls as she walked, tracing carvings as she went, feeling the faint heat on her damp face, following sighing breath and the animal scent of sweat not her own. The passage turned and twisted. Clare followed in the dark. She didn't peek. She didn't count the time. She didn't look back.

Over the next few minutes, the passage widened until she could no longer touch the walls on either side. The breathing sound grew louder, rasping and huffing spasmodically, and she could sense the great size of what huffed and rasped and sweated.

Her own eyes stayed closed. She put her hands, cold and trembling, out into the empty air before her. She could almost hear the beast's eye rolling in its head. She walked a few feet farther, stopped.

In the silence, Clare felt the heat from the beast's skin on her own; she was that close.

The creature took a sudden, wheezing breath, then gave a series of short, terrible cries of rage or anguish, so quick and furious they were like the barks of a mad dog.

Clare's eyes flew open.

A few yards away stood an enormous black shape, the size of a small elephant on its hind legs. Its head was the head of a great black bull, wide forehead narrowing down the muzzle to wet black nostrils. Beneath the two yellow, curving, sharp-pointed horns, his small eyes rolled in panic or fury, the whites wet and twitching.

The monster's head and shoulders were a bull's: but below the shoulders, the monster was made like an enormous man, arms twisted with ropy muscles, broad chest bulging. Above the waist his skin was shiny and black as a sea creature, slick as a whale or seal.

Below the waist he was covered in coarse dark hair. From head to toe he was a deeper black than the night sky, and instead of feet, he stood upon the hooves of a great bull.

Stumbling backward, Clare found her back pressed against a wall almost immediately. She turned, but the passage that had led her here had vanished. She and the monster were at the bottom of a high, circular stone enclosure, like a narrow, topless tower, or a dry well, nothing above them but the cloudless, pale blue-violet fairy sky. This was the center of the labyrinth.

All brave and strengthening thoughts of saving the tree and the fairy roads, of making it up somehow to Finn, all of those vanished. If she could have run, she would have, for she had no chance against this beast and was certainly about to die. But there was nowhere to run, and her legs felt too weak to run.

"Help," she whispered to the air. "Help, help, help."

As if in answer, a soft voice floated high above the heads of Clare and her monster—a soft, disappointed voice.

"But you're cheating," it said sadly.

Pressed against the wall, Clare laughed a single wild laugh. *Mad Clare.* Was she supposed to close her eyes again?

The beast gave a long, ominous bellow or groan.

She will fail.

She will die. Humans who try, die.

She is too young.

Oh well, thought Clare, straightening up. *Closing my eyes worked before. And I don't think I'm so young.*

She faced the beast, closed her eyes, and took a step forward.

His sweat. Her own sweat.

Another step.

His snuffling, chuffing breath, faster now; then a series of low barks. But now, with her eyes closed, Clare was no longer sure the barks were angry.

Another step.

Were the barks perhaps . . . fearful? But what could a beast be afraid of?

A last, smaller, frightened step. Her hand struck something: slick skin over hot flesh, muscle shifting under a huge, heaving side.

"Oh!" said Clare, aloud.

And now Clare did one of the most surprising things she had ever done: eyes closed, hands out, she put her arms around the beast.

Why? Because her eyes were closed, so her nose could smell sorrow's salt. Her ears could hear that the heaving breath was crying. Her hands felt the trembling beneath the smooth flesh.

She remembered the fairies saying: *It is angry with you.*

But blinded, Clare knew they were wrong, they were all wrong. *My monster isn't angry. It's sad.*

"There you are," said Clare gently, eyes still closed. "I see you now. I'm so sorry. It's all right. It's all right now. I'm here."

The beast wept and wept.

Face pressed against the beast's hot, smooth side, Clare felt the heaves of the sobs, then felt them slow, and become the rhythms of rising and falling breath. She smelled the zoo smell of animal sweat and animal body.

She knew, with sudden certainty, that the fairies were wrong: Balor wasn't conquered by his beast. He stopped listening to it, he stopped seeing with it, and his beast went mad from loneliness and grief. She took a few steps backward, and opened her eyes again.

The beast gave a low, rough snort and shook its great bull head, back and forth, back and forth. Clare fought down the fear that came with opening her eyes.

"Beast," she said, hesitant. "Can you talk?"

Clare's beast rolled its frightened or angry eye, and huffed its breath out again. It held its huge arms out from its side; it rocked back and forth on its hooves.

Those who try, die.

No. You choose the story you make.

"Beast," she said. "I don't know what's right to do."

The beast gave several desperate, wheezing grunts, then lifted one enormous arm in the air. *It's going to hit me*, thought Clare . . .

and then, with a shocked pang, she remembered that gesture. "It was you at Finn's Cap," she said. "It was you."

The beast huffed again and rolled its huge head, the horns slicing a double yellow semicircle in the half-light. A speck of white froth appeared on one black lip.

"I don't understand, and I'm afraid," she cried. The beast turned angrily, clawing at himself, and Clare saw something glinting on his broad, midnight chest, something silver and spiky.

Something familiar.

From around his huge neck, the beast lifted a heavy, thick-linked silver chain. Dangling from the center was a silver star: her mother's star, the star she had lost at Finn's Cap. Only somehow—the *only somehow* of dreams—the star was much bigger now, with a bright diamond at its center, like a drop of rain in the center of a flower. Bigger, transfigured, but unmistakably her mother's star, and her own.

And somehow to see the beast wearing her star transformed the creature, for a moment, from a monster into a friend. Now, seeing the beast's raised arm, she remembered Finn's raised arm in the dreadlock and dancing dream. She saw the beast's gesture for what it was: not a threat, but an invitation. The beast was inviting her to dance. He was inviting her now, just as he had invited her as she woke from her dream at Finn's Cap.

"I do love to dance," Finn had said. "They say I get it from my father."

"Oh, *that* was the key!" said Clare, almost laughing. "*Dancing* was the key, and you were trying to show me!"

The beast made a long and slow sound, like someone blowing into a glass bottle. He took a step toward her, his hooves raising dust in the empty circle. He held out the silver chain. But when Clare stretched out her hand for it, he did not give it to her, but instead wrapped it carefully around her right wrist. The other end he wrapped around his own left wrist.

And somehow (somehow), the chain around her wrist was delicate again, the chain she had known all her life, while the chain around the beast was thick and heavy-linked still.

Between them, the diamond-hearted star twisted and dangled like a child between its parents.

Again, now, the beast stretched a long arm out to Clare, and she put her palm against his. The moment stretched long between them, and anxiety rose up in Clare like the clouds of dust raised by their feet: *Midsummer comes so soon.*

Then, from far above them, came singing: a high, girlish voice, pure and sweet as spring.

For the rest of her life, Clare often tried to remember the words the yew-girl sang. She could recall certain phrases, and sometimes almost remembered more, but never quite. They slipped away as a dream does. The one line that stayed with her, like a fragment of poetry, was this: *Know what roots know: there is only one tree.*

Palm in palm, eyes closed, great bull head hung to one side, small red head hung to the other side, the beast and the girl bound together danced a circular dance, a fairy dance, in the violet light at the center of the labyrinth. They danced first facing each other, until their breath become one breath, and they knew they were one dancing creature. Then they turned and danced with their backs to each other, their eyes closed, their hands lifted to the clear sky. And Clare surrendered herself to the dance in a way she never had before, even with Finn, or even alone.

Because Clare's eyes were closed, she did not see that their dancing made a circular track, which became a circular dent in the dusty ground. She did not see that the dent became deeper, and the dirt inside the circle fell away.

But when the song stopped, and the beast and girl bound together opened their eyes, their dance had opened a door in the earth, into which a spiraling path descended out of sight.

"Clare, Clare," called the high, sweet voice from above. "It's almost your birthday!"

Clare's stomach contracted. Her birthday, her first birthday, was the day she must return with the flag. "We have to go," she said to the beast, and took his hand more firmly in hers.

Together they descended the twisting, stony path, into a darkness as dense as black bread. Clare's eyes were open, though they might as well have been closed. But it seemed as though the beast could see, or found its way some other way than seeing.

As the spiraling slope descended, the floor became less rocky, became hard and smooth, and the walls around them had that same hard, warm smoothness: the walls were wood. She was just thinking, *What does that remind me of? Oh, my tree, my in-between, mine and Finn's,* when the path leveled off. It was as simple as that: Clare put out her foot to step down, and found level ground.

Now she and her beast moved together down a pitch-black passage, and she had the sense that the smooth wood passageway was contracting around them, growing lower and narrower the farther they walked. It was the darkest of all the tunnels she had known. *Oh please let us not be back in the labyrinth*, she thought. *Oh please let us be going the right way. Oh please let us get there soon.*

Wherever *there* was, and however she would know it, when they reached it.

But if the passageway was contracting, then Clare and her beast must be getting smaller, too, for the passage never closed on them entirely. At its narrowest point, when there was barely room for her and her beast to stand together, the passage turned sharply and stopped.

There was light here—not a lot, but enough to see her horned and bull-headed beast, the dull gleam of its skin. Enough to see that their way was blocked by an iron gate. No lock, nor lever, nor any way at all to open it, as far as Clare could see. Her hand in the beast's tightened in despair. Had they been going the wrong way this whole time? Was there time to trace their way back?

Clare put her hand to the gate and tried to shake it. The gate—its iron elaborately wrought into dozens of little crowned figures, vine-wreathed kings and queens bowing, offering one another flowers, in ornate repeating patterns—did not move even a quarter inch. "It's iron," she said, "so we must not be in Timeless." Though where they were, she couldn't guess.

Now the beast, too, put his great, hairy hand to the gate, but lightly, not gripping. He caressed the iron delicately and gave a low, almost musical moan.

The gate began to move. No: the gate began to liquefy. The little iron kings and queens elongated, bent, bowed, straightened. They began to move backward, pulling the scrollwork back with them, like stagehands pulling back curtains.

Clare felt a familiar chill: a Strange chill. She paused at this threshold, looking at her beast.

"That was a fairy-making," she said. It was not a question. Then, with slow understanding: "Oh, but . . . oh. It was you. You made that totem out of fireflies. You were warning me."

Although she was never sure he understood her words, the beast turned to her gravely and inclined his huge horned head.

My beast can make the way the fairies do. Someone had said that a beast can only speak through pain or pleasure or making. The question, she saw, is whether it will make alone in fear and confusion, or together, in a sort of dance with you.

"You probably don't understand this," Clare said to her beast, "and I don't have time to say it the way I ought to. But I'm so sorry we've been apart so long." Then she took up his hand again, and together they walked through the gate,

They found themselves in a dimly lit forest clearing, surrounded by ancient, bent trees with dark green leaves. Clare looked to the sky for a clue, but above them the dimness simply disappeared into darkness. She could not even tell if they were inside or out.

The beast pulled at her hand, and they took a few steps farther in. At the center of the clearing stood a low stone well, choked with dead leaves.

Above the well, hanging upside down from the branch of a tree, was a little girl with long green hair.

15

The Yew and the Beast

The upside-down girl was brown as a tree, dark brown, except for the dark green hair that dangled into the well. Her rough pants and shirt were the color of olive leaves. Skin the color of wood, hair flowing evergreen—but her eyes: her eyes were white as clouds, pure white. She was blind.

Clare and her beast, still bound at the wrist, walked through the clearing to the well. The closer they came, the more familiar everything seemed to Clare, till by the time she was standing near the girl she almost laughed, or maybe cried. She knew this girl, of course she did. But her heart was so full and so tender, all she could say was, "You're my yew."

The yew-girl smiled radiantly through swollen eyes and dried tears. She had been crying for a long time. "You came," she said. "You came, I knew you'd come, but then I thought you wouldn't, but then you did."

"Are you all right?" asked Clare. Her heart felt wet and gold as a sunrise. "Can I help you down? Did Balor hang you up here?"

The yew-girl laughed a hoarse, crying-too-long laugh. "No, of course not. I like to hang upside down. I'm good at it." She reached past Clare and put a small hand to the beast's arm. "Hello, Asterion," the yew-girl said. "I missed you a lot."

The beast bent low, and pushed his head against the yew-girl's hand. She pulled gently on one of his horns.

Asterion. He had a name. Clare looked up at the beast and squeezed his hand. Then she sat at the edge of the well, lightly stroking a lock of the girl's green hair with her free hand. "I'm so glad I found you. Because, listen, I'm going to help you, and help—just everybody. That's why I'm here. I need to unlock this gate—do you know what I mean by that? I think you do—and get to the in-between. In the tree. And I have to really hurry."

During this speech, the upside-down girl's face fell. At the end, she shook her head vigorously, so that the long green hair flew around her face. "No," she said. "No. You just got here. You can't leave already. Don't you want to play first?"

Clare hesitated. "I do want to play," she said, "only I don't have time right now. I'm sorry."

The yew-girl's lip trembled. "But you haven't been here in so long. You used to come all the time, but you haven't come in so long. And since that bad thing happened . . ." She stopped, and her arms wrapped around herself, her small shoulders drew together as if to protect her heart. "Since that bad thing happened, I've been all alone. I can't find anyone. Everywhere my roots try to go is a wall. I can't find all my other trees, I can't even find my ocean grandma. I was all alone!" And now she was crying, big round tears spattering down to moisten dead leaves. "And no one was here but Asterion, and we missed you! And then he was gone, too!"

"I'm sorry," said Clare miserably. "I'm sorry, I'm so sorry, I didn't know. I'm trying to fix it. That's why I have to get into the—"

"Well, anyway you *can't* go to the in-between," said the yew-girl, her wet face darkening, "because the well is dry." Without warning, she grabbed the branch she hung from, flipped over to land on her feet, and walked blindly and surely around Clare to take the beast's—Asterion's—free hand. "So I guess you might as well stay and play. Or at least tell stories. I know a good place for that."

Clare sensed she had met someone as stubborn as she was. Defeated for now, she followed the beast and the child to one of the ancient trees surrounding the clearing.

"If I had the key to this gate," said Clare as they walked, "then I could get to the in-between. Do you know the key? Could you maybe just, tell me?"

The girl dropped to the ground and made herself comfortable against a broad trunk. The beast lowered himself beside her, and Clare sank to her knees on his other side.

"If I could tell you," said the girl primly, "I would not, because that would be cheating. But how could I? Keys cannot be said. Do you not know *keys*?"

"I know a little about keys," said mortified Clare. To herself: *Then remember: Hurrying doesn't help.*

So Clare made an effort to slow her racing mind. She listened to the girl croon, "Asterion, Asterion," as she stroked the beast's arm. And when the beast bent his great head to lay it gently on the girl's lap, Clare slid closer, her hand still in his, their wrists still bound, and curled against his obsidian-black side.

The girl stroked the beast's horns. "He is tired," she said, "and so are you."

"I didn't know he had a name," said Clare. She repressed a yawn. She was tired, and this slowing down to listen, the only way to find a key, had made her so much more aware of how tired she was.

"His name means 'star,'" said the girl. She turned a wide smile and pearly eyes to Clare. "And so now, stories. I love this tree for telling stories. First I will, because mine will be a bedtime story, and you will fall asleep."

"Oh no," said Clare, sitting up. "I don't have time to sleep. I really can't."

The yew-girl's mouth turned down and her blind eyes shifted down. "Yes," she said. "You have to sleep."

"But why?"

"Because you're *tired*."

"But if I don't get through this gate in time, the gate could be closed forever. Then you'll be lonely forever," added Clare, feeling that this was mean to say, but that she had no choice.

The stubborn yew-girl simply turned her back. "I'm going to tell my *bedtime* story," she said. "So you have to go to *bed*."

Clare tried to persuade the girl, who would neither turn to Clare, nor answer, nor give any sign of having heard. After several minutes, in a frustration near despair, Clare said, "All right, all right, I can try to sleep, but only for a little bit, okay? A very short nap. Is that okay?"

The yew lifted her head and smiled. "You will sleep as long as you must," she said, "because it's a very good story."

So Clare curled up again, her head against the side of her great beast, smelling the salt and pleasant sweat of him. His side moved slowly up and down, because he was already asleep, Asterion was. And almost as soon as she lay down, Clare's body too felt heavy as sand, and she listened to the girl's story in a kind of drowse.

"Once upon a time," the yew-girl began, "a tree stood in a forest. It was an old, rich forest, rich with death: with fruits dropped and decayed on the ground, and bird messes, and dying grass—all the deaths large and small that make a forest rich, and make the roots beneath it strong and supple."

Weird beginning to a bedtime story, Clare thought sleepily.

"One day, a hunting party came through the forest. As they passed beneath the oldest and wisest tree, a child trailing behind the others picked up a stick from the ground and threw it at a squirrel sitting underneath the tree, guarding a cache of nuts. The stick was aimed too well, and put out the squirrel's eye."

Something inside Clare twisted, and her eyes opened.

"The child did not even notice that the stick had hit so true, and ran to catch up with the hunting party. But the tree heard the squirrel weeping and said, 'Why don't you borrow the moon for your eye?'

"The squirrel replied, 'There is no moon tonight, only a black hole against the sky, like the hole where my eye should be.'

"'That's right,' said the tree. 'But when the moon turns again, as it must, then you will have a new eye.'

"The squirrel said, 'I am not tall enough to reach the moon.'

"The tree said, 'I am tall enough. Climb to my highest branches and see if you can reach it.'

"In those days, squirrels lived on the ground and didn't climb trees. So this was hard for a squirrel, especially one so recently injured. But the tree urged him on the whole way, saying, 'Don't delay—once your eye has healed over the wound, it will be too late.'

"So the squirrel climbed the highest branches, and plucked the tiny sliver of moon from the sky, and placed it in the wound where his eye had been. And it worked! The squirrel had two eyes again. Afterward he and the tree became best friends, and the squirrel learned to scramble among its branches as easily as squirrels do now. And ever since, trees and squirrels . . ." The yew-girl trailed off. "Clare?" she said. "Are you crying? It isn't a sad story."

"No," said Clare damply, her face hidden.

"*Was* the story sad?"

"Only I wish it were true," said Clare, her words muffled into the warm side of her beast, her hand still clinging to his open, soft, sleeping hand, "oh, I wish it were true, and not just a story."

"Oh well, it is true," said the yew-girl confidently. "All my stories are true."

Clare choked out a small laugh. "I don't think so," she said. "A tree tall enough to reach the moon is definitely just a story, I'm sorry. But if it did exist," she added with passion, "I would find it, I would."

"It *does* exist," said the yew-girl, with exaggerated patience. "It's in my *story*. And anyway you wouldn't need a tree like that, to reach the moon. You have Asterion." She yawned prodigiously. "So that was a bedtime story; so now let's go to sleep."

Clare, with her own painful wound no moon could heal, and with her terror of the clock ticking away somewhere, the clock she couldn't see, knew with certainty that she would never sleep.

But the long, soft sighs of the girl and the beast nestled around her slowed her own breathing, and called back the drowsiness. Little stabs of anxiety jolted her from time to time, but soon even those faded away, and she was dreaming.

And, as had been true all her life—only she had never known it before—Clare and the beast dreamed together, hand in hand.

Clare and the beast dreamed that they were an old woman and a golden lion who walked together along a river at dusk.

The old woman wore a long green coat with wooden buttons. Her white hair moved lightly around her face, and her breath came in puffs of white. She felt taller and bigger than she had as almost-fifteen Clare, also softer in some places, harder in others. Her hands felt knobby and stiff. Her right shoulder ached sharply, and her legs felt thick and slow beneath her. But she also felt great calm.

Old-woman Clare stopped beside the dark, swirling river. The golden lion stood on its hind paws, its huge warm face above her face like a great sun. They stood that way for long moments, a kind of embrace, the lion's forepaws crossed behind her neck as if he were placing something there. Clare felt the sweat and heat of the lion's flesh under the rough hide.

When the lion dropped back to its haunches, Clare found around her throat a soft collar of golden fur, surely part of the lion's own mane. She stroked his head in gratitude. They looked out at the evening sky, translucent green and indigo, scudded with shadow-clouds. Old-woman Clare thought to herself: *I am old, and I have almost learned to ride the wind, like the birds, instead of plowing against it.* Old-woman Clare laughed. *But not quite.*

An old man walked toward them, once-black hair now mixed with slushy gray. His hand rested on the neck of a tall white stag beside him. The old man wore dark glasses and a wry half smile. His half smile matched the half smile of the old woman.

"You found the inside," said the old man.

"I did," said the old woman, in her voice that was Clare's, yet rougher and lower than Clare's.

"There is deeper still to go," said the old man.

"I know," she said. "There always is."

"There always will be," he agreed.

Then he took her hand, and she put her other hand on his shoulder, and they danced. The lion and the stag sat side by side, watching them. His black coat was rough under her fingers, and the bones of his shoulder hard beneath it. His face was softened by time, but still and forever, from the day she was born, no face more familiar than his.

With no music to move to, they found a music between them. The dance swung outward, wide, so that they barely touched; and the dance swung in close, so that they danced heart to heart. They swung each other off their feet, into the air, and they didn't come down, but rose dancing into the evening sky, and danced there as night fell around them. Clare saw the stars come out behind Finn; she saw that his hand as it moved left a brilliant, curving trail of stars from each finger.

She saw that Finn was made of stars.

She looked at herself, and saw that she was made of stars, too. *Oh,* everyone *is made of stars*, thought Clare, *of course they are, how funny I never noticed.*

They danced together, trailing stars.

Clare woke up, eyes still closed, still made of stars.

The stars drained away as the world returned. Labyrinth. Yew-tree girl. Beast.

The Hunt that could not go on without the fairy flag.

Her own gate, closed to her.

Finn, with her arrow in his eye.

All these things—her own poison arrows of remorse and fear—wrenched Clare from the sweetness of sleep. She pushed against the beast's sleek hide, pressed herself to sitting, and opened her eyes. Surprised, she lifted her right hand. It was no longer bound to the beast's. Instead, her mother's silver chain and star were back around her neck. The beast slept on, but Clare saw heavy links of silver around his neck as well.

The yew-girl was hanging by her knees over the well again. "Your turn," she said. Her long green hair dragged through the dusty dead leaves of the well.

"How long was I asleep?" said Clare. "Was it long, do you know?" She felt anxiety mounting again. Unbelievable that she had fallen asleep, with less than a day to save everything that mattered.

The yew gave an upside-down shrug. "I don't know. Come by me. Tell your story up here." She stretched out delicate brown fingers. "Hold hands with me, Clare."

Clare rose, feeling strange and light without the beast's warm hand in hers. She put her hand to her star, and watched how, in his sleep, the beast put his hand to his own great star. "I don't know if I have time . . . ," she began, and saw the pain in the yew-girl's face. "All right, yes, all right," she said. "Sorry, and I do want to hold hands with you. I really do. Only I'm just so worried."

"It's harder to worry upside down," said the girl.

At the rim of the well, Clare dipped her hand into the leaves, then a whole arm, to see how far down they went: much farther than she could reach, at least. She said, "It actually doesn't seem safe, hanging over this well."

"Oh no, it isn't safe," said the yew-girl reassuringly. "There is no *safe*." (And Clare remembered Her of the Cliffs saying those words, in a rather different tone.) "Outside the seed-husk, no safety at all. But that's good! You know how that old story says, 'The seed does not like to leave its little home. It holds the shell around itself, crying, "No, no, no!"'" She laughed.

"Um, I don't know that story," said Clare.

"Well, the point of the story is, that the seed is so glad, when the husk is gone, to find it must fall and fly, touch and be touched. Oh, Clare," she added, with an extra dollop of delight. "Come *see* how not safe it is up here!"

Reluctantly, Clare climbed up the edge of the stone well, awkwardly hooking one knee, then the other, on the overhanging branch, her knees beside the girl's, holding tight with both hands. It had been a long time since she'd hung from monkey bars.

Carefully, slowly, she let go her grip, until she hung straight down. Her star hit her in the face, so she tucked it inside her shirt. Clare was taller than the yew-girl, but the girl's hair was longer, so their tips of their hair tangled together, red and green, in the dry and dusty well.

The girl reached over and took Clare's hand in her own small, fine-boned one. At the touch, Clare felt herself open and soften, so much that she had to consciously tighten her knees on the branch so as not to slip off. It was what she had felt when her tree-roots had touched the yew's: cracked open, flooded with light.

The yew-girl put her other hand tenderly to Clare's face and caressed it, more like a mother than a child. "Clare, we missed you," she said. "Asterion did, and I did. You were gone so long, so long. You were gone a million years, I think."

"I'm sorry," said Clare, with her whole heart. "I'm really, really sorry. How can I make it up to you?"

"Tell me a story," said the girl. "A very, very good story that is yours, that you have made. I know you are still a maker, for you would not be my guardian, if you were not. Trees were the first makers, the first of all."

"Trees were?"

The blind eyes blinked twice, and the girl laughed. "Clare," she said. "We made this *world*. We take air and light and bring it underground, and turn it into food and life. Then we give our making to the world. We painted this whole dead and rocky world in pretty blues and greens. This whole world is our painting, our making. And so . . . ," she added, cleverly, "what is *your* making? What story will you tell?"

Clare went silent, trying to think of one.

"Your *own* story, that *you* made, or make for me now," the girl reminded her.

"I don't know if I . . ." Clare trailed off. She felt a hot flush, or maybe it was just that she was hanging upside down. She'd never made a story.

"Have you no makings at all?"

Clare was cut by the disappointment in her voice. "No, I'm so sorry. I mean, yes, sort of, but not really, just these . . . these sort of poetry things . . ."

The brown-and-green girl ran a hopeful thumb across Clare's knuckles. "Say one?"

Clare gritted her teeth and reached into her pocket for the commonplace book. "They're not very good," she said, trying to wiggle it out of the pocket one-handed. "There are lots better poems in here, by other people, if you want to hear a real poem."

"I want to hear *your* poem," said the yew-girl, adding rather sadly, "though really I want to hear your story. I wish you could think of one."

Regretfully, Clare released the yew-girl's hand. "One second," she said. She pulled the pencil stub and the commonplace book from her pocket. On one of the right-side-up pages she wrote, with some difficulty, *Know what roots know: there is only one tree.*

"I didn't want to forget that," she said. "From your song."

The yew-girl smiled and arched her back with pleasure.

Clare turned the book the other way and flipped to the back, where she made another note, this time for a future poem: *The secret makings of trees: pulling air and light from the world into their laboratories below the ground, creating food and breath and color for the world.*

"That was because you gave me an idea for a making," said Clare.

The yew-girl smiled, but added, with a little impatience, "Your poem, though."

Clare looked at the poem she had been working on in her loft—a few days ago, she supposed, but it seemed like three lifetimes ago. She penciled some quick changes, then shoved the stub back in her pocket, and took the yew-girl's hand again. Her face felt heavy and strange with the weight of the blood running into it, but her spine felt light and free.

"Read," said the girl.

Holding the book upside down in front of her face, Clare read.

Along the sea, the moonlight spills

A kind of path

For one with feet, not fins.

Bare feet and cold

Splash along this radiant road.

On water and light she runs

Toward stone and tree,

Toward home.

The finless girl flies to her Finn

Wrapped in the roots of the in-between.

"Oh," sighed the yew. "'Wrapped in the roots' is just how he was for so long! I *like* that making. And, Clare," she added, both shy and sly: "Do you think I could have this book? That has your makings? Would you leave it here?"

Clare hesitated. It was hard to say no—and what if this was somehow the key? But it was her book, it had been her mother's book, and she couldn't find a way to open her hand and let it go.

"I can't," said Clare, holding the small brown hand tighter. "I'm so sorry, sweet."

The yew-girl turned her face away so Clare could not see her expression. Anguished, Clare asked, "Isn't there something else I can give you instead?"

"Well," said the yew slowly, face still turned away, "you could tell me a moonlight road story. Would you? It's been *forever*. Say yes."

"A what?" said Clare. She had tucked the book back into her pocket, was now reaching for the yew's hand again. A few feet away, the beast groaned and turned in his sleep. "What's a moonlight . . . Oh, *wait*." A little waterfall of memories. Her mother sitting at the edge of her bed—her bed! the same bed she had now—telling her bedtime stories.

"Oh, *that's* where I got that moonlight path," Clare said, soft. "I knew it was familiar. My mother used to tell me that for a bedtime story. It was always different, all these crazy adventures, but it always started the same way, with this girl running down the moonlight road."

"Yes, that story," said the yew. She turned to Clare now, and her face glowed. "The story all the mothers and daughters and granddaughters have always told, in your house. I haven't heard it in *so* long, Clare."

"I haven't, either," said Clare.

And she began the story.

"This is the story of the Moonlight Road. The moonlight road doesn't always come to your door, and when it does, it's not always at a convenient time. But the rule of the moonlight road is that when it comes, you must always take it."

"What if you're scared to?" asked the yew-girl dreamily. Clare suddenly heard her own voice, asking that same question in that same dreamy way—it was part of how the story was told, a call-and-response. And it came to her, how her mother would answer.

"Then you take that fear, and you kiss its face, and say, 'I'm so sorry you're scared, but I can't take you with me. You can tell me how scared you are when I get back.'"

"What if the journey just seems too hard and you don't want to try?"—and Clare remembered this question, too, and how the storyteller must answer.

"Then you take that feeling, and you kiss its face, and say, 'I know how you feel! But, sorry, I can't take you with me on this trip. You stay home and relax!'"

"And what if you think you'll fail? That's the worst one," added the yew, in a small voice, and Clare's heart was touched and torn at the idea of her yew, afraid she might fail. She knew the right answer to this one, too.

"Then you take that feeling of doubt," she said, holding the yew-girl's hand tighter, "and you kiss its face, and say, 'I know you're worried, you sweet worrier. But I can't take you with me on this trip. Stay home and worry for me. See you soon!'"

"That's right!" cried the yew. Her face glowed like burnished wood. "That's what you have to do, isn't it, Clare? Run away without them, run away, run away, down the glorious, wonderful, UNsafe—"

"—moonlight road," Clare said, finishing for her, and squeezing her hand back.

Clare spun the story on. She spun the girl onto a ship manned by tall, silent people the color of eggplants, whose eyes were sunflowers. She spun the girl onto an island where trees grew whole rainbows of fruit sweet as candy, but every night at dusk an enormous creature climbed out of the waves, its skin shiny and mottled as a fish, but with two legs and long blue horns and monstrous fangs. Every evening the creature ate fruit until it was sick, then slept on the beach, groaning. One night the girl crept up on the creature and pulled out its fangs, so that it woke up crying, with a bloody mouth. The girl gave the creature her handkerchief, and they became friends, and had adventures together.

Clare spun and spun. Some bits she remembered from her mother's soft Irish voice, but most of it she made up. She spun the story out like a thread from her mother and grandmother and on and on, down to her and the yew.

And as she spun the story, she realized with certainty: *Oh, now I see. This is it. This is the key to this gate. This story is the key.*

At the end of the story—when Clare had the girl running up her own stairway at dawn, her adventures over for now—Clare felt a small, rhythmic tugging on the tips of her hair.

She craned her neck to look down. The well was bubbling and full. It was water, gently sloshing water, that dragged the tips of her hair back and forth.

"Clare," said the yew-girl.

"Yes," said astonished Clare.

"What do you want most, right this second? Most of anything. Say fast without thinking."

Fast, without thinking, upside down, Clare said, "I want to make up for what I did."

"Ahhhhh," said the yew-girl. "Then you better go in."

"Go in?" asked Clare. "What do you mean 'go in'?"

The yew-girl burst out laughing. "I mean let GO," she said, "and go in!" A brief, prim pause: "Unless you're scared."

So Clare held her breath, gave the yew-girl's hand a last squeeze, straightened her legs, and slipped headfirst into the clear, bubbling water.

16

The Moon in Her Mouth

Upside down, damp, snorting water from her nose, Clare spilled back into air. She found herself in a narrow space: cozy, dim, firefly lit. Pushing wet hair from her eyes, she righted herself and looked around.

The in-between. Just as one pool had taken her to Timeless, the yew's well had brought her home.

For a moment, she allowed herself the comforting beauty and scent of it. But only a moment. This was her chance to make up for what she had done, as best she could: to get the flag and bring it back to Finn, so that he could fulfill his life's task.

(If Finn could still shoot, with only one eye. But she wouldn't think of that.)

Everything depended on whether Balor was here, and if so, whether he was asleep or awake. She put her ear to the slender crack in the yew: nothing, not even a sleeping sigh (but would he even be sleeping? she had no idea what time it was).

Cautious as a cat, Clare thrust out her head and looked around. Nothing, still nothing. Not a sound or a sign. Could she be so lucky—was he gone? Would it be this easy? She slipped out as silently as she could, in case he was hidden, and as quickly as she could, in case he came back.

The light was cool. In the stone window, Clare was taken aback to see half-light, the magic hour of the Strange. But this light was changing, she reminded herself. If it was getting darker, then night was only just coming, and she had plenty of time. If it was getting lighter, then it was already morning, and she was almost too late.

In the dusty quiet of the great vaulted room, Clare darted behind the screen to the small bookshelf by her father's bed. She left damp footprints across the floor, and didn't care: no time to care, and she'd be back and safe in the in-between in a moment.

As she knelt at the shelves, her heart failed her: the book wasn't there. She knew it well, from bedtime stories, from long summer afternoons sprawled across carpets. She knew its old and peeling pale green jacket, with a pen-and-ink drawing of Skye itself, craggy mountains set into the sea.

But it wasn't there.

No, wait! Here it was, tucked in sideways and wrong ways out. Holding it, she was surprised by a stab of fear—her father's book, from when he was a boy, and now that boy was buried under thousands of tons of rock. Even if her making had managed to turn Balor's thoughts from him . . .

But she had no time for thinking the worst. Instead, she turned to the middle of the book and paged forward, looking for the Fairy Bridge chapter. Just a few pages in, and a few more—yes. Here it was, that thin, gray scrap of fabric. She held the bit of flag in her hand, as she had rarely been allowed to do. It tingled of Strange. She put it to her heart, and then to her face, to catch any scent of father or fairy.

She pulled out her commonplace book, once again somewhat damp, though luckily the pages were dry. She paused at a verse in her mother's neat girlhood hand:

Come away, O human child!

To the waters and the wild

With a faery, hand in hand,

For the world's more full of weeping than you can understand.

She laid the bit of flag on that page, and returned the book to her pocket. Now a glance at the darkening stone window told her that it was night, not morning, so she still had time. Heartened, full of intention, she stood and ran out from behind the screen that made her father's bedroom.

Outside the screen, she stopped short.

It was lucky she no longer held the flag in her hand, because if she had, it would have fallen to the floor.

Hovering in front of the yew tree, just a little above her eye level, was the totem: its faded, sickening yellow and red, its exploded eye, its ravenous mouth in a silent scream. It hovered, watching her.

Where are you safe? Balor had said. *Nowhere at all.*

In the silence and deepening darkness, it all came back to her, the despair of that terrible day and worse night at the castle. Now she understood—she thought she understood—that the despair had never truly left. It couldn't leave, because the despair was the truth. All her hopes of making it up to Finn, all her odds and ends of joy—finding the flag, dancing with Asterion, telling stories with the yew—those were stupid delusions and lies.

As if it had heard her thoughts—almost as if it were galvanized by them—the totem began to move. Slowly it scraped its tail along the stone wall behind it, back and forth, back and forth, charging itself, preparing to strike.

Clare sank to the ground, physically sick, knowing with certainty that all was lost. She saw—she thought she saw—the bleak and hopeless reality: that of course Balor would win. He had nearly won already, and she had helped him, by putting out the eye of the one person who could have stopped him. She was the teeth of the wolf.

She knew that Finn would never make again, would never be his own wry, proud self again.

She knew that the yew would remain walled off from the other trees, lonely forever, as long as Balor allowed it to live.

She knew that humans would never dream again, or make again, and that fairies would never be unsettled by love.

And she knew that she would never see her father again, a thought that bent her over with grief, face to the ground, as the totem scraped and ratcheted, and outside the sea sighed its own, uncaring sigh, back and forth. It was too hard, she was too small, and too afraid. And Balor would be back any minute.

Please, she thought, *I just want to close my eyes. No more, no more.*

The last light was leaking away. The room was dim, and the totem's ratcheting, scraping progress echoed across the stone. Clare turned her wet face to the small stone window, where a star had come out, and another. No moon, no calming yellow-green light; only a black hole, where the moon should be, like the moon in the yew-girl's bedtime story. A black hole, and a few cold stars too far away. Clare thought of the fairies who worshipped those distant lights that they could not see from their own world, and because of her would never see again.

And at that thought, she felt a tingling against her skin, under the pocket where she kept her commonplace book. As if in a dream, as if she had no choice, she pulled out the book. It fell open to the page where she had tucked her scrap of fairy flag.

Come away.

Lying on the ground, Clare began to think slowly, as if she were working out a difficult math problem. *My great-many-greats-grandmother on my father's side was a fairy herself,* she thought. *And she left this flag for my family's protection. It will protect me. And it will protect my father.*

The scraping noise across the stones moved faster.

What do you do if you're afraid, and you know you'll fail?

To watch Clare struggle to her feet, you'd think a weight were pressing down on her. She walked toward the tree, leaning hard into the malignant power surging from the totem, pushing her back. It was like the power that swelled from Her of the Cliffs, except this power was a poison that dissolved all confidence and hope. Once, she staggered back a step, almost fell, but pushed on.

Scrape, scrape, went the totem, swishing its tail against the rocks. Now its mad, chaotic eye had an almost electric glow, and its mouth looked ready to scream or sing.

"I can't take you with me," Clare said through gritted teeth. It was as if she spoke to the totem itself, rather than her own doubts. It was hard to find breath, its power pushed at her so hard. She raised her voice as best she could. "I'm not taking you with me! You can't come!"

And with her last bit of strength, she seized the totem by the throat, slid her hands down its long stick-body, and smashed it with all her strength on the hard floor.

In the in-between, her heart wild as a bird, Clare braced herself against the tree-walls on each side. She felt on fire, that she had done such a thing, had fought the worst of fear and despair, had fought that thing, had won. Her body felt charged with some ferocious electricity—she was almost sure her hair was floating around her head.

Tomorrow was Midsummer's Eve. That's what that black hole of a moon had meant. With the fairy flag, the fairies would ride, and Clare meant to ride with them. She put her hand down to a root, to feel her way toward the Strange.

And stopped.

After all, she had a whole night before she had to be back.

She stood like that, bent over, one hand on the root, one to her mouth, thinking hard.

The black hole where the moon should be.

She moved her hand from her mouth to the star around her neck. Now, finally, she moved her hand along the root, saying softly: "Asterion. Take me to Asterion."

Clare and her beast stood facing each other on a ragged mountain peak, silhouetted against a deep red-violet sky. It was dark: so this was not fairy. She didn't know if it was the human world, exactly, but it was not fairy.

A faint, chilly light silhouetted Asterion's vast, dark bulk against snow-spattered black crags. But it was a moonless night. Where did this delicate light come from? Clare looked up.

One star. Far above, one small, silvery star.

She picked her way over rough black rocks to Asterion, eyes focused on the uneven ground, using his wet, hoarse breath to find him. How that breathing used to frighten her, and now it was longed-for comfort.

"Asterion," she said, when she reached him. "The yew told me a story about . . ." And she paused. She wasn't sure how much the beast understood of words, but she was certain a long, involved fable would mean nothing to him. And yet they made their dreams together. What was the language they used in dreams?

Wanting.

Clare reached up, as far as she could, to embrace her beast. Her face rested against his chest, just below the star. Eyes closed in concentration, trying to put all her heart and will into each word, she began to whisper, though too softly for him to hear, at least in any normal way. "Asterion," she said. "I need the moon. I need it more than anything, more than *anything*. Please take me there."

Gently, Asterion pushed her away. She looked up, afraid he had not understood or was angry. He knelt beside her, and his huge, inhuman head, its elongated black eyes set on either side of a long, thick muzzle, came up to her shoulders.

An uncertain pause. Asterion gave a guttural growl that echoed as if from the bottom of a well.

"I'm sorry, I don't know . . ." Clare began. But he had extended one huge arm, pulling her closer, and—oh! onto his back.

It was awkward, at first, and prickly around his waist. She had to sort of shimmy up until she had one arm over his shoulder and down his chest, so she could see. When he stood, she kicked out a leg to keep her balance.

For a moment, they stood among the black crags. Then, without preparation, without even a running start, the beast leaped upward, legs kicking against the night air, and headed for the star.

Through the blackness they flew, Clare clinging hand and arm and leg, watching the night roar past from between Asterion's horns. They passed a flock of night geese whose bodies were one long, bent muscle. "Hello, birds," she shouted, a little crazily. "Isn't it weird, isn't it so strange, that one minute you're safe in your egg and the next minute you're flying."

They flew into deeper dark and saw creatures made of light, even stranger than the light-beings who haunted the in-between.

The single silver star grew larger as they approached. Soon it was not a star at all, but something more complicated: a thing with silver fingers reaching up, and silver fingers reaching down, like two hands, *like my beast and I, when we were joined.*

It was a tree, a tremendous, glittering silver tree, set like silver filigree against the velvet black of space. Each branch forked into new branches, and each of those branches forked, and over and over again, until the crown of the tree was a mass of forking silver twigs, each twig a miniature of the tree itself, a tree that replicated itself over and over.

And each of the roots divided, and each of those root-pieces divided, so that the roots of the tree were a mass of glittering, gleaming forking, too.

And between the roots and the branches was a gleaming silver trunk, veined with color.

"It's the Night Tree," said Clare, not knowing why she called it that, but knowing that was its name. The closer they flew, the vaster the tree, and the more detail she could see: that from every limb and twig hung, delicate as a Christmas ornament, a tiny glowing orb. The bigger orbs hung from the bigger branches, glowing fiery diamond-white, or yellow-gold, or tangerine fire, or flame blue. From the smaller branches hung dimmer orbs, red or misty gray, burnt black or dirt-brown or ocean-green.

And from the smallest twigs hung the smallest orbs, in stony colors, gray and moss, like gems before they're polished.

In these billion twigs and orbs, how would they find their own moon?

"It's there somewhere," Clare told her beast.

But as they sailed among the branches of the dazzling tree,

Clare's eyes were confused by the wild brightness, and she began to feel sick. "I'm closing my eyes," she said to her beast. "It's up to you. Please find it." Asterion continued, fluid and sure, his great legs swimming beneath them. With her eyes closed, it was harder to keep her balance, so Clare reached her arms farther around his neck, pressing her face close. She felt the muscles of his shoulders move in time with his legs. She set her breathing to breathe in time with the muscles, just as she had in their dance.

Eyes closed, she recalled with shame the pretty white horse of her hunting dream, her Balor-infected dream, how its heart beat under her calves, just as Asterion's heart beat strong beneath her. *But that horse was not my true steed, and how could I ever have thought it was?* She buried her face more deeply in Asterion's midnight shoulder, and sensed the heat or ice of each orb as they passed it.

The kicks slowed, and Clare opened her eyes. They were deep into the midst of Night Tree now. Her eyes dazzled at the spinning, glimmering, cool-or-fiery orbs.

Asterion hesitated, hovering in the air.

"I'm here now," said Clare. "I'll help. You're not alone."

Kicking his legs slowly, the beast she rode rose slowly up, sank slowly down, like a boat on the waves, like a horse on a merry-go-round. Clare squinted at the thousand orbs dangling around her. "Moon, moon," she sang softly to herself.

And then she saw—lit by a nearby sunflower-blaze, in the

shadow of a small, languorously turning orb that glowed sea-blue, pine-green, snow-white—she saw what she had come for: a tiny pearl of a moon. But it was far up on a slender branch, and many more tangled branches were between them, too tangled for her beast to move through.

"Wait for me," Clare said. She raised herself up with all the strength in her thighs, and seized a branch above. She locked one leg around the branch—a hundred glowing blue and silver balls spun dizzily around her—then pulled herself up to standing. She stepped up to another branch, then another, until, on tiptoe, reaching as far as she could, Clare plucked that little pearl of a moon till she held it cool in her hand.

To keep it safe, she placed the moon carefully in her mouth. Its cold radiance filled her bones. As she climbed back down among the thousand starry, spinning orbs, she held the moon in her mouth with reverence and stillness. Even when she slipped, once, and lost her grip, and almost fell: even then she kept the moon safe and cool.

When she was again clinging to Asterion's back, she said, "Let's go find him." Knowing it might be too late, she would still bring Finn the moon.

She wasn't too late; she arrived before noon—if Timeless had a noon—on Midsummer Eve. She leaped from the back of her beast, still careful of the moon in her mouth, and ran through the great, leafy hall. A crowd of unsmiling smilers followed behind, peering over her shoulder.

Finn sat on a chair, frowning, his flute on the floor beside his chair, as if he had dropped it there in weariness or impatience. Clare could only see the untouched side of his face, but as she approached he turned to face her. The bloody patch across one eye and the look of utter relief in the other made her catch her breath.

Her of the Cliffs stood beside Finn. Her face remained a mask, though a less terrible one, her mouth a flat line. She pulsed with tangible energy, like a bonfire. "The flag?" she said.

Carefully, Clare took the moon from her mouth. "This first," she said. "It's for his eye. It has to go in before it heals. It might—I don't know . . ." She looked at Finn now, his uncomprehending expression beginning to shift toward hope. "I don't *know* if it will work, for his eye, but it might. I think it might," she ended awkwardly.

Her of the Cliffs looked at the moon in her hand, then looked at Clare with an expression hard to read. She took the moon and washed it in rainwater. Then she planted it like a seed where Finn's left eye had been.

Today is my birthday, Clare thought: *the first of my two birthdays. And for this to work is the only present I want.*

But Finn's own blue-gray laughing eye did not return. The moon remained a faintly glowing white orb in his brown face. He was still half blind.

“I’m sorry, I’m so sorry,” said Clare, kneeling by his chair, facing the ground to hide the shame. “I thought—it was a stupid idea, but I thought—”

“Not stupid, never, we don’t use that word, now, do we?” said Finn, the teasing in his voice masking his disappointment. “No, kind and brave and clever it was, and who knows what may be, for the moon turns in its own time, not ours. But, Clare—sit here beside me, Clare—you met your beast and tamed him. You are a mad and remarkable Clare.”

“I did,” said Clare, making herself look at him, and smile at him, as if his face didn’t tear her heart in two. “I did, it was so strange, oh, I have so much to tell you. But we don’t have time.”

“After the Hunt,” Finn agreed. His smile faded a little. “That’s right.”

“Why hunt?” murmured a sulky voice from the crowd behind them. “Why ride to save a road we do not need?”

“We do have need,” said Finn quietly, not taking his eyes from Clare.

“Says the one-eyed hunter,” said another. “Who will not shoot straight even if we find Balor for him.”

Now Finn stood and faced them. “I will shoot straight.”

But the fairies ignored him and continued their conversation.

“We ride so the humans may make asleep and blind.”

“We ride so humans may weep and love.”

"No," said Finn, raising his voice. "We ride to keep close to change and death, to make our makings greater."

Bitterly, from the back of the hall: "We ride so that humans may walk past those makings, blind to their beauty."

"And we ride at what cost?" asked another.

"Yes, for look how the human girl chose," cried another. "At a choice between fairy and her father, she chose her father. And indeed she made him safe, but at what cost?"

Clare turned wildly to Her of the Cliffs. "Is that true?" she asked. "Tell me. Is my father safe?"

"He is safe," she said, unsmiling. "He has been drawn from the hole where Balor buried him. He is safe, he and the miners. But because you chose him over us, Finn will miss his shot. So all you care for, and all we care for, is already lost. It is a fruitless Hunt." Her voice had broken with disgust, and she turned to the crowd. "No Hunt!" she called.

They took up the chant. "No Hunt! No Hunt!"

The Strange young man with the starry hair was leaning against a nearby chair. "I hope you succeeded in your quest, Clare," he said, pointed and mild.

She understood. She pulled the commonplace book from her pocket, opened it to the flag, and handed the book to Finn. He took the scrap of cloth in his hand.

The crowd went silent. Every one of them, even Her of the

Cliffs, turned to watch as Finn examined the flag, turning it over in his hand.

Finally, still gazing at the fragment of cloth, Finn broke the silence, speaking in a conversational, almost absent tone. "I find myself wondering, now I hold it in my hand," he said: "Which of you was it?" He looked up at the crowd. "Which of you married the Macleod man of the changing world, and gave him this flag, and promised our protection when his family had need?"

Some shuffling of feet. Fairies glanced at one another, then back to the floor. The crowd began to shift, almost imperceptibly, some to one side, some to another, making a sort of narrow parting: and at the end of that corridor of color and feather and bone stood Her of the Cliffs.

"So I thought," said Finn calmly. "For who else had the power to promise our protection, but the Hunter herself?" He walked until he faced her directly. His voice was still gentle, but with force behind it. "With your permission, may I tell you why you gave this flag? For I believe you have forgot."

A murmur of shock at the boldness of this, but Her of the Cliffs's face did not change. She stood, silent, arms relaxed at her sides, like a gunfighter.

"You gave this flag for love," said Finn. "Humans come to our world to dream. And we go there to love. I have wondered if our love seems as blind and willful to them, as their dreams seem to us. The love that gave this flag, now: that was a wild and willful love."

Silence hovered over the room like an enormous bird.

"But you can only love what you must lose," said Finn, "and that is a hard knowing for Timeless creatures such as you." Finn gestured to the whole crowd, and smiled his wryest smile. "Well I know I am lovable beyond reckoning; but you'd none of you love me half so much, if you would not lose me one day."

A sound like a sigh of grief ran through them.

It was dawning on Clare, as slow as dawn itself, that she was descended—by how many dozens of generations, but still—from Her of the Cliffs. She looked at that fierce red hair, so close to the color reflected back to her by every mirror and still pool.

"This flag is a promise," Finn continued, "and a promise is a kind of road itself, like the fairy road, across time and peoples. Just as I am that kind of road. If you abandon the road, you abandon me. You cut me off from one of my parents.

"You know I honor the makings of Timeless. They are my joy and my life. But our makings live best in the only place they can die, in the human world. Ah, I have seen the makings you make in the human world, all of you, how precious and strange they are, how fine, compared to the cold toys we make here."

A murmur of assent from the crowd.

"We do not ride for humans," said Finn. His voice was rising now. "We ride for fairy. We ride for our best, most fearless makings. And we ride for love. I know you scoff at love, and I know you long toward it." Finn held the flag high above his head. "It is Midsummer Eve. We ride tonight."

There was a half second's hesitation. Then—whether because of the power of the flag, or because the flag's power was to teach Finn to lead, Clare would never be sure—Her of the Cliffs herself called out, "Tonight we ride!"

It was as if she had touched off a charge. The crowd exploded in all directions. It was like nothing Clare had seen before in this languorous place: the fairies were *rushing*. The intrusion of time made the fairies brighter, more energized; but also fearful and anxious. The Wild Hunt was near.

Finn stood at the center of the whirling crowd, his eyes on the book in his hand.

Clare ran up to talk to him—to say how moving his speech had been, how astonished she was to find she was descended from Her herself—but stopped short, aghast.

He had turned the commonplace book upside down and was reading a page in the back.

"Oh, but *no*," she moaned without thinking.

He looked up, startled, maybe even hurt. In the second or two of silence between them, Clare remembered both Balor's awful mockery, and the yew-girl's sigh of pleasure. She made two fists to hide her trembling fingers and said, "I'm sorry. I'm just shy. Look all you want. Wait, actually"—and with a deep breath, she flipped through the pages to find the moonlight-road poem—"look at this one."

As he read, Finn and Clare made a spot of stillness among the swishing silks and flashing colors of the Hunt preparations. She felt that her heart lay open in his palm.

But she also felt that whether he liked the poem or not, her heart would be all right.

When he raised his eyes, one blue-gray, one pearl-white, his expression was a curious mixture of pleasure, admiration, and some kind of happy sadness she could not quite identify. "I knew you for a maker, Clare, from long ago," he said. "I knew that, indeed, and I was right. This is well made."

Clare smiled stupidly, unable to think of what to say. Finn smiled. "I have a making for you, as well. I mean," he added, a little anxiously, "I don't say I believe you made this for me—"

"A little I did, and a little I didn't," said Clare.

Finn grinned. "Same as I. A little I made a making for you, and little for myself, and—well. Afterward. There will be an afterward, there must be, for that's a making you must see. But, sadly"—his odd, ironic smile crinkling his odd eyes—"for all I have tried, all my life, to think of other ways, I find the only way to win this battle is to fight it."

He handed her the book, and carefully folded the flag into his pocket. He leaned toward her, and she felt a single breath held between them, as if they might never breathe again. He kissed her on the cheek, and walked away.

The spot he had kissed glowed and glowed with the memory of it.

17

The Wild Hunt

Clare had a plan.

With Finn gone, she made her way into the crowd of bustling Strange. She had not said her plan to Finn, for fear of a fight, but she meant to make it real.

"I want to go on the Hunt," she said to the woman with ice-threaded eyes, who hurried along with her arms full of bridles in leather and silk. The woman did not so much as turn her head.

"I could help," she said to the dark man with the bright white hair, who led an enormous, snorting red stallion by a piece of black thread tied around its neck. He hurried on.

"It's my house we're protecting, and my tree," she said to the crowds who rushed past her. "It's my house, and I have a steed, there has to be some way I can help."

No one noticed her, and no one replied.

She followed them anyway, defiantly, listening hard, to find out the plan.

She learned that it was called the Wild Hunt both by humans and the people of Timeless. They hunted at the two solstices, Yule and Midsummer.

To the people of Time who noticed, the Hunt was pounding hooves and barking dogs that screamed across the night sky like claps of thunder—some people said it *was* claps of thunder, but others had seen the fairy host with their own eyes.

Clare gathered that the whole host would ride the fairy road, and reach her house just at sunrise. But Finn alone would ride the shaft of Midsummer sunlight through the window at dawn. He would have a single shot ("a single shot, with a single eye," muttered one), one chance to pin Balor down. If he hit, the rest of the fairies would follow, sweep Balor alive into the depths of the cold sea, and bind him there forever.

If he missed, Balor would surely turn and attack.

Clare pushed on until she found Her of the Cliffs, who sat in a carved wooden chair, adjusting the strap on her quiver to fit Finn's broader chest.

"I am coming on the Hunt," said Clare defiantly.

Her of the Cliffs did not look up. "So I thought you might," she said.

Feeling as if she had burst headfirst through an open door, Clare said, "Oh! Oh . . . well, good. But then . . . I mean, do I need to do something to get ready?"

Her of the Cliffs said, rather pointedly, "It is likely you need to sleep. You have a few hours." She tugged at a piece of leather, trying to free it from a wooden clasp.

Clare realized she was, in fact, exhausted.

"Not here," said Her of the Cliffs, through an awl in her mouth. "No dreaming-awake-making in the midst of our hall." She looked up, and Clare thought there was almost amusement on her face. She removed the awl. "What are you waiting for? Go. We'll fetch you if you sleep too late." At Clare's hesitation, the amusement vanished. "Do you doubt my word?"

"No, no," said Clare humbly. "I'm sorry. Thank you. Can I ask one question?"

Her of the Cliffs nodded, as she bored into the leather.

"At my house, I smashed Balor's totem against the floor."

Her of the Cliffs looked up.

"But I don't know if—do you think, do you think I might have killed it?" Her voice sounded foolishly hopeful to her own ears.

Her of the Cliffs smiled. "That is unlikely. But it was brave, Clare Macleod, to do that. It could not have been easy." She bent her head over the leather and wood. "It was well done," she added, "worthy of the Hunter's many-greats-granddaughter."

Clare left the hall as light as a leaf. Her father was out of the mine. Her of the Cliffs had said *well done*, had called her worthy.

Finn, too, Finn had said *well made.* And the spot on her cheek that he had kissed, it glowed warm and sweet as a Strange.

Tired as she was, she ran the last yards to Asterion, who lay under a tree, but not yet asleep, waiting. She took his hand, and curled beside him, and together they dreamed.

In the dream, they stood in howling storm, before a flood-destroyed bridge, which they had to cross.

"It's my dream," shouted Clare, into the howl of the storm. "I'll make a bridge." And she threw herself long, long across the raging flood, lengthening as she flew, until with feet still on one side and hands on the other, she was the bridge herself, and a group of schoolchildren—some of them blind, oh, it was a school for the blind—walked across her. She felt their shoes like little hooves across her back, and set her jaw against the storm.

Clare woke on her own in time. She and Asterion ran to the hall hand in hand, Clare half skipping to keep up with his hooved, thundering strides. She left him outside and slipped in, hovering at the edge of the crowd in hopes Finn would not see her.

He stood at the center of a great mass of fairies, more than Clare had seen altogether before. When he raised his hand, holding the flag, the hall fell silent.

A strong wind came up, a wind inside the hall, and blew out all the candle flames. The wind blew Clare's hair straight back, made her eyes water. The trees must have been thick around the leafy hall, because it was dark here without the candles.

In fact—and Clare felt a catch of joy when she realized it—it was night. They were no longer in fairy. It was night, a night permeated by a pale, cool light, a light that reminded her of the quartz light of her home. *What* was that light?

Oh: now she knew; now she saw. It was starlight. The new moon of Midsummer was a black disk against the black sky, and all around it the stars shone thousands-bright on their fairy host.

But how was it that the stars were not above her, but *beside* her?

And then she saw: she was in the sky. She and the crowd of laughers and smilers around her were in the sky, in the dark air, a hundred feet above the earth, perfectly still—at least it seemed that way—as the wind rushed past them, and the world rushed beneath them.

At least, that was how it felt to Clare: that she and the host had never moved from the leafy hall, only everything had rushed and changed around them; that it was the wind and the world that were moving.

The wind carried a cry back to her: "Host!" a fierce and familiar voice shouted. "My host! Mount your steeds!"

Instantly Clare felt herself lifted by strong arms, felt muscles pulsing beneath her. "Asterion!" she cried. Not clinging to his back this time, she straddled his shoulders. With one hand, she steadied herself on one of his horns; with the other, she leaned down to caress his face.

Far below, a woman rushed backward, carrying a bag of groceries. At least, it seemed that her feet moved forward, but the world carried her back, as the world itself sped backward beneath the fairy host.

Clare felt an ecstasy, a tightrope walker's ecstasy, poised so perfectly on the line between two worlds. Her blood surged with a Strange joy. She put her head back to the sky and stars. She saw that the whole host had their heads back, hair streaming, as they stood balanced on the edge of the flying world.

She felt the air pass through her, and the light pass through her.

"I love this," she cried out loud to the night. And all around her, she heard the fairy host, baying and howling and roaring their own cries of joy, the joy of the Hunt.

As the cry went up, the woman beneath them whipped her head up, and saw them. Terror swam across her face. Clare smiled down, remembering a poem in her mother's commonplace book:

The winds awaken, the leaves whirl round,
Our cheeks are pale, our hair is unbound,
Our breasts are heaving, our eyes are a-gleam,
Our arms are waving, our lips are apart,
And if any gaze on our rushing band,
We come between him and the deed of his hand,
We come between him and the hope of his heart.

All around her, the host took a thousand forms, on all manner of beasts. To her right, Clare saw a slim figure, man or woman or child she couldn't tell, more like a ghost, only not white, but some insubstantial color, mounted on a flying fish.

Beyond, she saw an enormous blue whale driving through the sky, whose rider—Clare saw only short, tangled black hair whipped around a dark and laughing face—looked like a mouse on the back of a horse.

She saw a gaunt man who unraveled a skein of many-colored yarn that streamed behind him like a rainbow. He stood balanced on huge snake that twisted and writhed against the stars.

She saw a tiger, its color the yellow and black of WARNING, straddled by a tiny chestnut-colored girl in a white dress.

(And if one of these had looked toward her, they'd have seen a pale, wild girl with hair red as an autumn leaf, exultant on the shoulders of a midnight-colored minotaur.)

At the head of the host, well ahead of the others, was a whirling cyclone of brilliant orange flames, at whose center Clare could just make out, amid the flickering white and blue, Her of the Cliffs.

"Her beast is *fire*," she said aloud, astonished.

"Is fire itself," agreed a voice beside her. "Which—now, steady on, girl—which makes her dangerous beyond predicting and warm as a kettle on a stove, both at once. As you have seen."

It was Finn, of course, with his pearly left eye, riding a white stag whose right eye was white as the moon. "Well, hi," she said.

He smiled. "Trickster Clare. But I knew you would come, of course I knew, for I know you. And I know now better now than to try to 'no' you. Who says no to she who smashed Balor's totem with her own hands?"

Clare rolled her eyes to hide the sunburst inside.

"Let's catch her up and lead them all," said Finn, and charged ahead. Beneath Clare, Asterion gave a kick. Led by the stag, Clare and her beast galloped the air fast, fast, until they were far ahead of the rest of the host.

Now Clare saw flowing beneath them the lake island, her own lake island, the heart of the Strange. Ahead she knew they would find a blossoming hawthorn tree, and beyond that a pale, stony cap, alone in a field. Farther still, a ruined castle sugared with starlight and flowers. And then her home, her home and her yew, to free them from Balor and his wicked totem forever.

Clare looked behind her once more. She saw a moon-white horse with yellowy froth on its teeth; she saw a tall pale woman in a lake-blue dress, holding a sword above her head; she saw a small man, all in green, his jaw dropped low in a roar of joy.

Then: "STOP!" shouted the woman wrapped in flames. "STOP!" echoed Finn, whirling to face the host. "Stop! Wait!"

Clare looked down. Far below was the little grove of trees where she had hammered her fists against the fairy thorn. She craned her neck—she could see no blossom-covered tree among the others now. Had all the flowers fallen so quickly?

"Balor has chopped down the fairy thorn," said Finn, his voice a shocked shadow of itself. "The road is broken."

Clare looked up. "Broken?"

"Without the fairy thorn, one part of road cannot not reach the next. The connection is lost."

Clare waited for Finn and Her of the Cliffs to begin to argue over a strategy, some way to meet this new crisis. But they didn't. There was only a terrible silence between them, and the murmurs of the fairy host behind.

In the end, because their silence was so painful, and because the glorious Hunt could not end this way, it was Clare who spoke, to ask what she was sure was a dumb question. "Why don't one of you just . . . make a making, and turn into a tree?"

Her of the Cliffs shook her head, and fire danced from her hair. "A good thought. But that tree would have no human in it, and it must have both, to be a gate. Were this another Hunt, then you might, Finn, you of all of us. But for this Hunt, you must lead."

Another, bleaker silence.

“So what about me?” Again Clare’s small, stubborn voice. “I was a tree before. So I know the trees. And I’m human. And I know the people of Timeless.” She looked uncertainly at Her of the Cliffs. “And I have at least some fairy in me, from you, ma’am,” (*ma’am!* she cursed herself) “and maybe from my mother, too, so maybe it’s more than just that little. I could become the tree.”

“She is a maker, I know her for a maker,” said Finn; but his voice sounded anxious. Then, to Clare: “Are you willing to try? It is try or give up our quest, and lose the bridges between our worlds forever. If you fail, the worst that can happen . . .”

“ . . . is that I fail, in front of you all,” said Clare. She said it with Finn-like irony, but her stomach felt sick. “Of course I’ll try. I won’t just try, I’ll do it,” she amended.

“I believe you can make this making, Clare Macleod,” said Finn. “But you must work quickly, do you understand? This is the shortest night of all. The sunrise comes soon, and when it comes, if we cannot ride it through the stone window and into your home, we lose our chance.”

“I understand,” said Clare. “Don’t worry. I will make my making.”

Finn gave a strange sort of half bow from his stag. “Thank you, Clare. We all thank you.”

There was a pause.

“So,” asked Clare in a small voice, “how will I get down?”

In answer, Asterion moved closer to Finn, and gently slipped Clare off his back until she sat upon the back of the stag. She felt unmoored without her beast; the starry night felt colder, and she herself much smaller.

For a moment, the four of them hung against the stars like strange new constellations—a great bull-headed beast, a boy and a girl on a white stag, and a woman wrapped in flame. Behind them glowed a frozen river of curious, silent creatures.

Asterion removed the great silver chain from around his neck, the one that matched her small and delicate one, and wound it around her waist. He held his end—the end with the star—and looked down.

"But I don't think it's long enough," said Clare.

Asterion looked up at her, but his eyes were too dark to read in the dark night.

Finn leaned over to put his own brown hands on the chain beside Asterion's. "We have you, girl," he said.

So holding her breath, clinging to the chain, she slipped off the stag. For a moment she dangled there. Then, hand over hand, they slipped her down. Somehow the chain was long enough, or it got longer, somehow (the *somehow* of dreams, again, always the somehow of dreams among the Strange), gently twirling Clare down through the dark. As she lowered, more hands appeared to hold the chain: pale ones and dark, silver-blue, dimpled-fat or withered claws, lizard-skinned, long-taloned—all these hands held on as Clare spun down, down, down on Asterion's chain.

On the grass, she stepped out of the chain, and watched it fly back up into the night. Now she saw what the white-faced woman had seen: a great host of people and creatures, all colors and sizes, roiling the sky like silent thunder.

This is the shortest night of all. No time to waste. In the starlight she ran toward the grove of trees where the fairy thorn had stood, boots in the grass loud in the night-silence. The closer she came, the stronger the familiar sense of Strange.

But the Strange had altered. There was still a sense of *springtime*—but now it was also piercing *grief.* The lovely white-blossomed tree had been maimed. She put her hand against one stump, felt sap drip like sticky blood.

Time to begin.

But in the predawn silence, the Strange eyes watching her from the sky felt . . . loud. They would all be watching, and most likely they would watch her fail. Her stomach knotted. "Just *try*," she muttered to herself. "Just shut up and *try*."

But it was hard not to imagine Finn's face, turning away in embarrassment at the ugly awkwardness of what she *tried.* Hard not to imagine him seeing her for what she was, not a maker but a pathetic faker. For a moment she had a mad impulse to run, run somewhere, run where?

Then a cool, firm voice inside her, a voice that sounded something like Her of the Cliffs, but also like her own voice, said, *Clare. Stop it. Think.*

She thought.

It's just like making in a dream. *Just know what you truly want, and use the desire to make.*

"But Asterion always begins it for me, in dreams," Clare murmured to the mutilated tree. "I don't know how to begin on my own."

You must find your beast in yourself and work that way.

Clare put her hand to the star at her throat. All right. How do you find your beast?

Well: how did she find him in the first place?

Close your eyes. No cheating.

Clare closed her eyes. The chilly, humid air clung to her face. The night was a perfect silence.

Asterion, how are you? she asked in her mind. And she thought she could see, inside herself, near her heart, Asterion's black and glistening eye. *A beast can only speak in pain or pleasure or making.* She noticed that her shoulders were hunched in, and thought—*Oh: that's Asterion, protecting himself from my fear.* She let them relax.

She felt her feet pigeon-toed, all her weight on the right, and how that pushed Asterion off balance. She righted herself, and felt his presence steadier inside.

A bird chirped, two small tweets, somewhere in the distance.

A *bird*? Clare's eyes flew open. At the edge of the sky, just the beginning, only the beginning, of gray. Only enough to catch the notice of a bird, or of a girl whose world depended on her completing a making before dawn.

Something, do something, and now. Well: she only had the one way, really. She spoke to the dying tree.

"I know the key to this hawthorn was singing," she said. "And I am not a singer really. But I am"—the words were so hard to say, especially under the thousand cool eyes, but she said them—"I am a poet. I will make a poem. A sort of prose-poem. A poem that calls a tree to me, or calls me to a tree."

Then in one reckless leap, she began.

"A tree is a girl who is not cheating. A tree keeps her eyes closed." She closed her eyes.

"Trees are the first makers. We turn sun and breath into blue-green life." She lifted her face, eyes still shut, to the just-graying sky, feeling the damp air caress her skin.

"Whatever the world gives me, I bring it deep into my secret roots to make with. Then I bring what I have made out again. In this way, I make a world.

"So I am both," said Clare, eyes closed, her face up, understanding this for the first time as she spoke, "I am both root and branch, earth and light"—*and human and fairy*, she thought, *and dreamer-asleep and maker-awake, and girl and beast, all of them*—"I am rooted where I stand, and I face the changing sky, and I make."

She felt how close she was, how she almost had the last ingredient, so she reached out with her deepest desire, and found it.

"And I don't make alone," she said. "Trees speak through knotted fingers, knitting the world together beneath its skin. We never pause for breath or silence, and our conversation is unending."

Thinking, as she spoke, with curious clarity: *humans, too, we make in conversation. Every song or invention or dance is secretly knitted together in one great making.*

The beast inside her glowed like a black sun. Clare stopped talking, rooted her feet, and threw up her arms. She did not care that she looked like a child playing "tree." She gave the gesture her whole desire. Her feet planted strong in the earth, and her arms raised up to the sky.

And now it was happening. Wood grew across her eyes and ears, and Clare exulted inside. Just before the silence came, she heard above her a wild cry, carried over a thousand voices: *We hunt! We hunt! We hunt!*

Then she did not see; she did not hear. But she felt, and she saw with some inner eye, as the fairy host rushed through her, one by one, every strange creature, as if she herself were an open gate.

Of all the strange things Clare saw and did on that strange night, the strangest of all was this: that when the fairy host flew through her, it didn't feel strange at all. It was like a memory, or a dream. With each strange creature that passed through, she thought, *Oh yes, oh yes, I remember, I remember now, that's me, that was me, I did that*—the way you remember in dreams.

She remembered, somehow, that she herself was a young black man with bright white hair and an impatient smile, riding a snorting red horse.

And she herself was a woman with ice-threaded eyes, sitting lightly on a flower-covered hawthorn branch that sailed through the air as she threw back her head and laughed.

And she herself was the fierce, pale girl, teeth sharpened to points, who rode a snake and screamed in a wild and alien tongue.

And she herself was the fat, thin-haired man with cold gray eyes, holding a handful of playing cards, whose steed was a gray mule.

And she knew herself in the violet-haired man in the shabby jacket, and in the naked woman who leaned over a winged gargoyle, urging it on. She knew herself in the three dark women bound together by a silk scarf at their waists, riding a dragonfly—she knew them, she was them, just as she was the white dog with bright green eyes leaping behind them. They all passed through her, and she found herself in them, and she found herself in the black-eyed man who sat cross-legged on a roaring, crashing green wave, and in the one-eyed, molting cat, and the slender young ankle-tufted buffalo, and the woman holding an old brass lamp, and the blind child standing on top of an elephant, and the great golden-furred pig.

Then she felt afraid, and said: *But if I am all of these, then who am I? Where am I, where is the I, if I am all of these?*

The other trees entwined their fingers in hers below the ground, they held her fingers close, and said, *You are yourself, you are also yourself, unlike any other, your own unique self contains all these others safely.*

Then she felt the touch of her own yew, the electric sweetness of that touch, and the joy and calm that came with her root-finger twining with hers. The twining continued, the yew-root seemed to grow and stretch, until it wrapped behind the Clare-hawthorn tree.

All at once, Clare had the distinct impression that her pocket—if a tree could have pockets—was being picked. *My commonplace book.*

Clare felt rather than heard a familiar, musical laugh as the root of the yew pulled back again, and the commonplace book was gone.

Oh no, oh yew, thought Clare the tree. But because she was a tree, knitted into the conversation that makes the world, she understood that the book remained with her even while it was with the yew, and was not really lost at all.

Still, even her woody heart felt a stab of loss.

The last of the host passed through her just as the sun began to crest the edge of the earth. It was dawn at Midsummer. It was Clare's second birthday.

Tree-Clare waited. A tree is content to stay. Blind and deaf, she waited in the tree-hush of noiseless wind, with upstretched fingers, with tangled roots in rich, silent communion.

A scream ripped through the silence. Not a human scream—tree-Clare could not have heard a human scream. But her roots felt a pain as piercing as a scream would feel to human ears.

It was the scream of a tree.

It was the scream of a yew, her own yew, her own brown-and-green tree girl, ancient and new, who had given her back her making and her heart.

Her yew was being struck and sliced and torn.

All of Clare's true self—the human, and the filaments of fairy, the self born to be the guardian of the yew—came roaring forward. *Run*, she told herself. *Run to her now. Save her.*

The girl-tree's roots withdrew from the other roots, her long branches withdrew from the air. Her single trunk became two strong legs, and she ran, and ran, and ran.

18

No Safety, There Is None

Something was wrong.

As Clare neared her hill-home, she saw that the fairy host was not inside. They circled the green mound, around and around, a flock of huge and many-shaped birds riding the wind from the ocean that crashed and surged just out of sight.

But Finn was not among the circling host. He must be inside alone. Why had the rest not followed? Why were they not inside?

In a few more stumbling yards, Clare saw what was wrong. Something was blocking her home's stone window from the inside; the new Midsummer sun couldn't get through. That was why the host was trapped outside.

At the same moment, she realized that the crashing, surging noise was not the ocean, or not only the ocean, but fairy calls and cries over and among the ocean sounds.

The Hunter missed his shot, they cried.

His eye.

The one-eyed Hunter missed the shot.

When the host saw Clare, the clamor rose in pitch, became a sort of weird, singsong chant—*His eye, his eye, she took his eye*—as the crowd whirled and spun around the hill, looking for a way in.

Flushing in furious shame, Clare opened her mouth—to defend herself? to apologize? to ask how Finn had even got through the blocked window?—then stopped, mouth still open. Of course: the fairies could only enter by riding the Midsummer sunrise through the window. (Her mother's words in her ear: *That window must always stay open for the fairies to travel through.*)

But not Finn, thought Clare. *He's half human. He can walk through the door, and he did.*

With stubborn fury: *And so will I.*

She ran up the hill straight through that keening, hateful cry—*there she is, she took his eye, she took his eye, the teeth of the wolf*—pushed open the heavy, silent door, and ran inside. Bursting out of the narrow passage and into the main room, she stumbled to a stop.

Before her was a tableau, like a photograph, like a stage picture after the curtain rises, but before the action begins.

In the center of the room: Finn on his knees, one hand on the floor, his bow on the ground beside him. His shirt was torn open, and a red triangle burnt on his skin, the mark of the totem. Though Finn was not unconscious, he seemed stunned: his moon-eye pale, his gray eye wet and furious and frightened, jerking in a way that reminded her of her lonely, frightened beast in the labyrinth.

To Clare's left: Balor, holding an axe, standing by the yew that bore the marks of his hacking and hewing.

To Clare's right, as she raised her eyes, was the final piece of the tableau. Blocking the window—*blocking the window*—as it switched its tail across the stones, recharging: the hideous, screaming face of the totem.

"Hello, Clare," said Balor, low and calm. "I thought you might turn up. I forgot that this young Hunter"—gesturing to Finn, dazed on the ground—"could just walk through the door. An unfortunate lapse on my part, and it might have been very bad for me." Balor smiled. "But the Hunter has only one eye. Must have been some terrible accident—I wonder how it happened?" He bared his yellow teeth. "So he missed his shot—didn't you, boy? And my totem did not miss his shot, not by any means. In a few moments, it will take another shot, and that will be enough to kill even a half fairy." His wolfish smile broadened, as if he were recalling something from a favorite nightmare. "Your father's dead, you know. His corpse is already rotting."

He turned back to the tree, the huge black bulk of him, swinging his axe deep into the tree, in horrible, thudding *chunks*.

My dream-making worked! thought Clare. And perhaps that knowledge gave her the courage to see this new nightmare with clear eyes.

Finn on his knees, struggling to stand as the totem prepared to strike again.

Clickclickclick, the totem along the wall. One of its upper corners was broken off; she must have done that the day before. If only she had done more.

Balor sweating in his dark suit, the power of his swing, the sickening, horrific *chunk* as the axe cut into the yew. Clare thought of her yew-girl, the axe sunk in her flesh.

She had no idea what to do. But she knew what she could *not* do: she could not overpower Balor; and she could not reach the totem.

Clickclickclick, the totem faster and faster, dragging its long stick along the wall. Balor cursed to himself as he struggled to pull the axe from the tree.

Finn tried to push himself up to his feet, but his arm collapsed, and he fell again.

Clickclickclickclick—and then, worse: the noise stopped. The totem that darkened the window was ready to strike Finn again. Balor's axe stopped, and from the corner of her eye Clare saw him straighten, as if waiting for the pounce.

All this in seconds, and in her rising desperation Clare still could not see what to do.

"The sun," said Finn, and Clare's head snapped around. He was groping the floor around him, still on his knees. "The sun," he said again. He looked up at Clare for the first time. He was so dazed that she was not sure he even recognized her. "The sun," he said a third time. And then, with difficulty: "It's almost too late."

And now Clare knew. She ran to Finn, and almost without stopping, took up his bow from the ground, pulled an arrow from the quiver slung over his shoulder, and swept across the floor and up the ladder to her room.

Below her, a booming, cruel laugh. "She dreamed she hunted once, and now she believes she's the Hunter!" said Balor. At least the blows of the axe had paused.

Clare fit the arrow to her bow. It was true: she had only shot an arrow once before, in her dream. *But I can do it, I know I can*, she thought: *You made me the teeth of the wolf—you taught me how to bite.*

She pulled the bowstring back behind her ear.

Balor had walked across the room for a better view. He leaned on the axe, smiling. Above him, the totem seemed to crackle with power near release.

"Only the Hunter can strike the wolf, stupid girl," he called. "You are not the Hunter, no matter how many eyes you've put out." He spread his arms out mockingly. "See how I fear you!"

Clare's face flushed. "No, I am not the Hunter," she agreed. Finn had struggled to his feet. She looked at Balor, the bowstring drawn back and perfectly steady.

Then she raised her aim above Balor's head, and let the arrow fly.

And now Balor no longer laughed—now he roared, a roar of fear and rage. Because Clare's arrow flew true, straight through the swirling chaos-eye of the totem.

The totem dropped like a stone at Balor's feet.

A shaft of sunlight pierced the room, straight into her eyes, briefly blinding Clare—but through half-closed eyes, under the arm she had thrown across her face, Clare saw that much more than sunlight was streaming in. The fairy host poured through the gap.

Balor saw, too. *Only the Hunter can strike the wolf*—true, but he had lost his weapon, and Finn was on his feet now, and the host had power to bind.

Balor ran to the entranceway and out the door.

"Bring the bow!" shouted hoarse Finn, as he followed Balor, stumbling, catching himself, and stumbling forward again.

Clare slid down her ladder with the bow, right behind.

But even pushing open the heavy door was too much: Finn fell to his knees on the ground outside. He slammed his hand to the ground in frustration.

"It's just you're really hurt," said Clare. "Let me help you."

"The others cannot follow out the door," he said. "They can travel the roots of the tree, now, but they can't come out the door." He coughed—it was almost a laugh. "I'll live," he rasped. "But I hear him on the shore. Go to the cliff and tell me. Tell me what he's doing."

She ran. Green waves crashed and frothed against the dark rocks of Clare's cliff. On the narrow, rocky beach below them, Balor was talking—almost as if he were talking to the waves themselves—but fast, too fast to understand, and moving his hands.

"He's talking to the ocean," called Clare.

"Saying?" said Finn. He was standing now, wavering, stumbling toward her.

"I can't tell," said Clare, "but he—"

She broke off. At Balor's feet, the sea was churning harder, and the dirty white froth swelled higher and higher. Clare had the odd sense that someone must have poured soap in the water, for the foam to bulge up so unnaturally. It rose so high above the green water that it was taller that Balor himself.

"The water . . . the foam is so high," said Clare. "I'm sorry, I don't understand what's happening."

"I do," said Finn, stumbling toward her, unsteady, head down. "Give me my bow."

Balor chanted faster, and the foam began to shape itself—a torso, a long neck, four legs, a tail—until the dirty foam had somehow become a creamy, foamy horse, snorting white froth and tossing its head wildly.

A split second later, Balor had leaped onto the back of his froth-horse and charged off to sea.

"Ah no!" cried Clare. Finn was aiming, but both of them could see that Balor was already too far. He lowered his bow. "If we had a boat, or . . ." She trailed off. After all this, Balor would escape, and it would be for nothing. "Where is he going?"

"Of that I'm not sure," said Finn. "But I go there, too."

"But how?" The wind blew Clare's hair into her mouth, and she pushed it aside.

"Ride the wind," said Finn. He stood on the cliff edge, leaning into the wind, breathing hard at the effort to stand. "I did it once before." His eyes were focused on Balor, not on the ground, but Clare glanced down to the jagged rocks below. They no longer looked like a ruined chocolate cake, but like death itself.

"Finn. Don't. Even if—I mean, can you even shoot straight?"

He winced. "In your house I could not. Better light outside. I have more arrows."

"But, Finn—"

His unreadable blank white eye turned toward her. "I've no choice, and no time for choice." A sardonic grin. "Which makes the moment easier." He turned toward her swiftly, almost angrily, seized her wrist, and kissed it. "Clare Macleod, mad maker, never cease your madness and making."

Then he turned to face the wind, and fell.

Clare watched, hands over her mouth in horror, because she

didn't want to frighten him with a scream. He plunged down ten feet, twenty—until an updraft caught him, and he flew.

He *flew.*

"*Finn,*" cried Clare, with wild admiration. Then a thought like a thrust knife: *But he'll never hit him, he can't, his aim is off, because of me.* She sank under the weight of remorse as Finn wafted up and out over the ocean.

Then her posture changed. Her head drew out of her shoulders, and her arms dropped to her sides. It was as if her body had realized something before she did. Finn couldn't shoot straight alone. But with help, with another eye to guide his aim . . .

Her thought was interrupted by the sound of a motor. She turned and saw, pulling slowly around by the door of her home, her father's car.

Her father's car! She took a couple of running steps toward the car before she stopped. Once she had almost sacrificed the whole world to run to her father. Once. Not twice. Finn needed another eye. She darted back to the cliff's edge.

Green spumes dashed up around the dark, jagged rocks below.

She thought: *I will fall, and I will die.*

She thought of the fairies' Strange and exquisite makings, their true and radiant selves, scattered over our world like shells on a beach. If Finn failed, the tide would bring no new fairy-makings, and the old ones would be trampled and broken by the years until they were dust, and the beach of the world was only sand again, and never again a lovely or terrible Strange to stumble across.

She thought: *But I don't know how.*

She thought of never dreaming again. She thought of the great beauty of her own world—every flaming yellow autumn, every riot of green and yellow in spring, the changing blue of the sky behind it all—she thought of all that loveliness fading to the colorless gray of a filing cabinet under fluorescent lights: fading not just for her, but for everyone. A world without beauty, because without dreams or makings, all their eyes would forget how to see.

She thought of Finn, born too soon and parentless, whose mother had found love even when locked in a tower.

She thought of Finn caught in Timeless, never again to make his changeful, artful makings.

She thought of never seeing Finn again.

The yew-girl said: *There is no safety, and so we must touch and be touched, and we must fall and fly.*

Behind her, a car door opened.

Without another thought, Clare put her hand to the star at her throat, said, "Oh, Asterion," and leaped out over the rocks.

She fell like a rock herself: graceless, plummeting, and hard. Then a wind caught her, just the way you catch your breath, and swept her into the sky.

A few seconds later, Clare's father ran to the edge of the cliff and looked down. Nothing there but rocks and churning foam. Confused, he murmured, "I'd have sworn I saw someone jump . . . ?" But all he saw now was a strange bird in the distant sky, a huge bird in autumn colors, heading out to sea.

The yew-girl had been right: to abandon safety, to ride the wind, was cold and wild and glorious. She rode the wind like a sloop rides wave after wave, up and down, up and down. Sometimes the surging sea below sent a spray of cold salt water into her face.

Perhaps because she was smaller than Finn, and unburdened by bow and quiver, she caught up to him quickly.

"You need me," said Clare, breathlessly, and almost laughed at his expression as he turned to see her. "You can't do this alone. You know you can't."

"Mad, mad, mad," said Finn. The wind blew his words back and up.

"You need me," she said, grabbing the edge of his shirt, pulling even with him, "you know you do. And I need to make up for what I did."

Finn said nothing, only looked at her, rueful and admiring.

The low eastern sun cast handfuls of glitter across the waves as Balor galloped west on his froth-horse. Finn and Clare flew behind, side by side, closing the gap. Birds fly faster than horses can run, especially horses made of froth and foam, and they gained on him quickly.

"Flying feels like dancing," said Clare, giving herself to the air, letting it swing her up, down.

"It feels like making," Finn said into the wind. "For how you trust your desire to know the way, and ride that desire and ride."

Clare did not say, but thought to herself: *Flying feels like being with you, Finn. Throwing myself on my every fear and letting them carry me into the sky.*

Already, they were within an arrow-shot's distance from Balor. "We're at your back," Finn cried. "Turn and face me, Grandfather!"

And to Clare's surprise, Balor spun his foamy horse around. His face was a mask of fury and fear and—but how could this be right?—and *grief*, somehow: fury, and fear, and old grief.

"You killed her, boy," Balor said to Finn. "You look like her. And you killed her."

Clare felt Finn beside her hesitate, lose his ease in the air. He stalled for a moment, tumbled, almost losing his arrows, then found the air again and swung back around. From his quiver, he pulled a black-tipped arrow with a long red thread streaming from the shaft. The other end of the thread was fastened to his own belt.

Balor's face, seeing the arrow, went whiter than before. He

looked from right to left, as if to see where he could run. "It is her fault," he cried, suddenly, "it need never have happened, if only the grandmother would have let me back in." He pulled his horse around in a circle, he shouted to the sea: "Let me in!" He kicked at the water, he leaned down to beat it with his hands. "Grandmother!" he cried. "Let me in! Let me back into fairy! Let me be safe again!"

Clare felt what she had never expected to feel for Balor, a terrible pity, and more than pity: a kinship. She saw that even she and Balor were as tangled as roots are. She knew what it meant to want to return to safety and seed-husk again.

But you cannot get back into your seed-husk, once it is cracked open and no longer yours.

Balor turned his face to the sky and gave a roar of rage and sorrow. Finn hesitated, then re-aimed his arrow. Flying behind and above him, Clare could see that the aim was off. *The one-eyed Hunter.* "Wait!" she cried. She caught him from behind, riding lightly as a bird, put her face to his face against his moon-eye, and put her hands over his hands on the bow and string.

For an instant, they held poised on a current of air, like some strange, ancient seabird hovering over a fish.

Then Balor showed Finn his yellow teeth. "Your mother deserved to die," he said, "she was a—"

The arrow struck him in his seeing eye.

Without its rider, the sea-foam horse rode on a few steps, then dissolved back into the sea, as Balor sank under the waves. The red string spun into the water after him. In a moment it would pull taut and yank Finn into the water behind his grandfather.

"Finn, you'll drown," said Clare. Her voice sounded high, panicking to her own ear. "Let me cut it, give me an arrow, Finn—"

He turned to her with an unreadable expression: "Clare: you don't drown because you can't breathe," he said. The red thread was spinning out and out, it was almost taut. "You don't drown because you can't breathe. You drown because you try to breathe what is not breathable. We'll be fine."

We?

The thread tightened, and Finn disappeared into the green ocean.

And so did Clare: because at the last second, she grabbed for his hand. *We.*

The morning sun cast another sparkling handful on the ocean, as water smoothed over the hole that Finn and Clare had made.

If you had looked, you would have thought nothing had happened there at all.

Clare didn't breathe. It was hard to remember—she closed her eyes and said it over and over in her mind: *don't breathe, don't breathe.* But it was impossible, it was surely impossible, she had to draw a breath, and panic rose wild inside her.

But soon her body began to believe that it needed no breath. Slowly, then, she opened her eyes, and looked around.

Green and blackening water flowed past, colder and blacker the deeper they were pulled below. What would happen when they reached the bottom? She held Finn's hand tighter.

Below, through the murky, salt-stinging water, came a stream of color, like a liquid rainbow. But as the thread drew them closer, she saw it was the fairy host, driving through the ocean just as they had driven across the sky, as if air and water were the same to them.

The yew tree, thought Clare—*The fairy road leads through the yew tree to the ocean itself.*

Without warning, the thread slackened; now Finn and Clare floated gently down on their own, no longer dragged by the stone of Balor's body. Finn's hands were finding the bloodred thread that tied him to his grandfather, untying it, letting it loose.

The fairies had settled to the ocean floor; they were crowded together, working on something. The something was Balor. They bound him down with Finn's red thread—only the water slowed their busy hands, so that they seemed to be nursing him tenderly, as if they were dream-doctors, binding him as slowly and gently as you bind a wound.

Next, each of the fairies produced another thread, and Balor was bound in all of them. The colors wove together, at first like a tangle of many-colored grass, then even more closely, to make a brilliant cocoon, a kaleidoscopic shell, around Balor—whose empty eyes stood open still, whose mouth stood open, arrested in a cry.

Balor was bound to the ocean floor in blackness, and the creatures of light left him there, streaming away the way they came. Finn and Clare stayed. They bobbed gently in the green water as bubbles left by the departing host rose up around them. They watched as seaweed crept around Balor; as the sand washed over him; as he was covered up for a long, long sleep by the gentle, inevitable waters.

They watched until Balor's eyelids finally closed.

Then Finn and Clare rose up together, through water that warmed and lightened, until their heads broke free, gleaming and slick, and they blinked and spit the salt out, and took in air again.

When her own eyes cleared, as she floated and kicked in the salty water, Clare saw something that made her put her hand to her mouth in happiness. Finn's white eye had turned a pale and lovely green. It was no longer a cold moon, but the bud of a flower. The moon in the sky was growing again, and the moon-seed was growing in Finn's face.

"Oh, my grandmother," Finn cried, treading water, spitting salt from his mouth. "You might send us home now."

The water stirred a little near them. Slowly, a green and glowing road—a moonlight road—glowed up from the sea. How, with the moon outshone by the morning sun?

Then Clare saw: tiny luminous plants just beneath the surface had made a path, a path that spiraled outward like a seashell unfurling, like the road that uncurled for Dorothy, only instead of yellow brick, it was green and living light.

Clare and Finn both scrambled up until they were standing on the path of lights, the lights they knew so well from their in-between, now furling and unfurling across the waves.

She looked at wet and dripping Finn, and he at her, and they both laughed. Trusting the green path, but not trusting it to remain forever, they ran.

Soon they were out of sight, if there had been anyone on the wide and empty ocean to notice.

19

Those Lovely Ashes

When Finn's and Clare's feet found the rocky beach, and the glowing road disappeared behind them, she heard a voice, the best and most familiar voice, calling her name.

"Dad!" she cried, and ran slipping up the rocky cliff path. Then she stopped and turned to Finn.

He smiled, looking exhausted, pushing half-dried, salt-caked hair from his face. "We'll meet in the in-between," he said.

So she flew up the path to her father. He had arrived home to find the door swung open, and the totem shattered to splinters on the floor, and the yew with pieces hacked from it, and Clare nowhere to be found. He had walked all along the beach and the forest, calling for her, calling and calling.

"I'd been calling your phone to no answer on the drive here, and calling Jo the same, and was about to call the police, had the phone in my hand to call, when I saw you. And you were in the water? Tell me you weren't swimming, you mad girl, it's far too cold, and look at you, salty and damp as—"

"Dad," said Clare, and then her arms around his neck made it hard for him to talk, so they just laughed and slightly cried.

He was thinner and paler. He made light of his time underground, and told her a funny story about how the men decided who should go up first, when the rescue came. But his hands shook more than a little. Soon they were walking into their house, arms around each other.

"It's your birthday," he said. "Well, it's the second one, anyway. I didn't miss them both, at least, though I'm sorry I have no gift."

"You're *here*," said Clare as they emerged from the passageway. But when she saw the yew, her face fell. She ran to kneel beside the tree and put her hand to its wounds. "Do you think . . . Will the tree be all right?" she asked.

Her father joined her, squatting down, picking up a chunk of yew. "I think so, in fact," he said. "It's an ancient tree and a strong one. I believe it will heal. But we'll have an arborist around to see what we can do to help it heal."

Clare remembered the upside-down girl, her maddening stubbornness about the story, and almost laughed to herself. As if an axe could make a serious dent in that ancient, lovely willfulness.

"Clare?" Her father rested a hand on her shoulder. "How did this happen? Tell me your adventures, now." His face looked anxious, though he said it lightly.

Clare sat back against the tree, unsure what she could tell him, or how to start. She was quiet for a while, feeling stuck every time she thought to begin. "There's a crack in the yew tree that makes a place between human and Timeless, and everything made of light visits there"—no. "Our home is on a fairy road"—no. "There was a terrible man named Balor, and he tried to hurt us, but he's tied with threads at the bottom of the ocean now." None of these seemed like things she could actually say.

But then Clare remembered her father's dream. She began tentatively: "Dad."

"Yes, love."

"Do you remember . . . do you remember, that you dreamed about me one time? When you dreamed of digging?"

He stopped stirring eggs in the pan, and turned to look at her. "I do, girl," he said. "I do remember. So, but . . . that was you indeed? I thought . . ." But he did not finish the sentence.

"Yeah, it was me," Clare said. "You said . . . Well, in the dream you said Mam could do that, too?"

He smiled as if some happy memory was hurting him. "Did I say that? Ah, well. She could. She could indeed. She would visit me in a dream, of a time." He smiled again, a better smile, then threw back his head and laughed. "She was a trickster, in a dream sometimes. She did love a joke." He looked at Clare in a new way.

Clare saw she could ask him something she thought she would never know. "You didn't see me as myself at first," she said. "Do you remember? When you fell in the pit, in the dream? You saw me as some other thing. What was I?"

He smiled, remembering. "You seemed like a calf to me," he said. "A white calf, with red ears, bellowing at me in the rain, licking the mud from my face. But then suddenly and out of the blue—and it was quite a startle, I can tell you—the calf spoke to me in my daughter's voice."

They both laughed; the laugh became a shy silence. Clare took a deep breath: "Do you remember, in that dream . . . Do you remember saying something about 'the people of the tree'?"

Her father did not turn to look at her, but he stopped stirring eggs in the pan, and straightened a little. "No," he said. "I don't remember saying that. But I know that phrase. I do know about that, at least . . . Your mother told me some, about the people of the tree." Now he did turn to look at her. "She didn't call them that. That was my word for them. What do you know about that, Clare?"

So Clare told him a little of what had happened—not everything, but more than most parents would believe—and then, because he only listened, and never said, "I don't believe you, sweet," she told him even more.

But when she told him about Balor, his face crumpled into something wrong, and he said, "Love, will you ever forgive me for leaving you here alone?" And Clare, who had never thought of it as her father's fault, or even thought to think that—who, in fact, had thought he might be angry with her, for running away—threw her arms around him and said all of those things, until his face looked more itself.

Clare met Finn in the in-between that night and many nights thereafter. The yew-tree's axe wound healed a little more every day, much faster than any ordinary tree could heal.

Over the next two weeks, as the moon in the sky grew fat, Finn's moon-seed eye blossomed into a white flower, one that was half closed in the day, and open at night. "I can see through my eye again," he said with pleasure and relief, "for all I see through a flower." Clare was visiting Timeless and was curled up beside Asterion.

"It's a moonflower," said Her of the Cliffs. She had a new face now, still fierce, but also tender.

"Your face is kinder now," said Clare, shy, stroking Asterion's fingers. "You're not wearing the angry mask."

"I have always had the same face," said Her of the Cliffs, "and, my girl, I never hated you. Indeed, I felt at fault, for letting you go into danger before you were ready. It's the story you told yourself that changed my face. It's your story that made the mask."

"How did my story make a mask on your face?"

"Seeing is making, whether you see with your mind or your true self. Try to see with your self, your self and your beast together, and not your busy, frightened mind."

"When I see with my self, do I see your real face, your true face?"

"Ah: the true face. Someday you may see that. Someday, we may all see each other's true faces. But for now, this is close enough."

Later that night, Clare thought about faces and masks. She remembered the moon over the castle that turned its face away. *I think the moon wears a lot of masks*, she thought sleepily. *Maybe Her of the Cliffs is one of the masks of the moon. And the moon in my mouth, that was the moon. And Finn's eye, Finn's eye. That's the most beautiful moonflower of all.*

One morning, Clare's father took her to the hospital to visit Jo. They found her sitting up in bed among a nest of tubes and wires.

"Ah, she's fine now, just looking for your pity, such a layabout she is," said the nurse, and Clare knew this was a joke and meant the opposite of that, but that the joke meant that Jo would be all right.

Jo said, "So it's herself. But I believe I already saw you, quite *late* one night, in fact *asleep*, one night. Is that possible, girl?"

"Yes," said Clare, shy. But the nurse was paying no mind as she fussed over a needle in Jo's arm.

"Did you hear what I said, that night?"

"I did," said Clare, remembering the stream of cheerful bad

language from the dream-Jo hung in a tree. "But I won't repeat it, ma'am."

Jo laughed out loud. "Good girl yourself," she said, smiling from her white bed, and Clare knew she would be fine.

Over the two weeks that followed, as the full moon died into darkness, the petals of Finn's moonflower eye dropped away, revealing what had been hidden at their center: Finn's new eye. But it never looked like his other blue-gray eye; ever afterward, it was as brilliant green as new grass, and ran with thick, sweet sap instead of salty tears.

One night, Clare found Finn in the in-between in a strange excitement. "Come with me," he said, and would say no more.

He took her to a green place, a mountain meadow with sweet, thin air. Young grass swept across the meadow, soft and lemony-gold at the tips. White flowers crowded above the grass, each a cluster of white bells hanging from a long green stalk. A slushy stream slipped slowly across one corner, and along the edges of the meadow stood forest firs, dark and tall, like night closing in. The meadow looked like young spring, but the air was cold, and the sky was heavy and white-gray.

"This is somewhere in my world—" Clare began, but Finn put a finger to his lips—quiet, quiet. He pointed to one of the white flowers. Clare wrapped her arms around her thin white pajama sleeves and looked closer. From the bending stem of the flower hung a small dark packet, like a little Chinese temple. Straightening up, she saw that almost every flower dangled the same small, dark temple from its stem.

The wind was high and low: the tops of the trees bent and sighed, and the dark packets trembled from the stems. The sound of wind was like breathing, and the slow stream hummed underneath it like a child.

Then the wind stopped, and the water stopped, and the world went silent. The silence was like the lights that darken before a movie, or the *tap-tap-tap* of the conductor before the symphony begins. The silence was the frame around a painting. But what was the painting? Clare's heart opened up in readiness. This was a fairy-making, Finn-made, she could tell.

The dark packets trembled. The wind had stopped, but they trembled still. They rocked back and forth, moved from the inside.

And then a sound rippled across the meadow, a tiny splitting or tearing sound, catching and repeating from flower to flower. Each dark packet split open, each dusky egg cracked, and from each one, a white wet thing pushed its way out.

Now, on the stem of each flower, each white creature stood, tremulous, waiting. And as the creatures dried in the deepening cold, each one blossomed billowing white wings.

Clare shivered, watching them, and pulled her arms more tightly around herself.

The wind silent, the water silent, the cold dropping deeper. Each white butterfly shook its wings and spread them to dry in the cold, heavy air. The meadow was a field of wavering white about to take wing: and then they did, the white butterflies did rise up, and it was as if the field of white flowers were ascending into the white sky.

And just at that moment, it began to snow. The snow fell in gentle flakes, like white petals falling from the sky. The butterflies rose to meet the snow, like white flowers fluttering upward. The air was a mass of snow and white wings like white petals.

Clare's face was wet, not only from the snow, and her head felt full of space and light. "But no one will see this," she whispered, almost no more than breath.

"I see it," said Finn, just as soft. "And you see it. This is my making, that I have meant so long to show you. My making that I made a little for you to see."

He faced her, took one of her hands, and put the other about her waist. Her red hair was spangled with white crystals; his face was dusted with snow. In the white, fluttering silence, they danced to a melody they heard not with their ears, but somewhere deep inside.

"We started in all colors," said Clare, as they swayed together among the snowflakes and white wings. It was a silly thing to say, but she didn't think of that at all, because she no longer thought that, with Finn. "We started in all the colors, in the earth rainbow. And now we've come out in whiteness."

"Ah," said Finn, "but have you never seen a prism? White is the work of all the colors. Our colors made this white."

Clare thought of a line in her commonplace book—she could see it in her mind, in her mother's looping blue: "Life, like a dome of many-colour'd glass,/Stains the white radiance of Eternity." Maybe it was something about human and Timeless? Maybe that poet had known.

She felt a familiar pang for that lost book; and then she let it go, let the pages of the book flutter away with the butterflies.

The unheard melody rose as the snowflakes fell. And the boy with the moon in his eye and the girl with the star at her throat danced and danced and danced.

That night, when Clare returned home and climbed up to her loft to go to bed, she noticed something dark and square tucked among the branches of the tree. Turning on her bedside lamp, she plucked it out.

It was a small book, its cover thickly overlaid with lovely, eccentric drawings—tangled green vines, roots writhing among one another, and tall trees with entwining branches.

When Clare opened the book, she said, "Oh," aloud, with gratitude and awe, and sat down on the bed. It was her own commonplace book. But every page had been illuminated with gorgeous drawings: dark green needle-fronds, and winding vines, and tangling roots the color of cinnamon sticks. Every line in the book bore some decoration, including her own poems.

She held it to her chest. She put her hand to the tree beside her. She said, "Thank you, thank you. It's beautiful."

A month or so later, when her father's hands were their strong steady selves again, and his sunken cheeks had filled back up from the food he cooked for them both, they stood on their rocky beach with the box of Clare's mother's ashes.

Clare had never told her father the end of the story, with Balor buried beneath the ocean, so she could not ask him if it wasn't strange to send the ashes out onto the same water beneath which Balor lay buried. But it didn't feel wrong somehow. Because she knew that the ocean was the grandmother of the whole world—even of Balor, just the same as of her mother—and was big enough to contain it all.

The color of the sea that day was a brilliant blue, with only a bit of gray beneath, and the water cast a million bits of brightness back to the sun. The air was windless and waiting.

Clare and her father each took a handful of those lovely ashes.

"To your home, your home, back to your home, my dearest love," said her father, and flung his handful as hard and far as he could.

"To the arms of the kindest grandma," said Clare, and threw hers, too.

And the ashes were caught on an upsweep of air, like a surge of joy, and they spread and dissolved on the sudden breeze, and Clare felt a familiar scent of wild orchid and roses and joy sweep past her along with them. "Oh," she said, and turned to her father to see if he had felt it too, and he was smiling, and his eyes were full and wet.

Clare and her father lived together for years in their stone egg, tucked under the earth by the side of the sea. When she grew up, her father moved not far away, and her mother's and her grandmothers' house became her own home. She lived there all her life, though she often left to travel in Timeless and other places. But she always came back, because the sea is always both home and destination, the root and the flower, the source and the endpoint of every road, if you travel long enough, even fairy roads, as Jo had said. And although she grew tall enough to take the bed downstairs, and had a daughter who took her old loft room, Clare somehow never grew too tall to slip inside her yew tree. Or perhaps it grew along with her. At any rate, she never left her home and its in-between for long.

All her life, Clare felt the Strange. But now she no longer drew back from it—she ran to it, because she knew it was a friend, a friend who was making, or dreaming awake. And more often than not, it was Finn's making, Finn who stayed her best and truest companion all her life.

Clare never stopped making: in the poems she wrote—and she became known for her poems—but also in her garden, in the meals she made, in drawing and singing and stories, all those ways of dreaming awake. And whenever she made, she tried to make true: as true as Finn's butterfly snow; as true as the endless conversation of the trees; as true and as changing as the moon.

Acknowledgments

If you want to see what I think fairy-makings look like, look for the art of Andy Goldsworthy, whose work greatly inspired this book.

My other inspiration was something my niece Emma told me about her dreams when she was eight or nine. But I'm not going to tell someone else's dreams, so you'll have to ask her.

The character Jo was based in part on my aunt Jolene, who died while this book was in edits. I miss her.

Two borrowings I must acknowledge:

When Jo says, "Those that are away among them never return. Or if they do, they are not the same as they were before"—that's something a woman of the Irish Burren once told the poet W. B. Yeats, as quoted in the excellent book *Strange and Secret Peoples: Fairies and Victorian Consciousness.*

Also: as a child I loved an old book called *Maida's Little Shop.* At one point late in that book, someone tells a story in which a lady in the moon throws a golden carpet across the ocean for a girl to walk on. Only quite recently, just before I began writing these acknowledgments, did I remember that story; and just like Clare, I said, "Oh, *that's* where I got that moonlight path." The girl in the story's name is Klara, too. It's funny how the stories you read in childhood become part of you.

And now my many thanks:

Thanks times a billion to my sister and brother-in-law Nancy and Gene Matocha, whose generosity in letting me stay at their gorgeous mountain cabin gave a huge boost to both the writing and revising of this book.

Thanks to my yoga teacher Steven Ross for teaching the practice called "the moon in your mouth," and for being Scottish, so that I got that accent stuck in my head.

Thanks to Jeanne Frontain, my brilliant first reader, whose thoughtful comments helped more than I can say. I'm also grateful to her for pointing me at the wonderful book *Meeting the Other Crowd*, a collection of modern reports of Irish fairies.

Thanks to my excellent agent, Dave Dunton; I still feel lucky he signed me.

Thanks beyond measure to my superb editor, Julie Strauss-Gabel, whose story edits made this book so much better, and me so much happier with it. Thanks also to Andrew Karre for his super-smart and insightful line edits, and to all the generous talents at Penguin Young Readers who made this book more precise and more beautiful.

And mainly thank you to Ken, whom I love, and who teaches me how to be brave.